OUTRAGE

ROBERT K. TANENBAUM

OUTRAGE

G

Gallery Books

New York   London   Toronto   Sydney

Gallery Books
A Division of Simon & Schuster, Inc.
1230 Avenue of the Americas
New York, NY 10020

First Gallery Books hardcover edition June 2011

Manufactured in the United States of America

ISBN 978-1-4391-4925-6

To those blessings in my life:
Patti, Rachael, Roger, and Billy;
and
To the loving Memory of
Reina Tanenbaum
My sister, truly an angel

ACKNOWLEDGMENTS

To my legendary mentors, District Attorney Frank S. Hogan and Henry Robbins, both of whom were larger in life than in their well-deserved and hard-earned legends, everlasting gratitude and respect; to my special friends and brilliant tutors at the Manhattan DAO, Bob Lehner, Mel Glass, and John Keenan, three of the best who ever served and whose passion for justice was unequaled and uncompromising, my heartfelt appreciation, respect, and gratitude; to Professor Robert Cole and Professor Jesse Choper, who at Boalt Hall challenged, stimulated, and focused the passions of my mind to problem-solve and to do justice; to Steve Jackson, an extraordinarily talented and gifted scrivener whose genius flows throughout the manuscript and whose contribution to it cannot be over-stated, a dear friend for whom I have the utmost respect; to Louise Burke, my publisher, whose enthusiastic support, savvy, and encyclopedic smarts qualify her as my first pick in a game of three on three in the Avenue P park in Brooklyn; to Wendy Walker, my talented, highly skilled, and insightful editor, many thanks for all that you do; to Mitchell Ivers and Jessica Webb, the inimitable twosome whose adult supervision, oversight, and rapid responses are invaluable and profoundly appreciated; to my agents, Mike Hamilburg and Bob Diforio, who in exemplary fashion have always represented my best interests; to Paul Ryan, who personified "American Exceptionalism" and mentored me in its finest virtues; and to my esteemed special friend and confidant Richard A. Sprague, who has always challenged, debated, and inspired me in the pursuit of fulfilling the reality of "American Exceptionalism."

OUTRAGE

PROLOGUE

"ALL RISE!"

At the command of a rotund, jowly court clerk, those people still sitting in the gallery pews of the courtroom jumped up and stood at attention like soldiers waiting for the commanding officer to enter. The lawyers on either side of the aisle—prosecution on the right, closest to the jury box and witness stand; defense on the left—were already on their feet and now turned their attention to the front.

Slowest to rise was the defendant, a slightly built young man with wavy dark hair and large, luminous brown eyes. Head down, defeated, he appeared incapable of committing the horrendous crimes for which he'd been convicted a few weeks earlier. But the big man standing at the prosecution table just a few feet to his right had convinced the jurors otherwise. Now his life hung in the balance.

"Oyez oyez oyez," announced the clerk, an Irishman named

Edmund Farley, "all those who have business before part thirty-six of the supreme court, state of New York, New York County, draw near and ye shall be heard. The Honorable Supreme Court Justice Timothy Dermondy presiding . . ."

As Farley droned on, Dermondy swept into the courtroom, bringing a black cloud of judicial decorum. The somberness of the moment was etched into his intelligent, angular face. He had never been one to tolerate fools in his courtroom, and it was clear to everyone present that he wasn't about to start now. His dark eyes swept across those assembled within the confines of the dark wood–paneled room as if daring any one of them to disturb the sanctity of the proceedings as he stepped up onto the judge's dais and sat down.

"Representing the People, the Honorable District Attorney Roger Karp and Assistant District Attorney Ray Guma; representing the defendant, Stacy Langton and Mavis Huntley," Farley said, continuing as he had for some thirty years without missing a beat. He looked at the judge and said, "Your Honor, all of the jurors are present and accounted for; counsel and the defendant are present. The case on trial is ready to proceed."

Dermondy gave Farley a quick nod. The clerk then turned back to his audience, smiled, and invited them to be seated.

"Thank you, Mr. Farley," Dermondy said. "Good morning, everyone, especially you jurors—your task has been arduous, but it is coming to a close. I would like to ask something more of you. I know you're tired, but I urge you to focus now, more than ever, on this sacred task because a man's life is at stake."

The judge allowed the comment to sink in as he studied the faces of the twelve jurors. "As you are aware, this is a death penalty case, and what you decide may eventually reach a finality that cannot be undone for the defendant. He sits here convicted by you of two counts of murder. The People are seeking the death penalty and both sides have presented their evidence to you over the past couple of weeks for why, or why not, the defendant should be put to death for his crimes. Yesterday, you heard Ms. Langton present her summation on behalf of her client, the defendant; today you will hear from the district attorney, Mr. Karp."

Again Dermondy paused to allow the jurors to keep up. They looked worn out, their faces set in stone—they just wanted to go home to their families. Murder trials were tough enough on jurors, especially when they had to be sequestered, but death penalty cases were particularly emotionally and physically draining. Still, he needed them to hang in there a little while longer.

Then we'll all get to go home, Dermondy thought. But he also knew from his lengthy prosecutorial background and distinguished service on the bench that this was a case no one would ever forget.

"Let me remind you once again that during summation, the attorneys will tell you what they believe the evidence shows. However, what they say is not evidence, and it will be up to you to decide what weight, if any, to give their presentations. Do you understand?"

He was pleased to see them all nod. "Will you promise to focus one more time on what is said today, and then after the lawyers give their final arguments, their summations, and I charge you on the law, meaning simply give my legal instructions to you, you will deliberate and render a fair and just verdict?"

Again, twelve heads went up and down.

"Good. I thank you." Satisfied that the jury was in the proper frame of mind, Dermondy turned his attention to the prosecution table and said, "Mr. Karp, are you ready to proceed?"

Roger "Butch" Karp, all six foot five of him, tapped the yellow legal pad he'd been making notes on and rose from his seat. "Yes, Your Honor."

"Then, please, the floor is yours."

Dressed in his usual off-the-rack, bar mitzvah–blue suit, Karp came out from around the table and walked over to stand in front of the defense table, limping slightly from having aggravated an old basketball injury to his right knee. He looked down for a moment at the defendant, who quickly averted his eyes, his face drained of what little color he had left after several months incarcerated in the Tombs, the hellhole otherwise known as the Manhattan House of Detention for Men.

Shaking his head, Karp then turned to face the jury box, fixing his gold-flecked gray eyes on each juror for a moment before moving to the next. He nodded when he reached the last face, then began. "As you now have experienced, a capital murder trial has two separate phases. In law we say it is a 'bifurcated' proceeding. In phase one, the guilt phase, you the jury determined that the defendant is guilty of the murders for which he was charged. Phase two, the sentencing phase, deals with whether in your opinion, and based on the law, the defendant should be sentenced to death."

Karp let the finality of that sink in before continuing. "For the past couple of weeks, on behalf of the People, my colleague Ray Guma and I have presented evidence—what we call 'aggravating factors'—that more than justifies sentencing this defendant to death. For example, you were shown additional crime scene photographs and heard from the People's witnesses who graphically described the vicious nature of the defendant's merciless attacks on the deceased, Olivia Yancy and Beth Jenkins. But other than a brief few minutes in which Olivia's husband, Dale, spoke movingly, you heard very little about these women as real, living, breathing individuals."

Turning to point at the defense table, Karp said, "And as you know, the defense then presented its case, arguing that there were mitigating circumstances for why the defendant committed these crimes. The defense hopes this will persuade you to vote against invoking the death penalty. As such, you listened to a great deal about the defendant—his abused childhood, the violence he may have witnessed at an early age, the absence of convictions for other violent crimes, and how he *may* have been sexually assaulted while serving time in a juvenile detention facility some five years ago."

Karp walked slowly over to the defense table until he was standing in front of it. "If these things are true, then we certainly agree that no child should be abused or traumatized, and we may even come to understand what demons drive this defendant's evil nature," he said, fixing the defendant with a hard look. "But I also ask you to remember the testimony of Moishe Sobelman and the horrors he survived at the Sobibor death camp. And then remember that understanding does not mean that we forgive or excuse the brutal, vicious, methodical, and inhumane horrors that evil men perpetrate on the innocent—that the defendant perpetrated on two innocent women, Olivia Yancy and Beth Jenkins."

Without bothering to conceal the look of contempt on his rugged face, Karp stared down at the defendant. "He certainly doesn't look like he's capable of such horrors, does he? He's young. Cleans up well—"

"Objection," said Langton, an attractive thirtysomething brunette. She didn't need to address the issue further. While a defendant may have been arrested looking like he'd been living in a sewer, the prosecution was not allowed to comment when the defense team cut their client's hair, shaved and showered him, put him through detox if necessary, and then dressed him up like a preppy Dartmouth premed student.

"Sustained; continue, Mr. Karp," Dermondy said.

Karp nodded to the judge and then turned back to the defendant. "Here in this courtroom, the defendant hardly looks like the killer we all know him to be. He even wept for you on that witness stand with those big, brown eyes blinking away the tears. Listen to his tragic story, look at him frightened and demoralized in his seat now, and it's easy to feel sympathy for him."

Karp whirled and strode over to the prosecution table, where he picked up two eight-by-ten portrait photographs depicting the murder victims as they'd appeared in life. He held them up for the jurors to see. "But I would suggest that such sympathy is misplaced. It rightfully belongs to these two women. A young wife, Olivia Yancy, eager to move into a better, safer neighborhood, so that someday she could feel comfortable raising her children there. But she was instead ambushed by an evil and manipulative predator, the defendant, who stalked her because she was defenseless and vulnerable and lured her into his murderous trap under the guise of friendship."

As he spoke, Karp handed the photographs to the jury foreman and again pointed at the defendant, who quailed but did not look up. "And her mother, Beth Jenkins, a sixty-year-old widow, who went to help her daughter pack her family possessions for the move but walked in on Olivia being brutalized by that man here in this courtroom sitting so meekly at the defense table."

Stepping back from the jury rail, Karp allowed his voice to rise along with the genuine emotion he felt boiling to the surface. "So often evil men are made to seem like victims—they say they were only 'following orders' in Nazi Germany, or hitting back at the oppressors of Muslims everywhere . . . or they were abused as children. At the same time, it's almost obscene how quickly we forget who the real victims are, that they weren't just the numbers tattooed on their arms, or nameless, faceless office workers, or merely photographs to be passed around a jury box. Take a good look at the women in those photographs, ladies and gentlemen, and remember, they were real and they were the victims."

Karp pointed at the defense table. "Yes, ladies and gentlemen, we can understand that outside forces may help lead a man to commit evil deeds, but it does not justify or excuse the sort of horrors and suffering he may inflict on other human beings . . . as this defendant inflicted on Olivia Yancy and Beth Jenkins."

He paused, looking up at the ceiling for a moment. "You may ask, 'Aren't all murders horrible?' And 'Isn't the taking of any life equally reprehensible?' Good questions. So how do we differentiate between a murderer who deserves life in prison and one who deserves to be executed? And isn't it enough to remove the offender from the population and lock him away with no hope of ever getting out?"

Karp rocked slightly on his heels and leaned on the jury rail, facing the jurors eye to eye. "Make no mistake, my colleague, Assistant DA Ray Guma, and I considered these very issues before deciding to seek the death penalty in this case." He then stepped back and continued. "And we decided that because the defendant's outrages were so cruel, unspeakable, and inhumane, if there is to be a death penalty, then beyond any and all doubt, this defendant's evil qualifies. Let me suggest that perhaps the best way to demonstrate to you how we reached our conclusion, and the conclusion we are asking you to reach, is by going through the same process we did of reviewing the evidence and recalling what happened on that terrible day a little more than a year and a half ago."

The courtroom hushed; all eyes were on Karp. Even the defendant felt compelled to look up. "It was early afternoon when the deceased, Olivia Yancy, finished packing for the move to her new apartment and walked three blocks to her neighborhood grocery store. That night was to be the Yancys' last in the old apartment, and to celebrate, she was going to make a special dinner. She was happy. Her husband Dale had just been promoted to full professor at Columbia University. And the new apartment had two bedrooms, one for the child she intended to conceive. . . . Life was good."

1

IT WAS ONE IN THE AFTERNOON ON A SMOKING-HOT JULY
day in Manhattan with the humidity and stench of the city hovering above the asphalt and concrete as a noisome translucent
vapor. Ahmed Kadyrov wiped the sweat from his forehead as
he watched the pretty young woman struggle with two stuffed
paper bags, one in each arm, as she exited the mom-and-pop
grocer on 110th Street on the Upper West Side. He waited
until the auburn-haired beauty started off down the sidewalk
and then hurried to catch up.

Despite being a methamphetamine junkie beginning to
show the signs of his addiction—a deteriorating complexion
with dark circles under his large brown eyes—Kadyrov was
still a decent-looking young man of twenty-two who was often
mistaken as Hispanic with his neatly coifed black hair and
trim mustache. But he was Chechen, having immigrated to

the United States at age twelve, and still spoke with an accent, which women found attractive.

However, the only thing Ahmed Kadyrov liked about women was terrorizing and raping them, and then robbing "the bitches" to feed his demanding drug habit. Lately, he'd been getting a kick knocking them around a little too, and the last time had been particularly gratifying when he used the switchblade he carried in his pants pocket to draw a few drops of blood from his victim's neck.

As a boy he'd watched as a Russian army squad raped his mother and sisters. It was an event the psychiatrist at the Horizon Juvenile Center in the Bronx, where he'd served a year for his first sexual assault, had told him was at the root of his "issues with females and predilection toward sexual violence." But he didn't give a shit what some "fag shrink" thought; if anything he identified with the Russian brutes. Women, especially pretty ones like his mother and sisters, were whores and got what they deserved.

Kadyrov found the areas around the colleges in the five boroughs to be good hunting grounds. There were lots of pretty young women, especially in this neighborhood near Columbia University, which increased his odds of finding one in need of a "Good Samaritan," the ruse he used to win their confidence. They could be so incredibly gullible. For instance, he usually struck during the day, when such women thought they were safer accepting help from a neatly dressed stranger in a short-sleeved button-down shirt and khaki pants with a nice smile and friendly attitude.

"Excuse me," he said as he moved slightly in front of the

young woman, forcing her to slow her pace and adjust her heavy bags, "may I help you, please, to carry?" He laid the accent and foreign word groupings on especially heavy when on the prowl; he perceived that for some reason, women also thought polite-seeming European types were less dangerous.

The young woman smiled but shook her head. "Thank you, that's very kind," she said. "But I'm only going three blocks, and I wouldn't want you to go out of your way."

Kadyrov was ready for the expected response and reached for what appeared to be the heaviest bag before she could protest further. "Is no problem, I am going this direction. Please, I help." He turned up the smile a notch with a look in his eyes that indicated his feelings would be hurt if she refused his generosity.

"Well, sure, if you don't mind," the young woman said with a smile. "I'm Olivia."

"Very good to meet you," Kadyrov said. "I am Stefan."

They talked as they walked. He said he was a prelaw student at Columbia University, an irony that made him smile inwardly. She told him that her husband, Dale, taught English lit there. "He just made full professor," she said proudly. "It means more money, so we're going to be moving into a nicer apartment. I'm supposed to be packing now."

They reached the entrance to her apartment building, a ten-story, 1950s-era edifice of dingy yellow brick with graffiti scrawls on the walls as high as the "artists" could reach. Olivia stopped and turned to Kadyrov with a smile and reached out for the bag he carried. "I can get it from here, Stefan, thank you so much."

Kadyrov shifted the bag away from her outstretched hand. "Is no problem I take in for you, then I go," he said with a grin. "Job is, how do you say, only half-finished. No?"

Olivia hesitated, but she looked again at his smiling face and shrugged. "Well, sure, that's very nice of you." She stepped in front of Kadyrov so he wouldn't see the access number that she punched in. There was an electronic buzz and click and she smiled over her shoulder as she pulled the security gate open. "Come on up."

Kadyrov smiled. He loved this period of stalking just before he pounced, when his prey still didn't know that she was about to be savaged. Beautiful women, like so many pampered, stupid sheep, could be so oblivious to the fact that the wolf was walking among them dressed in a Brooks Brothers shirt, khaki pants, and loafers.

Olivia led the way to the elevator, which they took to the fifth floor, and then walked down the hall to a corner apartment. Kadyrov was pleased that there were no sounds from the closest neighbors' apartments. He slipped his free hand into his pants pocket and grasped the handle of the switchblade.

Olivia turned the key in the lock and opened the door. "Would you like a glass of water?" she said. "It's all I have. The fridge is empty and—"

Whatever the young woman intended to say next was cut short by the hand that went across her mouth and the feel of the wickedly sharp knife blade held against her throat. "Don't scream, *sooka*, or I'll cut your fucking head off," Kadyrov whispered in her ear as he kicked the door shut behind them. "Now we're gonna get busy."

2

SITTING ON THE D TRAIN AS IT RATTLED NORTH FROM Manhattan into the Bronx, Amy Lopez lifted her copy of the *Post* so that the young acne-scarred man with the peroxide-blond hair sitting across from her couldn't see her face. He'd been staring at her since getting on the train at the 125th Street subway station, and she'd caught him glancing at her purse, which she had tucked closer against her hip. She read the headline that screamed from the front page.

DA'S WITNESS COLLAPSES ON WITNESS STAND
AT IMAM'S TERROR TRIAL

She turned the page to read the report about the murder trial of a Harlem imam named Sharif Jabbar. It was one of those stories that had the city riveted to the various tabloids and the evening television news. A young woman had been decapitated in the basement of the al-Aqsa mosque in Harlem during some sort of frenzied buildup to a narrowly thwarted terrorist attack on the New York Stock Exchange the previous fall. And now, in April, the imam was being prosecuted for her murder.

According to the story, New York district attorney Roger "Butch" Karp, who was prosecuting the case, had called an unindicted co-conspirator, Dean Newbury, the senior partner of an old, established white-shoe Wall Street law firm, to the witness stand the day before. And while testifying against the imam, the old man had toppled over and died. The "official" word from a court spokesman was that Newbury had succumbed to "an apparent heart attack."

However, the *Post* was reporting a more sinister possibility. According to a reliable source who was not authorized to speak on the record, Newbury had shown signs of having been poisoned. The source was quoted as saying, "He took a sip of water and kablooey, he's on the ground frothing at the mouth and kicking around to beat the band. Then nothing. Nada. Dead as a doornail."

Amy finished the story and turned the page, dipping the paper ever so slightly and just in time to catch the young man watching her before he quickly averted his eyes. She looked down at the paper and a chill ran up her spine. The previous night, April 10, a woman named Dolores Atkins had been murdered in an apartment off Anderson Avenue in the Bronx. The police weren't saying much, but according to another officially anonymous source, she'd been raped and "cut up pretty bad" by her attacker.

"There were no apparent signs of a break-in," an NYPD

spokesman was quoted as saying. He'd declined to answer a question posed by the reporter, Ariadne Stupenagel, regarding the possibility that the murder was related to a double homicide that had occurred the previous July on the Upper West Side of Manhattan near Columbia University. The article had gone on to note similarities between Atkins's death and the murders of the other two women—Beth Jenkins and her daughter Olivia Yancy. The cases remained open with no arrests made or imminent.

When the train reached her stop at the 161st Street station near Yankee Stadium, Amy stayed in her seat as if she intended to continue riding. Then at the last moment, she jumped up and stepped through the open door. Hurrying along the platform, she glanced back just as she reached the stairs leading down to River Avenue. She cursed; the stalker had been quick enough to beat the door and was following her.

She walked down the stairs as quickly as she could and started zigzagging through the late-afternoon crowd on the sidewalk. This time when she looked back, she didn't see the young man and sighed with relief. She took him for a purse snatcher, and that would have made her a victim twice in two months. There wasn't much money in her handbag, but replacing her driver's license again, as well as having to put a stop on her checking and credit card accounts, would have been onerous.

Oh, and my engagement ring is in there, she thought. She'd gained a little weight with her last pregnancy with baby A.J. and the ring had been uncomfortable, so she took it off and put it in her wallet. *I'd hate to lose that. . . .*

Amy's last thought was interrupted by a violent tug on her arm. The young man suddenly materialized at her side and grabbed her purse. She tried to hang on as he took off running and screamed as she was pulled off her feet, losing her grip on the purse. "Help! Thief! Somebody help!" she cried as she scrambled to her feet.

A few bystanders yelled at the purse snatcher, and a couple of men gave momentary chase, but the thief knew his game and that the pursuit would not last long. He dodged between the traffic on River Avenue and kept running until he was on the west side of the soon-to-be-demolished old baseball stadium. He slowed to a walk and began rifling through the purse, oblivious to the looks he got from passersby. This was the Bronx; asking a tough-looking, acne-scarred young man what he was doing pulling out the contents of a woman's purse could only mean trouble.

Only fifteen lousy bucks, he thought. He could probably get a little more for the credit cards and checkbook, though his victim was sure to report them stolen and close the accounts. He was well aware that sometimes victims didn't act as fast as they should, and he might be able to make a few quick purchases posing as the husband of Amy Lopez. He'd eventually sell the cards to those who had ways of using them still—mostly knowing which businesses didn't run them through electronic billing. He stared down at the driver's license dismissively—it was worth only a couple of dollars.

He opened the coin purse of the wallet. Seventy-three cents

and a ring with a small diamond. *Less than a half carat*, he thought. *Maybe worth a few hundred brand-new.* He looked at the inscription on the inside of the ring: *Always, Al.* The sentiment could stay, but he'd file the "Al" out of it. *I might get thirty bucks, if I can find the right loser.*

The thief found a buyer two hours later, standing with a dozen others in Mullayly Park near 166th Street and Jerome Avenue. He'd seen the Puerto Rican teenager around the neighborhood but had never talked to him. Skinny and awkward, with long, wavy dark hair and soulful brown eyes, which looked even larger behind the thick glasses he wore, the young man wasn't like the others who hung out at that particular part of the park.

Mostly loud punks and their slutty girlfriends, the thief thought. His target was shy to the point where he couldn't look anyone in the eye for more than a second, even if the conversation was friendly. And he constantly shifted from foot to foot when nervous, as if he wanted to run away.

I think somethin's wrong with his brain, the thief thought, but he had to admit that the young man did seem to have one talent that got him tolerated by the others: he could repeat word-for-word seemingly every hip-hop recording ever made. Except for a slight Puerto Rican accent, he even sounded like the originals, although he had none of the attitude or hand gestures. *I think his name is Felix*, the thief thought as he watched the young man finish his improv rap and fall silent.

"Felix, my man, you look like an hombre who needs a ring for his girl," he said, sidling up to his target. "I got just the thing." The thief produced the ring. "It's worth four hundred, but since we're compadres, I'll let you have it for a hundred."

"I . . . I . . . I don't have that much money," Felix stammered, surprised that the acne-scarred man had spoken to him at all.

"Hell, Felix ain't got no money, and he ain't got no girl-friend," said a large black youth standing close enough to hear the exchange, guffawing.

"I . . . I . . . I have a girlfriend," Felix replied, looking down at his feet.

"Hell yeah, Raymond, haven't you heard, Felix is the dude that knocked up your cousin Cherise," a short Hispanic girl with too much makeup said. "Ain't that right, Felix? You the daddy?" She laughed. The locals hanging out at the park teased Felix, an easy target, every chance they got.

"No . . . no no," Felix replied, shaking his head swiftly from side to side and turning red as he shifted faster from one foot to the other.

The large black youth, Raymond, scowled. "That right, Felix? You im-preg-nate Cherise?" He moved over so that he was only a few inches away from Felix and towering over him, then turned his head to the side and winked at the Hispanic girl. It was obvious: there was no Cherise, pregnant or otherwise.

But Felix didn't know that. He was beginning to look desper-ate. "No! It wasn't me!"

"You sure?" Raymond growled. He looked over his shoulder to make sure the others were watching and grinned. "Now, tell me the truth, is you the one who diddled Cherise?" he asked belligerently, turning back to Felix, his face set as if he was about to fly into a rage.

Suddenly, Felix nodded so vigorously he had to push his

glasses back up his nose. "Yeah, sure . . . okay. I . . . I . . . I did-dled Cherise. I'm sorry. I didn't mean to—"

"You didn't mean to?" the big youth roared. "What did you think you was doing with that little pecker?"

As the other youths laughed at the joke, Felix looked behind him as if he'd heard somebody call his name from a distance. "I . . . I . . . I got to go," he stuttered.

"You . . . you . . . you better," Raymond said, mimicking Felix. "Cherise is trying to figure out which one of you peckerwoods forgot to use pro-tec-shun. Now that I know, she'll be comin' after your ass."

Felix looked like he might cry, then he turned on his heel and began to walk quickly away.

The purse snatcher, who'd been laughing along with the others, saw his opportunity leaving and hurried after him. "Yo, Felix, wait up," he said. "That was just plain wrong back there. You didn't really get Cherise pregnant, did you?"

Felix shook his head again as he continued to walk at a fast clip. "No. I don't even know her."

"Then why'd you say you did?"

Felix shrugged his shoulders and slowed down. "That's what they wanted me to say."

"Well, it was wrong of them, dude," the thief said sympathet-ically. "So, tell ya what I'm going to do. I know you got a girl-friend stashed away from those jokers, and she ain't no whore like Cherise. Fine-looking young man like you—and by the way, I like the mustache you're trying to grow there, brother, makes you look older, classy. Tell you what, I'll sell you that ring for fifty bucks . . . and that's a steal, bro."

Felix stopped walking. His face twisted with doubt. He reached into his pocket and pulled out a wad of crumpled bills and coins. He counted what he had and shook his head. "I only got twenty-three dollars and sixteen cents."

"Oh man, you trying to rob me?" the thief said, rolling his eyes. He paused before adding, as though reluctant, "Well, 'cause I don't like what those *pendejos* was doing to you, I'll take it." He held out his hand and accepted the cash, and then handed over the ring. "You gonna make some bitch happy, she gonna take care of you reeeaaaal good."

Felix smiled shyly as he inspected the ring, then frowned. "It says, 'Always, Al.' Who's Al?"

The thief thought fast. "Why, I am. Al Guerrero. My bitch decided to dump me and I got the ring back. That's how come I knew it was a five-hundred-dollar ring."

"You said it was worth four hundred."

"Whatever, now it's yours," the thief replied. "All you got to do is get a little file and take off my name and you're set with your lady friend. Now I got to go."

Felix felt a pang of guilt as he watched the man trot quickly in the opposite direction. He knew that his parents wouldn't approve of what he'd just done. Especially his dad, who never approved of *anything* he did.

His mother was always worried that others would take advantage of him and get him into trouble. It was true that they sometimes liked to play jokes on him—like committing some minor offense and then saying he did it, knowing he'd confess under pressure. Like the time at school when Raymond flushed firecrackers down the toilet, wrecking the pipes. Or when the police were called in to investigate when some other kids broke the front window of the Korean market on Anderson Avenue. Confronted, Felix had admitted he was the culprit in both instances even though he'd been nowhere near either scene.

Felix didn't know why he confessed to things he didn't do. He was, his mom always said, "a people pleaser," but more than that, he didn't like it when people were angry with him, especially the people in charge, like his dad, teachers, and the police. He'd discovered at an early age that it was easier if he just went along and did and said what other people wanted him to. In the case of his dad, if Felix denied some transgression and waited for the old man to really get worked up, the beating was much more severe than if he confessed quickly and just got slapped around a little bit.

Plus, as in the cases of the school prank and the Korean grocer, the authorities had quickly determined that he wasn't involved. So other than a mild strapping with a belt from his dad "for lying," which wasn't out of the ordinary, nothing had ever come of his confessions.

Felix reasoned now that he'd paid the owner for the ring and got a good deal, and that there was nothing wrong with that. Still, his parents would never believe that it was an honest transaction, so he was just going to have to keep it a secret.

He wasn't quite sure what he was going to do with the ring, but he was tired of everyone making fun of him because he'd never had a girlfriend. There was this one girl he liked. She worked as a waitress at the Hip-Hop Nightclub on West Thirty-eighth Street in Manhattan. Maria Elena. He was going there next week to perform for open mic night at the invitation of his friend Alejandro Garcia, who was a big-time rap artist.

Maybe she'll notice me, he thought happily as he stuffed the ring in his pants pocket and headed for his family's apartment on Anderson Avenue.

3

"Mr. Karp, that newspaper reporter Ariadne Stupenagel is here to see you. She says she has an appointment," Karp's receptionist, Darla Milquetost, said over the office intercom.

"Tell her I'm not in," Karp replied, loud enough that Stupenagel could hear him not only through the intercom but also through his open office door. He winked at his wife, Marlene Ciampi, who was visiting and waiting for her old friend Ariadne.

Karp was kicked back in the leather office chair with his size-fourteen feet up on the ancient battle-scarred mahogany desk that had occupied the inner sanctum of the New York district attorney's office since the days of his mentor, the legendary district attorney Francis X. Garrahy.

He stood and stretched his still-trim, six-foot-five frame. It had been a week since the jury had come back with a guilty verdict in the murder trial of the Harlem imam Sharif Jabbar, and he was still enjoying the release of all the tension that came with such an undertaking.

There was no gloating over the verdict. The way he saw it, the advantage was with the prosecution. As the chief prosecutor, he knew he would prevail if he did his preparation and was certain of the defendant's factual guilt going into the trial, and if he had legally admissible evidence to convict beyond any and all doubt. *Otherwise, the defendant never should have been charged in the first place,* he thought.

However, with Jabbar convicted, it was as if Karp had passed through the perfect storm. Now the sky was blue, the ocean a lake, and he was relaxed and starting to catch up on some of his administrative duties, as well as what was going on at the DAO while his focus had been fully occupied by the terror trial.

The only thing rocking his boat at the moment was the impending court battle to make sure that Jabbar served his sentence of life without parole in New York and wasn't whisked off by the feds into a witness protection program in exchange for information, thus escaping punishment. Even if he could keep Jabbar in a New York state prison for the rest of Jabbar's life, Karp was still torn over whether the punishment fit the crime. He thought back to some of the discussions he'd had with several of the senior members of his staff over whether to pursue the death penalty for Jabbar.

There was no doubt in Karp's mind that Jabbar had deserved the death penalty—the victim had been cruelly tortured for hours before her execution, which had itself been painful, horrific, and slow. However, there'd been other considerations. One was that there was no evidence to prove that Jabbar knew about, or participated in, the victim's torture—one of the aggra-vating factors necessary to warrant the death penalty. And two, witness testimony and the evidence clearly showed that the terrorist Nadya Malovo actually wielded the murder weapon; Jabbar had been more planner, facilitator, and cheerleader than executioner.

This had not stopped Karp from prosecuting the anti-U.S. firebrand imam. For his role, Jabbar was just as guilty in the eyes of the law as Malovo. But when deciding whether to seek the death penalty, Karp had to weigh the possibility that jurors would make a distinction between Malovo and Jabbar.

On the one hand, it wouldn't make a difference; if they found Jabbar guilty but refused to vote for the ultimate punishment, Jabbar would automatically be sentenced to life without parole. However, in the past there had been death penalty cases in which jurors knew that a conviction might subject the defen-dant to an execution they didn't believe the defendant deserved specifically because he or she wasn't the "real killer." Jurors finding themselves in this position sometimes balked at render-ing a guilty verdict. And all it took was one holdout for a hung jury.

Unwilling to take that chance in this case, Karp knew he had to be satisfied with the life-without-parole sentence . . . as long as it was served in New York. However, if he got the chance, Karp knew he would pursue the death penalty against Malovo, the always elusive, daring, and vicious assassin. She'd been apprehended in Manhattan by U.S. Marshal Jen Capers after murdering one of his star witnesses, Dean Newbury, near the end of the Jabbar trial. But for the moment, it looked like he wasn't going to get the chance to prosecute her in a New York City courtroom. She was locked away in a federal maximum-security penitentiary awaiting trial on a variety of federal charges and he couldn't get at her.

The situation made him uneasy on a personal level, too. Malovo had a grudge against him and his family, and he'd be able to keep better tabs on her if she was locked up in New York.

In the meantime, the Karp-Ciampi household was in a state of flux. His wife was casting about for "something fulfilling" to do as she contemplated the last of their children leaving the home in a couple of years. An attorney herself, she'd recently successfully represented "Dirty Warren," the vendor operating the newsstand in front of the Criminal Courts Building at 100 Centre Street. He had been charged with murder in Westchester County. Flush with victory, she was considering taking on the occasional case in which she felt an injustice was being perpetrated; however, she wouldn't take on cases in Manhattan to avoid any perceived conflict of interest with her DA husband.

Meanwhile, his daughter Lucy's summer nuptials had been postponed—apparently indefinitely. The reason given when Lucy showed up suddenly in New York from her home in New Mexico was that her fiancé, Ned Blanchett, had been called away on "business," which was code for an assignment with the antiterrorism agency they both worked for. However, Karp had been told by his wife that Lucy was having second thoughts about getting married.

On a brighter note, their twin sons, Isaac and Giancarlo, were at long last going to have their bar mitzvah, a rite of passage that had been interrupted and delayed by a seemingly constant stream of "mayhem," as Marlene referred to it. Although a couple of years beyond the usual age for the ceremony, they were now aiming at late summer/early fall.

The boys were currently working on a Jewish history report that the rabbi of the bar mitzvah class was requiring, as well as the traditional reading of the Torah. Karp was pleased that they'd decided to interview his friend Moishe Sobelman, a Midtown bakery owner, about his horrific experiences as a prisoner in the infamous Nazi death camp at Sobibor, Poland.

Karp leaned forward and pressed the button on the intercom again, smiling as he did at Marlene, a petite beauty with dark curly hair who carried herself with a grace and charm that still enraptured her husband. "Send her in, I guess," he groused good-naturedly. "And thank you, Darla."

"You're welcome, Mr. Karp," his receptionist said with a tone that indicated she would have rather told the visitor to take a hike.

The door to the office opened and a tall, redheaded Valkyrie in a lime-green dress blew into the room like a force of nature. "Very funny, Karp," Ariadne Stupenagel said, rolling her eyes at Marlene. "You really know how to make a girl feel welcome. . . . Oh good, I see that your only redeeming feature—your wife— is here." She crossed the room and embraced Marlene, giving her a kiss on each cheek that left a smudge of her trademark crimson lipstick.

Marlene laughed. Loud, abrasive, and one tough investigative journalist, Stupenagel had been her roommate in college at Smith and they'd remained friends ever since. She reached for the reporter's left hand, whistling at the diamond ring perched there. "That's some rock," she said. "You and Gilbert set a date yet?"

Karp groaned loudly, drawing glares from the two women. Gilbert Murrow was Karp's office manager. He kept his boss's appointment calendar, tried to steer Karp away from political pitfalls, and handled most of the administrative duties so that his boss could concentrate on his office's efforts to mete out justice to the guilty and ensure that the unjustly accused would be exonerated. Bookish, pear-shaped, balding, and four inches shorter than his fiancée, Murrow had surprisingly won the heart of Ariadne, who by her own estimation had amorous relations with the Fidel Castros of the world if it helped her get a story.

The reporter held the ring up to be admired. "It is a beaut, isn't it? The poor dear probably had to save for a year, considering the wages his miserly employer"—she gave Karp a sharp look—"pays him for all his hard work and loyal service. We are thinking a winter solstice wedding."

"Then there's still time for Gilbert to recover his senses," Karp said hopefully.

"Watch it, buster, I know where you live," Stupenagel answered, turning back to Marlene. "And don't worry, honey, I also know *lots* of good-looking, eligible, and civil men, should some unfortunate accident befall your husband."

After a little more of the pointed but friendly verbal jousting that was the hallmark of the relationship between Karp and

Stupenagel, the three sat down. A freelance writer at the moment, Stupenagel wanted to pen a feature story for the *Gotham City* weekly magazine, tentatively titled "New York's Number One Crime-fighting Couple." Karp had cringed at the concept, and only Stupenagel's blatant appeal to his sense of fair play and Marlene's intercession had convinced him to go through with it. He'd been a little surprised that Marlene had been willing to do the interview—she'd never been one to seek publicity—but he was sure that Stupenagel had twisted her arm using whatever means she had available.

Of course, he'd set some boundaries. He wouldn't discuss open investigations or current cases, except in the most general terms. Nor did he want her writing about his children except in passing.

The interview lasted nearly three hours. They discussed several of his most recent cases, including that of a college professor who'd killed her children because she said God told her to, a famous theater producer who murdered an actress and tried to claim she committed suicide, and, of course, the case against the Harlem imam Sharif Jabbar. They also covered several terrorist plots that, despite being outside the realm of their "official duties," Karp and Marlene, as well as other members of their family and friends, had a hand in thwarting.

Finally, Stupenagel appeared to reach the end of her questioning by asking Marlene about the case of Dirty Warren and her possible new career as a crusading defense attorney/private investigator. After Marlene answered the questions, Karp pointedly looked at his watch. "Anything else?" he asked.

Stupenagel smiled. "Well, since I've got you here, I am working on another story about unsolved murders in the greater New York area," she said.

"This sounds like a story more for the police than the DAO, but go ahead," Karp said.

"Oh, I'll be talking to the cops, too," Stupenagel replied. "But I'd like your opinion as the chief law enforcement official in Manhattan. To start, I think there's something like ten thousand unsolved murders in New York City going back to 1985, and roughly two hundred more go cold every year. In fact, at a rate of six hundred or so murders a year, almost a third of them will go unsolved."

"I'm aware of the statistics," Karp replied. "More than half of all homicides committed are solved within a year; after that, the chances diminish. Still, with an overall clearance rate of about seventy percent, which last time I looked at statistics compiled by the FBI beats the national average by eight percentage points, New York's finest are to be commended."

"Yes, but many of the unsolved cases are the unusual ones," Stupenagel said. "And by that I mean most of the time the killer and the victim share the same background, come from the same neighborhood, and are even the same race and approximately the same age. Black gangbangers shooting other black gangbangers. Not only do the killers have criminal records, their victims usually do as well. More often than not, the killer and victim knew each other; only about a quarter of all homicides are between strangers. And of those, most are the result of a dispute—somebody gets pissed off when someone cuts him off in traffic, pulls a gun, and shoots. Granted, stranger-to-stranger homicides have nearly doubled from what they were fifty years ago, but still, if you're not involved in criminal activities, your chances of being killed by a stranger in New York City are small."

"You're well versed in the statistics," Karp said. He realized that the long preamble was leading to something, putting him on his guard. "So what's your point?"

"I'm thinking more about the sort of unsolved cases that don't fit the statistical pattern," Stupenagel said. "Those are the ones that the public remembers."

"Are you talking about any case in particular?" Karp asked, knowing that she was going there.

"Well, yeah," Stupenagel admitted. "I'm thinking about the Yancy-Jenkins double homicide—the so-called Columbia University Slasher case—from last July. Somehow a killer got into the apartment of Olivia Yancy, killed and raped her, and also killed her mother, Beth Jenkins."

"I'm well aware of the case," Karp replied warily. "However, this is one of those ongoing investigations that are off-limits in this conversation."

"Is it true your office has an ADA assigned to the case? One Raymond 'Formerly Known as the Italian Stallion' Guma?"

"Couldn't tell ya," Karp replied. "And why 'formerly'? He'd resent that."

"Couldn't or won't?" Stupenagel shot back. "And 'formerly' because that bout with cancer a few years back turned him into a gelding from what I hear."

Karp rolled his eyes and said, "That's out of bounds, even for you, Stupe. I thought you and Guma were old friends."

"Hey, Guma dishes it out as much as he takes it," Stupenagel said. "He as much as told Gilbert that he boinked me back when we were both young and dumb. Now he's just old and dumb, and he's messing with my love life, so if I want to spread rumors about him, I will."

Karp shook his head and said, "Let's stick to the subject. As I said, the Yancy-Jenkins homicides are part of an ongoing investigation, and I'm not answering those questions. What else you got?"

"Are you familiar with the Dolores Atkins murder in the Bronx about a week ago?" Stupenagel said, and then shrugged.

"Only what I read in the newspaper, why?" Karp asked.

"Because the killer was another slasher/rapist, which I know are a dime a dozen in these parts. But just like in the Yancy-Jenkins killings, this guy also struck in broad daylight, and it appears that Atkins had just returned from grocery shopping, like Yancy. And the killer didn't just cut her up and rape her; he tortured her and then took the time to clean himself up before leaving."

"So, Ariadne," Marlene said, interrupting, "what's your angle here?"

"Well, I've been doing some digging and I think whoever killed Olivia Yancy and Beth Jenkins also killed Dolores Atkins," Stupenagel said. "I think he already escalated, and I don't think he's going to stop."

"What makes you say that?" Karp asked.

"Like I said, I've been doing some digging into a series of violent rapes—mostly in Manhattan, but some also in the Bronx and Brooklyn. Same description of the perp: slightly built, dark hair, brown eyes . . . maybe Hispanic . . . talks with an accent.

Talks his way into the apartment by offering to help the women with their grocery bags or, in the case of a couple of students, their books. Pulls a knife and rapes them."

"You said he escalated," Marlene said.

"Yeah. If it's the same guy, and I think it is, the first couple of times he mostly threatened. Then he started hitting and kicking. Finally, there's a case where he actually cut the victim's neck—not seriously, but enough to draw blood. And according to the police accounts taken from the victims, he seems to get aroused by the violence."

"You believe that he's now gone from rapist to cold-blooded murderer," Karp said.

"I do," Stupenagel said. "It's my understanding that the Atkins crime scene was even worse than Yancy-Jenkins, which I heard was pretty gruesome."

"Couldn't tell you," Karp replied. "And wouldn't."

Stupenagel laughed. "Of course not. But whatever makes this guy tick, it's getting worse, and he will do it again unless he's stopped."

"Then let's hope he gets stopped," Karp said.

Stupenagel looked at him for a moment, then shook her head and closed her notebook. "Yes, let's," she said, standing to let herself out. "Well, if anything turns up . . ."

"You'll be the first to know," Karp said, finishing her sentence.

The reporter smirked. "Yeah, I'm sure you have my number on speed dial," she said, and turned to Marlene, who also stood. "At least it was a pleasure to see *you*, my dear."

"As always," Marlene replied, giving her friend a hug.

When Stupenagel left the room, Marlene turned to her husband. "You have to admit, she may be on to something there. Violent sex offenders do tend to escalate. Do you think NYPD has made the connection?"

Karp shrugged and pressed the button on the office intercom. "Darla, would you see if you can track down Ray Guma and ask him to come to my office please?"

Marlene smiled. "So maybe Ariadne Stupenagel isn't as bad as you make her out?"

Karp grinned back. "She's a reporter; she's still the enemy."

4

"MIERDA! WHO IN THE HELL TOOK MY LAST GODDAMN beer!"

Even shut up in his tiny bedroom with the door closed, Felix Acevedo cringed as if he'd been struck by the sound of his father's fury coming from the kitchen of the family's tiny apartment. He'd been happily dressing for the night's outing to the Hip-Hop Nightclub, trying to decide which hooded sweatshirt and baggy jeans looked best. He squinted at himself in the mirror and practiced the rap songs he planned to perform. But now he flinched as his father yelled again.

"Felix! Get your skinny culo out here, goddamn it, or I swear to God, I'll—"

The man's swearing stopped for a moment as a woman tried to calm him. She spoke soothingly but her voice was obviously tinged with fear. For good reason. She'd hardly said five words when there was the unmistakable sound of a slap followed by a cry of pain.

Felix clenched his fists in anger and for a moment imagined storming out of his bedroom to the kitchen and beating his father, Eduardo, unconscious, as he'd seen the old man do to his mother on more than one occasion. He hated Eduardo—he was a mean drunk who hadn't worked a steady job in years but drank and gambled all day, sometimes all night, before eventually coming home. If Felix and his mother were lucky, Eduardo would then continue drinking until he passed out. However, if they crossed him, or if he simply felt like it, he'd take out his anger on them with his fists and feet, and sometimes a leather belt.

Eduardo Acevedo had brought his family to New York from Puerto Rico when Felix was a young boy, but his sloth and drinking prevented him from ever realizing the American dream, and his wife and son paid the price. Felix's mom, Amelia, was the sole support for the family. She worked nights cleaning offices in Manhattan. She left each evening after fixing her husband and son dinner and then didn't return until early the next morning.

"Felix, I'm gonna count to three and if you're not . . ."

It was no use. Felix relaxed his fists and felt his shoulders sag in defeat. He did not have the courage to confront his father, much less attack him. He'd just have to take his medicine for whatever he had, or more likely had not, done.

"I'm coming," he shouted. He put his glasses back on and gave himself one last look in the mirror, contemplating the piles of secondhand clothes he'd left on the floor of his messy room, wondering if there was a better combination than what he was wearing. But another bellow from his father reminded him that the longer he took to respond the worse it was going to be.

As he approached the doorway leading into the kitchen, he considered bolting out the front door. If it wasn't for the fact that his mother would then have to take whatever punishment his father thought necessary, he might have fled. He certainly had no idea what his father was screaming about regarding beer. Neither Felix nor his mother drank alcohol, having witnessed its effect on the other member of the household for so many years. If the beer was gone, it was because the bastard drank it, but the truth wouldn't matter to him now.

Felix shuffled into the kitchen with his head down so that he wouldn't have to look into the angry, bloodshot eyes of his father. But as if against his will, he eventually glanced up.

Dressed in a dingy wife-beater undershirt with yellow stains beneath the armpits, Eduardo stood glaring at him from the open refrigerator. His hairy arms were covered with faded green-black tattoos from two stints in Rikers Island prison. His mother, a tiny woman with a strawberry-shaped birthmark on her right cheek, sat mutely in a chair at the small kitchen table, using a tissue to dab at the blood that trickled from her mouth.

Eduardo caught Felix glancing at his mother and the look of sorrow that passed between them. He pointed at his wife as he snarled at his son, *"See what you made me do, you little* hijo de puta*?!"*

Felix nodded his head. "Yes, sir. I . . . I . . . I'm sorry."

"Sorry? Sorry don't cut it. Where's my fucking beer, pendejo*!"*

The words slammed into Felix like fists. His father rarely spoke unless it was to yell with the occasional Spanish curse word tossed in. "I don't know," he said, lowering his eyes again. "I didn't take it."

"Liar!" Eduardo screamed, slamming the door and moving toward Felix with his fist raised. *"There was one more in the fridge when I left for work this morning! You took it, fucking thief!"*

By "work" Eduardo meant gambling and boozing, but Felix wasn't about to throw gasoline on the fire. "Okay, okay," he cried. "I took it. I . . . I . . . I'll go buy you—"

The attempt to mollify his father was cut off by the backhand blow across his face that knocked his glasses off. *"I'll teach you to steal my beer!"* Eduardo started to remove his belt.

Amelia Acevedo jumped up from her seat and darted behind her husband to look in the refrigerator. "Look, Eddie, there is another beer, it was behind the carton of milk," she said, holding up a forty-ounce bottle of cheap malt liquor.

Eduardo looked at her suspiciously. Then he nodded as if he'd just realized some great truth. "Puta!" he spat. *"You bitch! You hid it on purpose! What? You got some asshole over here doing you all day while I'm at work? You giving him my beer?"* He raised his hand again and started for the cowering woman.

"No! It was me, I hid it," Felix said. Without his glasses his dad's face was fuzzy, but he knew it would be a mask of rage. "I was going to the park, and I wanted to bring some beer so that the other guys would think I'm cool."

Eduardo stopped and looked back and forth from his wife to his son as if he couldn't figure out which one to hit first. With a snort of disgust, he reached out and grabbed the bottle from his wife. "You owe me a six-pack for trying to steal my beer," he snarled at Felix, though he stopped shouting. He then turned to his wife. "This ain't gonna last, bitch."

"I was just going to the store," Felix's mother responded with a look at her son that signaled it was time for them both to leave. "I'll be back in twenty minutes."

"Make it ten if you know what's good for you."

As quick as they could, Felix and his mother left the apartment and were soon standing on the sidewalk in front of the run-down tenement building. "You . . . you . . . you should leave him," Felix stammered.

His mother didn't raise her head. "Where would I go? This is my home."

"Home?" Felix cried. "A home for rats and cockroaches, you mean—at least until winter, when even they won't stay because we can't pay for heat. You could live better if he wasn't around to drink and gamble all your money away."

"He'd find me, and when he did . . ." Her voice trailed off but they both knew what she was going to say.

Felix flushed with anger. "Someday I'm going to be a famous rapper, and I'll buy you a nice house. And if he comes around, I'll get the dogs on him."

Amelia looked up at her son and smiled through her tears. She reached out and patted his cheek where a bruise was already beginning to show from the blow his father had given him. "You're a good son, Felix. Now, you be safe tonight and stay away from people who can get you into trouble."

Felix thought about the ring that was making a lump in his wallet. He'd filed the name Al off but left the "Always." He wondered what his mother would say about his dreams of someday giving it to Maria Elena, the pretty girl with beautiful dark eyes he hoped to talk to that night. "I'll be safe," he promised. "I'm just going to see my friend Alejandro."

Amelia looked worried. "Wasn't he in a gang?"

"The Inca Boyz over in East Harlem," Felix admitted. "But that was a long time ago, Mama. He doesn't do gang stuff anymore. He's a famous rapper now, and he's my friend."

"Well, he better take good care of my son or he will have me to deal with," Amelia said with another smile as she brushed some food crumbs from the front of his sweatshirt. "I should have washed this," she said. "You are so messy."

"Aw, Mom," Felix complained, aware that he and his mother were getting amused looks from some of the neighbors out enjoying the mild April evening.

"Do you know how to get where you're going?"

Felix blushed. He knew that he was considered "a little slow"—he had difficulty comprehending what he read and math just made him confused. He had been held back in the sixth and eighth grades, and despite being nineteen years old he had just graduated high school. If there was too much going on, his brain seemed to shut down. Sometimes he'd come out of it and not remember where he'd been or what he'd done, but such episodes embarrassed him and he didn't like to talk about it.

However, he could remember word-for-word anything he'd heard, so now his mother pulled out a piece of paper. "I got this off the Internet last night at work," she said. "Catch the Four train to Grand Central Terminal and then the Seven to Times Square. Walk south on Seventh Avenue and then west on

Thirty-eighth Street until you get to the Hip-Hop Nightclub. If you have any trouble, ask a policeman."

"Okay, Mom, I got it," Felix said, and kissed her on the cheek.

Amelia bit her lip and looked like she might cry again. "Are you sure? I don't like you going out so late at night. And how are you going to get home?"

"I'm fine. Alejandro said he'd give me a ride back," Felix responded, anxious to get going. She pulled a twenty-dollar bill from her purse and stuffed it in his front pants pocket over his protests. "Take it and have a good time. It's not often I can keep anything from your father. Buy yourself a soda and maybe something to eat."

"Thanks, Mom, I love you," he said.

"And I love you, *hijo*," she replied. "I always will, no matter what."

Felix walked across Mullayly Park to the subway station at 167th and River Avenue and caught the 4 train into Manhattan. Repeating his mother's instructions over and over to himself, he found his way to the nightclub, a former warehouse on West Thirty-eighth Street. He was pleased that he didn't have to ask for help and made only one wrong turn—heading east on Thirty-eighth until he realized he was going the wrong direction. He was not so happy that there was already a line of people waiting outside the door to get in, but he took his place.

He didn't have to wait long, however, before a limousine

pulled up to the curb and Alejandro Garcia stepped out. The crowd cheered the appearance of the big-time recording artist.

Then Garcia spotted Felix. "My man," the rapper said, which was followed by an embrace, "what you doing standing in this line? You're a performer, homes, come with me."

Garcia started to lead Felix to the front door but he pulled up short when he got a look at the right side of his friend's face. "Who gave you that bruise?" he said with a scowl.

Felix shrugged. "No one. I ran into a door."

"Don't lie to me, Felix," Garcia growled. "Was it your old man again?"

"It was an accident," Felix said with a sigh.

"Accident my ass," Garcia spat. "That fucker needs a lesson."

Felix looked up in fear. "Please don't," he begged. "It'll just make it worse later."

Garcia studied Felix for a moment and then nodded. "Okay, homes, let's forget about it for tonight. You ready for your big coming-out party?"

Felix smiled shyly. "I've been practicing a lot."

"Good," Garcia replied as he nodded to the bouncer at the front door who let them in. "Just try not to show me up tonight. Now, let's see what's shakin' in the VIP room."

The night went even better than Felix could have hoped. He performed raps by Common and Ol' Dirty Bastard to the delight of the crowd. However, the highlight was when Alejandro Garcia bounced onto the stage and talked him into doing a duet with his latest hit, "Spanish Harlem Sistas." As the crowd shouted encouragement, they traded verses, and although Felix had only heard the rap twice, he didn't miss a word or mess up the beat. But it was his perfect imitation of his friend's delivery that made the spectators go wild.

Flush with the praise of the crowd and his friend, Felix got the nerve to talk to Maria Elena, who was working the coat-room that night. She was short with long dark hair and full red lips, and he thought she was the most beautiful girl in the club. But she had just congratulated him on his performance when a large black man inserted himself between the two with his back to the girl and his angry face scowling down at Felix.

"What the fuck do you think you're doing?" the man demanded.

"I . . . I . . . was talking to Maria Elena," Felix said.

"I seen that. You hittin' on my woman?"

"No," Felix replied, beginning to wish he was anywhere else. "I . . . I . . . I was just talking to her."

"Bullshit, you was cozying up, real smooth," the man said accusatorily. "You're trying to get in her pants, aren't you?"

"I . . . I . . . I . . ."

"'I . . . I . . .' nothin', motherfucker, you're trying to hook up with my woman, ain't that right?"

Frightened and under pressure, Felix did what he always did. He agreed. "Yes. I was trying to hook up with Maria Elena."

"Why, Felix . . . ," Maria started to say with a smile.

But the black man's eyes widened and his lip curled up in a sneer. He shoved Felix backward. "Why, you little . . ."

Whatever he was going to say was cut off when someone grabbed his arm and spun him around. That someone was Alejandro Garcia, who, although six inches shorter than the other man and forty pounds lighter, looked like he was going to go for the bigger man's throat.

"You got a problem?" Garcia snarled, his eyes fierce.

"Yeah, this joker was messin' with my girlfriend," the man said, trying to sound tough, but his voice was guarded.

Garcia looked at Maria Elena. "Was Felix bothering you?"

Maria Elena shook her head. "No, we was just talking."

The rapper turned to the other man. "They were talking," he repeated. "No law against that. Now get the fuck out of here."

"Why should I?" The black man was looking around for support without seeing any.

"Two reasons, *pendejo*," Garcia said, moving forward until he was only a few inches from the other man. "One, you pushed and insulted my friend for no reason. Two, if you don't, I'm going to kick your ass up around your ears. *Comprende?*"

The black man scowled down at his smaller opponent but made no move. "Fuck this place anyway," he said. "Come on, Maria, we're leaving. You don't need this job."

"Screw that," she replied, shaking her head. "I ain't quittin' nothing but you, Perry. I'm tired of the macho bullshit."

Alejandro cocked his head and smiled a most unfriendly smile. "Guess you heard the lady; now get your ass out of here."

"Yeah," Felix added. "Guh . . . guh . . . get your ass out of here."

Garcia and Maria both looked at Felix in surprise. Then they both laughed as Perry turned and pushed his way out the front door.

"Watch out, Maria," Garcia said. "I think Felix is going gangsta on us."

"I don't know," Maria replied with a wink at Felix, who was blushing, grinning, and shifting back and forth from one foot to the other. "I like the new Felix. He's kind of sexy."

Garcia looked at his friend and was going to add to the teasing. But Felix had already spun on his heel and was racing for the men's restroom.

5

"I think we need to say something to Dad."

"Yeah, right, he'll go ballistic, heads will roll, and then everybody on the team, including the coach, will hate us. *You* don't have to worry about it because you're riding the pine anyway, but I'm a starter and I'll never get to play again."

"I got to play in the last game," Giancarlo said to his twin, Isaac, who was scowling at him from across the room they shared as they sat on their beds.

"We were ahead twelve-nothing in the bottom of the eighth," Isaac replied. Bigger, stronger, and faster than Giancarlo, "Zak" hated it when his deep-thinking sibling tweaked his conscience, which just made him get his back up and lash out. "Coach Newell felt sorry for you. And *I* was pitching a no-hitter. . . . But the point is that if we say something, it's all going to come crashing down—the team, our run at a state title, my stellar freshman year as the number two pitcher. My whole life will be ruined."

"You're being overly dramatic; your 'whole life' wouldn't be ruined," Giancarlo said, scoffing. "It's not like you're going to make the pros anyway."

"I might," Zak argued, "but not if I don't play every year just because some kid is getting a little shit from some of the guys. Most of us have been together as a team since elementary school. He's a new guy, and he doesn't fit in very well. They'll get tired of it. Just wait."

"They're making his life miserable because he's from Mexico," Giancarlo shot back. "And because he can play. You've seen him, he's good. He'd make a better shortstop than Max Weller, and Max knows it. But Max is Coach Newell's little pet, so Coach sits Esteban on the bench and then looks the other way while the team bullies the poor guy, trying to get him to quit."

"Not everybody," Zak replied sullenly. "I don't do nothing to him—"

"You mean 'I don't do anything to him.'" His twin was genuinely bighearted and fair, but Giancarlo knew that he sometimes needed a little prodding when wrestling with the devil of self-interest.

"Whatever, Miss Molly," Zak retorted. "But as I was saying, I don't do nothin' to him and neither do you. Lots of guys on the team aren't bothering him."

"But enough are, and the thing is, none of the rest of us are saying anything about it. I feel guilty, but I don't know what to do. I don't want to screw up your dreams, and if I say something on my own, everybody will deny it and I'll just end up sitting with Esteban on the end of the bench—and probably getting the shit kicked out of me by Max and his sycophants."

"Well, thanks," Zak said grudgingly. "And I wouldn't let Max and these sick whatever-they-ares kick the shit out of you. They'd have to go through me first, and that ain't going to happen. I'm already taller than Max and I weigh almost as much."

"Nice to know you got my back," Giancarlo said, "but not even Super Zak can take on six other guys at the same time. So I hope it doesn't come to that . . . I'd hate to see you get the shit kicked out of you to save this pretty face. But the point is, what do we do about the guys bullying Esteban? It's not just words anymore. Max tripped him as he was going down the stairs to the field on Friday. And Chris Worley threw that beanball at him the other day in batting practice on purpose. He's going to get hurt."

"Then maybe he should quit the team," Zak said, lying back so he wouldn't have to look at his twin. He stared instead at a poster on the ceiling of legendary Yankee pitcher Whitey Ford. "Or maybe he should transfer to another high school where he'd be more accepted."

"You mean a low-income, Spanish-speaking, public school," Giancarlo retorted, shaking his head. "Jesus, Zak, you're starting to sound like Coach Newell, who's just a racist with a whistle and a clipboard."

"We have black guys on the team," Zak said.

"Because they come from wealthy families with a lot of pull at the school," Giancarlo retorted, "and we wouldn't be vying for the state private school title without them. And they're outfielders and not a threat to Max. But Esteban's a scholarship student from Brooklyn, takes the train into the city every day just to attend Hudson; nobody's going to stick up for him."

"Look, I don't like it either, but it's not my job to protect him," Zak said.

"Then whose job is it?"

Zak's response was cut short by a knock on the door, which opened to reveal their father.

"Hey, boys," Karp said to his sons, "lights out pretty soon. Moishe's coming over tomorrow to talk to you about your project and I want you bright eyed and bushy tailed. Are you guys ready?"

Karp paused. His father sense detected the charged field of tension between his sons. That in itself was nothing new. The boys were identical twins mostly in name only. They shared some physical traits, such as the dark, wavy hair; beautiful, doelike brown eyes; and general Mediterranean facial features of their mother's Italian heritage. And since they were already more than six feet tall in their freshman year of high school, it looked like they might attain their father's height. But even the physical similarities went only so far. With his finer features, porcelain skin, and slighter build, Giancarlo was like a more polished version of his more masculine and athletic brother, Isaac.

However, it was their personalities that differentiated the twins and frequently put them at odds. Both were smart, though Giancarlo was more bookish, a better student, articulate, philosophical, and more likely to use his head rather than his physical assets to get himself out of a situation. He was an accomplished musician who played nearly a dozen instruments, including the banjo and accordion.

Brave, forceful, and extroverted, Zak, on the other hand, was always full steam ahead, preferring to go through obstacles rather than around or over them—or not deal with them at all if he could avoid it. He kept his grades up only through the valiant efforts of his mother, who cracked the whip, but all he really wanted to do was play sports.

Looking at them now, one lying on his back and obviously avoiding eye contact, and the other furrowing his brow as he stared at his twin, Karp felt blessed. They were both good boys and generally made good decisions, though Zak's impetuous-ness and sense of adventure sometimes led him and his brother, who was usually along to keep an eye on Zak, into trouble.

"Everything okay?" he asked. Both boys mumbled an affir-mative.

Karp followed Zak's gaze to the poster on the ceiling and smiled. *Whitey Ford,* he thought, *the Chairman of the Board. Yankee legend, ace pitcher in the fifties and sixties.*

As a lifelong Yankee fan, he knew everything there was to know about the wily southpaw. Born October 21, 1928, in New York City. Height, five-ten; weight, 180. Lifetime record: 236-106; .690 winning percentage, best of any twentieth-century pitcher. Received the 1961 Cy Young Award and still holds many World Series records, including ten wins, thirty-three consecutive scoreless innings, and ninety-four strikeouts.

"Elected to the Baseball Hall of Fame in 1974, same year they retired his jersey," Karp said. "I was at the game . . ."

"We know, Dad," Zak said.

"We've heard the story," Giancarlo told him.

"Hey, when do we get to go to a game?" Zak asked.

Karp recognized the attempt to steer the conversation away from whatever the twins were debating. Zak was anything but subtle. But it did remind him that one of the things he'd promised himself after the Jabbar trial was that he was going to spend more time with the boys. He'd even had to miss a few of their baseball games, which galled him. And it had been a long time since they'd played hoops together or just threw a ball around in Central Park. As Marlene kept saying, it wasn't going to be too much longer before they were out of the house.

"Let's compare calendars tomorrow and pick a day," he said. "I'll spring for the tickets, but you're on your own for beer."

The twins smiled at their father's lame attempt at a joke; the promise of a family outing to the ballpark lightened the mood in the room. "Oh, and I'd suggest that you bring your digital recorder for Moishe's talk," Karp said. "This is oral history, and there's fewer and fewer people every year who can tell us the truth about what happened."

Zak sighed heavily. "Okay, okay," he muttered.

Karp smiled. He knew that this was not going to be his outdoors-loving sons' idea of how best to spend a Sunday afternoon. "You chose the topic and asked Moishe to help," he reminded them. "And this was the time that worked best for him. By the way, make sure you thank him or forget the ball game."

"We will," Giancarlo promised.

"Okay then, see you dudes in the morning."

"Nobody says 'dudes' anymore, *Dad.*"

"Good to know, dudes," he replied, and closed the door.

6

THE SKY WAS STARTING TO LIGHTEN IN THE EAST WHEN the young woman climbed the stairs out of the subway station at 167th and River Avenue. She'd just completed an eight-hour shift at the Old Night Diner in Manhattan and all she wanted was a hot shower and to crawl into bed. But with a groan she thought about the hours she'd first have to spend studying the schoolbooks she was lugging in the satchel over her shoulder.

It was Sunday morning and traffic was light on 167th as she started to walk west past Mullayly Park. She kept an eye on the shadowy environs of the park. The police had still not caught whoever murdered the woman she'd read about in the newspapers. The sidewalks were nearly deserted, too, and she was glad that it was getting light enough to see and be seen by the few pedestrians who were out and about. It made her feel safer.

Then out of her peripheral vision, she saw a man in a hooded sweatshirt. He had been walking in the same direction as she was on the other side of the street but was now crossing at an angle and speeding up to intercept her.

The woman, Marianne Tate, increased her pace. But so did the man. His face was shadowed by the hood, but he appeared to be a young Hispanic in need of a shave. She fought not to panic when he jogged the last few yards to catch up. "Your bag looks heavy," he said with a slight accent. "We are walking in same direction, let me help you."

"No, thank you," Marianne said firmly, as she'd been taught in the women's self-defense class she'd taken at the YMCA. He was to the side and slightly behind her, and she avoided looking directly at him and kept her eyes straight ahead.

When he started to hurry to get in front of her, she walked even faster. "Leave me alone!" she shouted, hoping someone would hear or that her voice would deter him.

Instead, he grabbed her from behind; she felt the blade of a knife against her throat. "Don't scream, *sooka,* or I'll cut your fucking head off," the man snarled. "Now you and I are going to get busy."

The man started to drag her into the park. But at that moment, a man walking a small dog came around the corner from River Avenue. He saw what was happening and shouted, which caused his dog to start yapping excitedly.

Tate's attacker hesitated and she felt the knife move away from her neck. Summoning her courage and recalling her martial arts instructor's admonition to fight back "with anything you have," she stomped on the man's instep and heard him cry out in pain. She then twisted slightly and threw an elbow behind her as she'd been trained, and was surprised when it made solid contact with the side of the man's face.

His grip loosened and she dropped to the ground, where she scrambled away on her hands and knees. She heard her attacker run off and started to cry as she looked up into the worried face of her rescuer, whose dog danced around barking.

"Are you all right, lady?" the man asked, helping her to her feet. "Shut up, Roscoe. Sorry about him, he gets a bit wound up."

"I think so," she said. "And that's okay, Roscoe was a big help. Thank you, thank you so much." She wobbled and pointed to a bench. "Maybe I should sit down for a minute."

"Yeah, yeah, you do that," the man said. He pulled out his cell phone. "Dialing nine-one-one. Maybe if the cops aren't snoozing in their patrol cars somewhere, they can still catch this creep. I couldn't see him very well myself. Did you get a good look at him?"

"Not really," Tate replied to the same question from the detective a half hour later, sitting at his desk in the detective squad room at the Forty-eighth Precinct house. "I mostly saw him out of the corner of my eye and he had the hood pulled up on his sweatshirt. I know he had black hair and might have been Hispanic, maybe Puerto Rican or Mexican, but not too dark skinned."

"About how tall?" Detective Phil Brock asked, his pen hovering above his notepad. He didn't hold out much hope that they'd catch the guy. Muggers were a dime a dozen, and for all he knew, this one was probably holed up in whatever rat's nest he called home or accosting tourists in Battery Park.

However, the brass was all over violent attacks on women because of the Atkins murder. There'd been insinuations from some media outlets that the NYPD, in particular the detectives working out of the Forty-eighth's detective squad, had messed up because the murder happened during the day and the killer had gotten away clean. The case had received a lot of press—particularly from one Ariadne Stupenagel, who'd been nosing around through unsolved murders in the five boroughs and was apparently using Atkins as her story's centerpiece.

Brock thought the attacks were unfair. Actually, violent crime had dropped significantly over the past two decades in the Forty-eighth, an area of the Bronx described as "economically disadvantaged" and filled with a lot of low-income residents.

Rapes tended to fluctuate year by year, averaging three to four dozen. But robberies, which had numbered a thousand or more per year in the early nineties, were now a third of that. There'd been 137 murders in 1990, which dropped to a couple dozen ten years later and had been holding steady at less than a dozen for the past couple of years, and detectives like Brock were beating the national average at making arrests.

Still, the press barked and the brass sat up and listened. They wanted the Atkins killer and they wanted him bad. "Before he kills somebody else," the captain in charge of the detective squad said. "Or life around here is really going to get miserable."

So Brock and the other detectives were putting a little more into anything that sounded like a possibility. And this guy had attacked Tate during the day, even if it was a little early; he also used a knife and wasn't just trying to rob her. The problem was Brock had no idea what he was looking for; no one had seen a suspect in the Atkins case.

Tate shrugged. "He was behind me, but I'd say a little taller than me, and I'm five-seven."

"What color was his sweatshirt?"

"Gray. A light gray."

"What about pants?"

"Jeans. I didn't really look at him. I was trying to keep my eyes to myself."

"I understand," Brock said. "But sometimes you never know what question will stimulate a memory. Was there anything unusual about him? A scar you might have noticed? Maybe a tattoo on one of his hands?"

Tate shook her head. "I didn't see anything like that. . . . He had bad breath."

Brock laughed. "Don't they all? Dental hygiene is not a priority with most of the bad guys I meet. What was his voice like? Gruff? High-pitched?"

"He had an accent."

"Any particular kind of accent? Hispanic?"

"Yeah." Tate thought about it for a moment then added, "I think so. Or maybe something else. I'm not sure."

"No problem, you're doing real good," Brock said. "So he grabs you and says something. What was it again?"

"He said that if I screamed he was going to cut my head off," Tate replied. "And he called me a name. Something like 'sucka'" or 'sooka.' Then he said we were going to 'get busy,' which I guess meant he was going to rape me."

"Then Mr. Tierney shows up and yells. You fight with the guy and you think you got him pretty good?"

Tate nodded and demonstrated how she'd struck her attacker with her elbow. "I know I hit him hard because I heard him give like a little grunt and he sort of let me go. That's when I got away."

Brock made a note and smiled. "Good for you. I hope you cracked his friggin' skull, pardon my French." He closed his notepad. "I think that's all the questions I have for now. I have your number, and we'll call if we need you."

The two stood up and shook hands. "So what happens now?" Tate asked.

"Well, I'm going to get an officer to drive you home," Brock said. "And while he's doing that, I'm going to have dispatch put out a BOLO—that stands for 'be on the lookout'—for someone who looks like your guy. Dark hair, dark eyes. Maybe Hispanic. Five-nine or so. Slight build. Wearing a light gray sweatshirt and jeans. Maybe we'll get lucky and one of the patrols will see him."

"I'm easy, easy, easy like Sunday morning. I can kick a stupid nervous joint when I'm yawning." Felix Acevedo practically skipped down Anderson Avenue on his way to Mullayly Park while reciting the lyrics to Common's "Take It EZ."

As far as he was concerned, the previous night at the Hip-Hop Nightclub couldn't have gone better. Even his run-in with Maria Elena's boyfriend—*former boyfriend,* he thought—had been a blessing in disguise after Alejandro Garcia stepped in and then the girl had said she thought he was sexy.

When she said that he'd panicked and taken off for the men's restroom. He sat in one of the stalls to pull himself together and considered whether she was hinting that he should ask her out. But where would he take her? He didn't have much money. Then he thought about asking her to go for a walk and he'd give her the ring. But after some more thought he'd decided to talk it over first with Alejandro.

"A diamond ring?" Garcia asked when Felix told him hours later. "Where'd you get it?"

"I bought it," Felix had replied, fishing it out of his wallet and handing it over to his friend.

"Bought it, huh?" Garcia said, holding it up so that he could read the inscription. "It says 'Always,' but someone filed another word off of it. Who'd you buy it from?"

"A guy I know from Mullayly Park," Felix replied. "His name is Al Guerrero. He's a friend and sold it to me for twenty-three dollars and sixteen cents. It used to say 'Always, Al.' But he broke up with his girlfriend and she gave it back. I filed the 'Al' off."

"Yeah, I see that, homes," Garcia said. "But you know it's probably hot, Felix. Stolen. You shouldn't be buying diamond rings from guys on the street."

Felix looked crestfallen. "I know," he said. "I just get tired of being teased because I don't have a girlfriend, and I thought maybe if I had a nice ring . . ."

Garcia put his arm around his shoulder. "It's okay. You didn't know. But next time, say no."

"I will, Alejandro," Felix replied, then he brightened. "Do you think I should give it to Maria Elena?"

Chuckling, Garcia shook his head. "No, I'd hold off on that for a bit. She just got out of a relationship, and it's too soon. Especially for diamond rings. Maybe ask her to a movie or something first if you want."

Felix considered the advice and then nodded. "You're right. It's too soon. I'll wait until after our date to give it to her."

Unfortunately, he never got the chance to ask Maria Elena out. He kept watching for the opportunity, but she seemed to have other people around her the rest of the night. And then Alejandro told him he was leaving and that if he wanted a ride home in the limousine, they had to go.

Wishing there were more of his neighbors out and about at two A.M. so they could have seen him, Felix had stepped out of the limo feeling important for one of the few times he could remember in his life. The back window came down and Alejandro poked his head out. "If your dad gives you any more shit," he said, "I want you to tell me. It's not right he beats up you and your mom. Someday, somebody's got to put a stop to it."

Alejandro drove off and Felix crept into the family apartment. He paused at the door and was happy to hear his father snoring on the couch. Once the old man passed out, the fire alarm in the hallway, even if it had been in working order, wouldn't have awakened him.

In the morning, Felix got up early, pulled his light-blue Georgetown Hoyas sweatshirt over the T-shirt he'd worn the night before, and left the apartment. He wanted to miss his father's foul mood when he woke up hungover. Standing on the sidewalk for a moment, he decided to head to the park even though none of his crowd would be there yet. It would give him time on a park bench to rehash his recent victories so that he could tell the others, whose faces he pictured turning green with envy.

Lost in his daydream, Felix didn't notice the police car that passed him going the other direction. The car slowed and then, with a sudden squealing of tires, pulled a U-turn to come alongside of him. He turned just as the officer on the passenger side jumped out with his hand on the butt of his gun. "Hold it right there, I want to talk to you!"

Felix panicked. If he got in trouble with the police, his dad would beat the hell out of him. He turned and started to run but tripped over a crack in the sidewalk and fell to the ground. His glasses skittered away.

A moment later, the officer was on top of him, wrenching his arms behind him. "You're under arrest, asshole," the officer snarled.

Screaming in pain, Felix at first couldn't think why the police officer was attacking him. Then he knew. "The ring! The ring is in my wallet," he cried out.

"What ring?" the officer demanded.

"The stolen ring! It's in my wallet!"

"Thanks for the tip," the officer said. "Now, pay attention, 'cause I'm going to read you your rights, and then my partner and I are going to haul your ass down to the Forty-eighth."

7

MARLENE JUMPED UP FROM THE COUCH WHERE SHE'D been talking to Lucy when the security-door buzzer went off. "Sorry, honey," she said, looking back down at her daughter, who was dabbing at tears, "I think this is the Sobelmans. Can we pick this up later?"

Lucy nodded. "Sure. It's not something we can do anything about on a Sunday morning. I'm just having a moment."

Marlene hesitated. The "moment" was actually a continuation of the discussion they'd been having since Lucy had shown up unexpectedly from Santa Fe a week earlier. Given her new occupation as a translator and sometimes field agent for a secret antiterrorism agency headed by former FBI special agent in charge and family friend Espey Jaxon, the unannounced comings and goings were not unusual. However, this time was different; it was personal.

When Lucy called from the airport to say that she was in

town and would be coming home, Marlene thought maybe it was to get help in sending out announcements and other wedding incidentals. Instead, she got home, waited until she was alone with her mom, and then said she was calling off the wedding.

At first, Marlene assumed that Lucy and her fiancé, Ned Blanchett, must have had an argument. Made sense; Lucy could be pretty hotheaded and Ned was a stubborn cowboy, and planning a wedding was stressful. *She'll blow off steam, he'll call to apologize, she'll put him through the wringer, and then she'll be on the next plane to New Mexico. Wedding's back on, only now there's even less time to get everything together.*

However, Marlene had misinterpreted Lucy's reasons. She wanted to marry Ned, but "not now." The world and their roles in it, she said, were just too crazy and dangerous to be thinking about marriage, settling down, and having kids.

Ned Blanchett was a former ranch foreman and skilled sharpshooter. He had been recruited onto Jaxon's team, and having never worked for a government agency before, he was an "unknown" in spy circles. And although Lucy wasn't allowed to tell her parents about their work, there were indications that some of it took them overseas into dangerous situations.

Apparently, from Lucy's hints, Ned was on such a mission now and she didn't know when he would be coming back.

Marlene had tried to console her. "Ned's pretty tough, baby. Ever since he got hooked up with this crazy family, he's come through time after time in some terrible situations. He can take care of himself."

"Until something happens he can't take care of," Lucy

retorted. "He's not Superman, Mom . . . he's not faster than a speeding bullet, more powerful than a locomotive, or able to leap over tall buildings in a single bound. He can be killed, and for that matter, so can I, though he's in harm's way more than I am."

Marlene didn't quite know how to answer that. And it was clear that her daughter wanted to talk, not debate.

Lucy went on. "But it's not just that. We're both dedicated to what we're doing with Espey. We're willing to take the risks because we think it's important for our country and the people we love. But the only reason I see to get married is to provide that stability for children. Ned and I don't need a ceremony or a piece of paper to know that we're each other's soul mates. But who can justify having kids these days? The world is crazy—lunatics trying to blow up subway cars filled with innocent people, including children; unstable fanatical governments racing to create nuclear weapons and thumbing their nose at the international community that says they can't; self-serving and myopic politicians who would rather see us all go down in flames than work together for the common good."

Lucy had gone on for quite a while, but then she'd clammed up and didn't want to talk about it. She just lay around the loft reading books, hanging out with her family, going for walks, and avoiding serious conversations. Several times, Marlene had caught her crying, only to have her say again that she didn't want to discuss the wedding or Ned. "Not now. I need to think."

However, she'd appeared to be ready to talk again as they sat on the couch waiting for the Sobelmans. But the moment passed with the buzzing from the security gate.

Marlene crossed to the door and looked up at the small security monitor. As expected, an elderly couple stood on the steps leading up from the sidewalk on Crosby Street and was smiling pleasantly at the camera. She pressed a button to unlock the gate and spoke into the intercom. "Moishe, Goldie, welcome! You remember we're on the fifth floor. We'll be waiting."

Butch had joined her at the door by the time the elevator across the hall opened to reveal the Sobelmans. They were a cute couple. Neither was much over five feet tall, though the man had a couple of inches on his wife. He had gray eyes and a full head of kinky gray hair that looked like steel wool with two large ears protruding from it; her curly hair was ginger colored and framed an elfin face with merry blue eyes. Although they were both in their eighties, they were still spry and stepped lightly out of the elevator to hug their hosts.

Moishe was holding a bag from their bakery on the corner of Third Avenue and Twenty-ninth Street, Il Buon Pane. "You need me to take that for you," Butch said, reaching for the bag. But Moishe pulled it away from his reach.

"Not so fast, my friend," he said. "I want to make sure this arrives in the kitchen safe and unmolested."

"Then come in, come in," Marlene said, laughing as her husband chuckled and beamed at their guests.

The Sobelmans entered the living room, where they met Lucy and were soon joined by the twins. As they all greeted one another, Moishe surrendered his jacket to Butch, but Goldie kept hers on. The women were going to a new impressionist exhibit at the Frick Museum on Fifth Avenue while "the men" talked.

As the women prepared to leave, Moishe's hands made the sign language symbols for "I love you" to his wife. Also a concentration camp survivor who had been "experimented on" by Nazi doctors, Goldie had not spoken for more than sixty years, although there was nothing physically wrong with her. She had said her first words in that time only recently, as the assassin Nadya Malovo prepared to shoot Moishe—part of her plan to exact revenge on Butch Karp. "Please, child," she'd begged Malovo, her voice hardly more than a whisper from the self-imposed silence. "If you must shoot, then I beg you, me first. I cannot stand to see him hurt."

Although Butch later told Marlene that the last thing he would have expected from Malovo was mercy, the assassin had not shot. In hot pursuit, U.S. Marshal Jen Capers entered the bakery at that moment with her nine-millimeter pointed at Malovo's head. Although Malovo considered taking out Capers and the Sobelmans in what might have resulted in death to all, she instead gave herself up. Capers, who had lost a partner to Malovo's treachery, then escorted Malovo to a federal lockup to await trial.

They had all wondered if having spoken once, Goldie would now continue. But she reverted back to silence and communicated through sign language, which was part of the reason Lucy was going on the excursion. A polyglot who spoke more than sixty languages fluently and parts of a couple dozen more, she was also a master of sign language.

I love you, too, Goldie signed back to Moishe. *Try to be good.*

I'll do my best, Moishe signed back with a smile as Lucy translated for the others.

✷ ✷ ✷

When the door closed behind the women, Karp turned to Moishe. "Why don't we set up around the kitchen table if that's okay with you? I think the boys want to record this."

Moishe nodded and held up the bag. "But first we celebrate life's pleasures."

The little old man winked at Karp, who laughed. He'd already caught the scent of Sobelman's specialty, cherry cheese coffee cake, which he deemed to be the best in the five boroughs, and that probably meant the rest of the civilized world, too. "I'll fetch the plates; boys, you get the forks," he said, rubbing his hands together. "And make it snappy, my stomach is doing handsprings."

It was a half hour later when the four pushed back from the table with contented sighs and full bellies. With reluctance all around, they turned to the darker issue at hand.

"So, I understand you want me to talk to you about the *Sonderkommandos*," Moishe said, looking from one twin to the other. The boys nodded. "I will warn you that this will not be an easy story to tell or to listen to; it may even give you nightmares. But I will tell you the truth because I believe every young Jew should hear it before his bar mitzvah."

The old man paused. "Tell me first, what is the significance of the bar mitzvah?"

"Isn't it the rite of passage for Jewish males from childhood?" Giancarlo said.

"And from that point on, we'll be considered men," Zak added.

Moishe smiled. "No ceremony creates a man from a boy," he

said. "A man is defined by his actions. But that is the definition most people would give. However, as your rabbi will undoubtedly tell you out at some point, a bar mitzvah marks the time when a Jewish male is morally responsible for his actions. And in a sense, perhaps, your definition is apt, as to be a man, one must be morally responsible."

Moishe took a sip of coffee. "Myself and my family and friends had just celebrated my bar mitzvah in our little town outside of Amsterdam, where my father was a baker, when our world changed forever. For many generations, we Jews were welcome in the Netherlands; indeed, Christian Dutch welcomed twenty-five thousand German Jews who fled their native land ahead of the coming storm in the late 1930s. We thought we were safe.

"Even when stories began circulating that Jews in Germany were being rounded up and shipped off to 'relocation camps,' as the Nazis so euphemistically called them, we still felt safe."

Moishe paused and pulled out his wallet, from which he took a small old black-and-white photograph. "This is me with my father, Abraham, my mother, Sarah, and my little sister, Rebecca. It was taken in 1943, shortly before the German occupiers announced that all Dutch Jews were to be relocated."

The photograph was passed around until it came back to Moishe, who looked at it longingly for a moment and then replaced it in his wallet. "And you know what the strangest part of all is? We didn't resist; we went along like so many sheep to the slaughter. People acted as if we were all going on vacation together. Families packed suitcases and dressed in their best traveling clothes. The vacation would last until the war was over, our parents told each other, and then we would all go home.

"We were sent to a camp near the Polish village and rail station for which it would be named. A quiet place in the country called Sobibor. It was isolated, surrounded by forests and swamps, lightly populated but strategically placed near the large Jewish populations in the Chelm and Lublin districts.

"Construction of the Sobibor camp had begun in March 1942, and it was a model of German efficiency. It existed on a large rectangle of land, four hundred by six hundred meters in size, that was cleared and surrounded by triple lines of barbed wire fence, three meters high and under the watchful shadows of strategically placed guard towers. Tree branches were intertwined in the fences so that the casual passerby wouldn't know what he or she was looking at.

"The camp itself was divided into three areas, each also surrounded by barbed wire fencing and more guard towers. The first was the administrative area closest to the railroad station, with a platform that could accommodate twenty freight cars at a time. It could have been a train station like any other in Europe," Sobelman recalled. "We were told it was merely a transit point and that we would be moving on shortly. Only they would not say where we were going.

"This area also included the living quarters for the guards, SS soldiers, and Ukrainians who were forced to work in concentration camps, though in truth, many of them enjoyed their work; after all, their people had a long history of murdering Jews.

"The first area was also where prisoners used as the camp's labor force were housed, including the *Sonderkommandos*, whom I'll return to in a moment," Moishe said before continuing. "The second area, called Camp Two, was where the new arrivals were marched to be separated from their belongings and each other. The young children went with the women."

Sobelman spoke quietly as he struggled to form the words. "That was the last time I saw my mother and sister. They and the others were taken to a building where they were forced to undress before going into a special hut to have their heads shaved so that the Germans could make use of their hair.

"Most of those who arrived on the train soon passed from Camp Two to Camp Three through a walkway two or three meters wide and surrounded on both sides by barbed wire. It, too, was covered with branches so that the prisoners could not see out or be seen by those outside. The Tube, as it was called, ran for 150 meters—that would be more than one and a half of your American football fields—toward a group of trees," the old man recalled.

"Behind the trees was a large, ugly brick building containing three rooms, each about twelve feet by twelve feet. Into these rooms naked, frightened Jews were driven—as many as a hundred and sixty people, sometimes more, at a time, all crammed together and unable to move as they listened to the sound of diesel engines starting outside and then smelled the exhaust being pumped into the rooms."

Sobelman looked at the boys. "I want you to close your eyes and imagine what I tell you," he said. "Now, imagine that you are in one of those rooms. You cannot sit down or hide. You cannot smell the carbon monoxide in the fumes, but you know it is there. So you and the others begin to panic. You fight and claw and climb over one another's naked bodies, looking for an escape. But there is none and you know that you are going to die, and all you can do is scream and pray."

Moishe closed his eyes. "Ach, I still can hear the voices of the Hasidic women shouting the Shema Yisrael as they were stripped and forced into the killing rooms. *Shema Yisrael adonai eloheinu adonai echad!*"

"Hear, O Israel, the Lord is our God, the Lord is One," Giancarlo translated softly.

"Yes, the Lord is our God," Moishe said with a slight smile. "But for reasons known only to Him, He did not stop the evil done to His people in those years."

Moishe was quiet again. His eyes remained closed as his voice wavered. "The women did not shout very long . . . not long at all. In fact, from the time most of us arrived at the rail station to those final moments in the gas chambers, it was only two or three hours. That's all it took to process and murder four or five hundred people at a time. . . . Men, women, children, they spared no one."

Moishe let the image linger before he went on. "For the Jews the guards had kept alive to work, there were many jobs around the camp. In general, these workers were treated better—even allowed to keep and use medicine they found on the poor souls chosen to die—and given more food. After all, they had to maintain their strength."

The old man cleared his throat. "But the very worst of the jobs was as a *Sonderkommando*, which means 'special unit' in German. And their primary responsibility was to dispose of the corpses from the gas chambers." The old man paused as he looked at the boys. "For a time, I was a *Sonderkommando*."

"How did you become a *Sonderkommando*?" Zak asked.

"I was with my father when we were forced to strip and then herded toward those gas chambers past the smirking SS guards and Ukrainians who laughed and hit us with sticks to make us keep moving," Moishe answered. "We had just about reached the building when a German officer, Hans Schultz, reached out and grabbed me by the arm. . . . I wanted to stay with my father and held on to his hand, but he pulled away and said, 'Do not forget.' And then he was gone into the building, and I never saw him again."

Moishe paused and dipped his head in sorrow as tears filled his eyes and began to stream down his cheeks. They sat in silence. "I apologize for the emotion," he said finally, "but it happens sometimes and leaves me unable to speak."

"Do you want to continue some other time?" Karp suggested.

"No, no, for heaven's sake, I'm okay now," the old man replied. "As I said, I never saw my father again. But I was spared not through some kindness, but because the Germans and their Ukrainian dogs did not want to do the dirty work. We worked in teams. Some cleaned out the killing rooms, the bodies so tightly packed that even when they were dead, there was no room to fall down. Rail tracks ran up to the back of the building; bodies were hauled out the rear doors and loaded on trolleys to be taken to pits, where other *Sonderkommandos* stacked them like cordwood for efficiency, then burned and buried them."

Sobelman sighed and it took a moment before he could continue. "But there were many jobs for the *Sonderkommandos*.

Some gathered the hair in the shaving hut and sorted it by color and quality—most going to stuff mattresses, though the best was used for wigs. My job was to remove gold fillings from the teeth of the corpses before they were placed on the trolleys for the burial pits."

Zak scowled. "Why did the *Sonderkommandos* go along with this?"

"Zak!" Giancarlo snapped. "That's rude."

"No, no, it's a legitimate question," Moishe responded. He turned to Zak. "The simple answer is that we had no choice. It was do as we were told or be killed, or commit suicide—and there were those who chose either of those last two options as well. However, the urge to survive is very powerful. Some because they fear death. But for others, such as myself, it was with the hope that someday I might exact revenge on my family's murderers, as well as carry out my father's wish that I not forget, which is why I think it is important to tell you boys my story. So that you never forget, either."

Even being a slave laborer was no guarantee of staying alive, Moishe said. "Because of our intimate knowledge of their mass murders the Nazis and their minions considered us *Geheimnis-trager*—the 'bearers of secrets.' The *Sonderkommandos* were kept apart from the others in the camp so that we could not tell them what we'd seen and experienced. They did not want some escapee or survivor to tell the world about their evil deeds. In fact, they were so worried that the *Sonderkommandos* were regularly gassed as well—their deaths being particularly cruel because they knew what was going to happen even sooner than the others."

"Why weren't you gassed?" Zak asked, shooting a quick glance at his brother.

Moishe shook his head sadly. "Ironically, I was spared because of my father's occupation. One day, a German officer named Johann Klier, who had owned his own bakery before the war and ran the camp's, sought me out. Other prisoners who had known my father had told Herr Klier that I was an experienced baker. So I went from pulling the teeth of corpses to baking bread."

As he passed a hand over his eyes, it took the others a moment to realize that he was weeping. But when Karp offered another cup of coffee "and a chance to catch your breath," he waved him off. "Forgive an old man his tears. No matter how many times I have told this story, the pain and grief are just as raw."

He turned back to the boys. "By the fall of 1943, more than two hundred and fifty thousand people had been murdered at Sobibor and the Germans were starting to worry that the war wasn't going so well and that word of their crimes would get out. They planned to wipe out all traces of the camp and every inmate in it. When word filtered to the *Sonderkommandos* that they were to be gassed in October, we rose up.

"On the morning of October 14, led by a man named Leon Feldhendler and a Red Army lieutenant named Alexander 'Sasha' Perchorsky, the *Sonderkommandos* and some of the other prisoners who joined in lured the SS guards in the camp to their deaths. We cut the electricity and telephone lines and broke into the camp armory. Then we began to fight the Ukrainian guards before escaping, though many of us died in the minefields surrounding the camp.

"There were six hundred of us in the camp that day," Moishe recalled. "About a hundred and fifty were killed by guards or the mines. Three hundred of us escaped. Within a week, one hundred of us had been recaptured or killed. Everyone who'd been left behind at the camp was murdered and buried. The Germans then bulldozed the camp and turned it into farmland, as if it had never existed."

Moishe's eyes glittered now with anger. "But those of us who escaped and survived did not forget. I eventually met and joined up with Jewish partisans who were fighting the Germans. The ember of revenge burned deep in my chest, and I killed my enemies with great pleasure."

The old man continued. "One day I was leading a small company of men when they captured three German SS officers whose car had broken down. I recognized them from Sobibor, including the officer who had pulled me away from my father, Hans Schultz. When I forced them to their knees on the road, Schultz started crying and begging for his life. 'I was only doing as I was told,' he cried. 'You cannot imagine the nightmares I endure. The sound of people screaming and begging for their lives. The little children crying. And that horrible wailing and the sound of them crawling over each other to try to escape when the gas began to enter the room.' That bastard looked at me like I would understand. 'You were there, Moishe,' he said. 'You remember how sometimes when you opened the doors to remove them, some of them would be missing fingernails and have just bloody stumps because they had been clawing at the walls and each other.' Terrible. Terrible."

"What did you do?" Zak asked.

The old man sighed. "I played the part of judge, jury, and, may God forgive me, lord high executioner. With my anger raging inside, I decided that the punishment must fit the crime. I remembered how these men had laughed as all those innocent people had cried out and struggled to stay alive. So I had my men strangle them with cords, starting with Schultz's subordinates. And while they kicked and dug at the cords with their fingernails, their faces turning purple and the blood vessels bursting in their eyes, I demanded that Schultz laugh."

"Did he?" Giancarlo asked quietly.

"Remember what I said about the will to survive?" Moishe said. "Yes, he laughed as though at a great joke. And then I threw the cord around his neck myself and cried—which I still do at the memory—as I choked the life out of him."

8

FELIX SAT AT A BARE TABLE IN A STARK ROOM OF WHITE-
washed walls and linoleum wondering when the police were
going to let him go home. He was by himself and there were no
sounds other than the nervous tapping of his foot.

Having lost his glasses when he fell, he could only squint
at the large mirror set against one of the walls. He'd watched
enough television cop shows to know that it was probably one-
way glass and that he was being watched by police detectives on
the other side.

Felix had already been at the precinct house for two hours.
They'd taken photographs of his face, and his fingerprints. But
mostly he'd been left to sit in the room. He wished they'd just
tell him what they wanted him to say so that he could say it and
leave.

The door clicked and then opened. A large man walked in
and stood for a moment studying him. He walked over and sat

in the chair across from Felix, who could then see well enough to note that he was an older man with a big, wrinkled face and icy blue eyes.

"I'm Detective Brock," the man said. "I understand that you've waived your right to have an attorney present?"

Felix hesitated for a moment. The police officer who arrested him had also asked him if he wanted an attorney. He remembered that the police on the television shows asked that a lot, too, so he figured it must be important. But he didn't know why. He did know, however, that attorneys cost money, and if his dad found out he was spending money on one, he'd get hit. He shook his head. "I don't want an attorney."

"And you're willing to talk to me?" Brock asked. "No one is forcing you to answer my questions."

Felix's natural inclination to please kicked in. "Sure. I'll answer your questions."

"Good. Thank you, that helps," the detective said. "Felix, can you tell me where you were earlier this morning, before the police officers arrested you?"

"Yes," Felix answered, glad to start with an easy one, "I was home."

"Was anybody else there?"

Felix cringed slightly at the memory of his father asleep on the couch. He didn't want the police to bother Eduardo. "No."

"What were you doing out so early on a Sunday morning?"

"I was going to Mullayly Park."

"Why?"

"To meet my friends."

"Felix, what would you say if I told you that you look like a man who attacked a young woman this morning near Mullayly Park?"

Felix furrowed his brow. "I didn't do it," he answered.

"Then why did you try to run away when the police officer stopped you?"

"I was afraid."

"Afraid of what? That you'd be arrested for attacking that young woman?"

"No," Felix answered.

"Then what were you afraid of, Felix?"

Felix thought back to the moment he decided to run and pictured his angry father coming at him with a raised fist. "That the policeman would find the stolen ring and tell my dad."

"The stolen ring," Brock replied, "the ring we found in your wallet? The ring you told Officer Givens was in your wallet?"

"Yes." Felix nodded eagerly.

"Where'd you get the ring? Did you steal it?"

Felix shook his head. "No. I bought it from Al at the park."

"You bought it from Al at the park," Brock repeated.

"Yes, from Al. He gave me a good price because we're friends."

"Then how do you know it was stolen?" the detective asked.

"My friend Alejandro told me it was."

"Alejandro told you the ring you bought from Al at the park was stolen?"

"Yes."

"I see, and that's why you ran from the police officer?"

"Yes."

Brock quickly changed the subject. "Where'd you get that shiner?"

"Shiner?"

"The black eye," Brock said, pointing to Felix's face. "Looks like someone belted you pretty good. Did the young woman this morning hit you with her elbow?"

Felix didn't know what to say. If he told the detective that his dad hit him and it got Eduardo in trouble, there'd be a beating later. "I ran into a door," he said.

"A door?" the detective scoffed. He stared at Felix until the young man began to squirm in his seat. "You know what? I think someone hit you. I think maybe it was that young woman. In fact, maybe that's what made you mad. Maybe that's why you tried to pull her into the park. Maybe you were going to cut her with your knife. Is that it, Felix, she pissed you off so you were going to rape her and cut her with a knife?"

Felix started to panic. Brock's tone had changed. Now the detective was saying that he had tried to cut a woman and rape her. But the detective was asking so many questions along with the accusations; Felix thought he better answer the questions that seemed the most important. "No. The young woman didn't hit me. I wasn't mad at her."

"She didn't hit you, so you weren't mad at her," Brock said. "Maybe you just wanted to rob her?"

This wasn't going well. The detective couldn't seem to understand him. "I didn't want to rob her."

"Rape her then? Did you want to rape her?"

"No, I didn't want to rape her."

"Then who hit you, Felix? That doesn't look like you ran into a door."

Felix's shoulders sagged. "My dad."

"Your dad hit you in the face?"

Felix nodded. "Yes. He thought I drank his beer."

"I see," the detective said in such a way that Felix knew he didn't believe him.

Brock appeared to be getting ready to ask him another question when there was a knock at the door. The detective walked over to the door, which opened to reveal a uniformed police officer. The two had a quick conversation and then the detective turned back to Felix.

"I'm going to ask you to go with Officer Krysnowski here," he said.

"Where am I going?" Felix replied, frightened. He'd hoped that the interruption meant he could now go home, but apparently they weren't through with him.

"We're just taking you to another room where there'll be some other men," Brock said. "You're going to stand in line and then do what Officer Krysnowski asks you to do. It's really very easy. You okay with that?"

Felix didn't think that sounded too bad, especially if it got him away from Brock. "Sure, okay," he said, standing. "Can I go home after that?"

The detective exchanged glances with the officer. "We'll see. I may have some more questions."

Felix sighed. "Okay, but if I don't get home soon, I'm going to be in trouble."

Officer Krysnowski led Felix from the room and put him in a line with four other men. They were then led into another room by the officer and told to stand along a wall and face another large mirror.

❋ ❋ ❋

On the other side of the one-way glass, Marianne Tate stood with Detective Brock, as well as another detective, Scott Mc-Cullough, and Jon Marks, the sergeant of the detective squad.

"Do you recognize any of these men as the one who attacked you this morning?" Brock asked.

Tate studied the men one by one. "I didn't get a real good look," she said. "He was across the street when I first saw him and after that it was mostly out of the corner of my eye."

"So none of these men look like your guy?" the sergeant asked.

Catching an irritated tone, Tate looked again. "Well, the guy on the end, number five, and number three look kind of like I remember. But I'm just not sure. Could you ask them to speak?"

The detective nodded. "Sure. Anything in particular?"

Tate's eyes grew angry. "Yes. I want them to say, 'Don't scream, *sooka*, or I'll cut your fucking head off.' And then, 'Now you and I are going to get busy.'"

Brock pushed the intercom button again. "Number five, I'd like you to repeat after me. 'Don't scream, *sooka*, or I'll cut your fucking head off. Now you and I are going to get busy.'"

Number five, another detective in the Four-Eight detective squad who was working undercover, said, "Don't scream or I'm going to cut your fucking head off. . . . Uh, now let's get busy."

"That wasn't quite right," Tate said.

"You want him to repeat it again?" Brock asked.

Tate bit her lip and shook her head. "Ask the other guy first."

The detective pressed the button. "Number three, repeat

after me, 'Don't scream, *sooka,* or I'll cut your fucking head off. Now you and I are going to get busy.'"

"Don't scream, *sooka,* or I'll cut your fucking head off," Felix said awkwardly, "now you and I are going to get busy."

"That's him," Tate declared. "He said it perfectly. And now that I've seen him a little longer, I think he looks more like the guy."

"You're sure?" Brock asked.

Tate nodded. "Yes, I'm sure."

"Thank you, Ms. Tate," Marks said. "You've really done well. Can I ask you to step outside for a moment while I talk to my detectives?"

Tate glanced one last time at the lineup. A look of concern passed over her face, but she answered, "Of course," and left the room.

"What do you think?" Brock asked.

The sergeant pursed his lips and then shook his head. "I think it's pretty good," he said. "It's a positive ID, but a defense attorney is going to make hay with her hesitation. I sure would like a confession just to nail it down. And if he's good for the Atkins murder, we're going to need him to talk."

Brock looked back at the lineup. The men were being led out of the room; Felix was filing out with a smile on his face. "I don't know if he's good for Atkins," he said.

"Why not?" Marks said with a shrug. "This assault on Tate would match up pretty well—sudden blitz attack on a young woman, using a knife, during daylight hours."

"You're right there, Jon," Brock agreed. "But the guy who did Atkins . . . he was a pretty smooth operator. He gets into the apartment with no sign of a break-in, murders Atkins, cleans himself up, and then leaves—all without anybody noticing him or hearing anything. But our boy Felix here, he's sort of bumbling and not exactly the sharpest tool in the shed. Hell, he's half-blind."

"Maybe he was wearing glasses," the sergeant replied. "And despite what they try to portray on TV and movies, not all killers are masterminds. Sometimes they're just fucking animals; clever animals, maybe, and they only get away with it for so long before they mess up. Like your boy Felix did this morning. I'm not saying he's good for the Atkins murder, but let's not assume he isn't. I tell you right now, I'd love to get the captain off my back on this one. Anyway, let's get a confession out of him for Tate and use that for leverage; maybe it will get him to spill his guts."

Felix was escorted back to the interview room and told to sit down. As he waited, he fidgeted and tried not to look at the mirror. He could feel eyes on him, like he was being watched from the bushes by some unseen predator.

When the door suddenly clicked and Detective Brock walked back in with another man, Felix about jumped out of his seat. He looked nervously at Brock and then at the other detective, who appeared to be younger, though he couldn't make out his features very well due to his poor eyesight. The second detective introduced himself as Scott McCullough, but he moved around to stand behind Felix, who couldn't see him without turning.

"Felix, we know that you attacked that young woman this morning," Brock said matter-of-factly.

"No! That's not true," Felix whimpered. Frightened, he started to stand up. "I want to go home now."

"*Sit down!*" the detective behind him, McCullough, thundered. "You were just positively identified as the attacker. She even says you sound like him."

"She's wrong," Felix said, trying to turn to where he could see the detective, who kept moving to stay just out of his sight. "I was just walking to the park to tell my friends about my new girlfriend."

Brock slammed his fist on the table, making Felix jump and spin back around to face him. "Goddamn it, Felix, quit fucking lying to me. You're just going to make it harder on yourself."

"If I tell you I did it, will you let me go home?" Felix cried.

"Just tell us the goddamn truth!" McCullough barked.

"You'll feel better for it, Felix," Brock told him.

Breathing hard, his eyes bugging, Felix thought about what Brock said. He hated it when people were mad at him. He would feel better when these detectives stopped yelling at him. "Okay, I did it," he cried out. "I attacked her. Now can I go?"

Brock looked over Felix's shoulder at McCullough. He then looked back at Felix and smiled. "You did a good thing, Felix, to get that off your chest, but I have a few more questions I need you to answer. To start, I need you to tell me how you attacked her."

Felix thought hard about what he'd been told. Someone had said something about a knife. "With a knife?"

"You tell me, was it with a knife?" Brock asked.

Felix read the intonation of the detective's voice and nodded. "Yes, it was with a knife."

"How did you get that bruise on your face?"

Again Felix recalled Brock asking him if the woman had struck him with her elbow. "She hit me with her elbow."

Brock stood up. "When she hit you, was she standing in front of you facing you like this?" he asked, pantomiming the action. "Or were you standing behind her, with her back to you, and she hit you like this?" He then simulated her striking him with an elbow.

Felix couldn't remember anybody saying anything about this. "She was in front," he guessed.

Brock scowled. "Really? In front?"

Picking up on the detective's negative reaction, Felix changed his story. "No, I meant I was behind her. She hit me like you showed me the second time."

"That means she used her right elbow, like this," Brock said, demonstrating, "and caught you on the right side of your face?"

"Yes. That's right."

Brock frowned and made a note on his pad, which at first worried Felix. But then the detective smiled and seemed to relax. His voice was nicer when he asked, "Did you say something to her when you grabbed her from behind?"

Felix was happy that the detective seemed pleased. But he wasn't sure what was expected of him next. Then he remembered what he'd been asked to say in the other room. "I said, 'Don't scream, *sooka,* or I'll cut your fucking head off. Now you and I are going to get busy.'"

Brock furrowed his brow but then shrugged. "Just like in the other room."

"Yes."

"What does *'sooka'* mean? Is it Spanish? Or are you saying 'sucker'?"

Felix had no idea what it meant, but it wasn't Spanish. "Sucker."

"And is that something you like to say, like when you attacked the other woman?"

Felix frowned. "What other woman?"

Brock shrugged. "You know, Dolores Atkins, the woman you killed a couple of weeks ago?"

Felix blinked. How had the conversation turned from a woman he attacked this morning to one he had killed weeks ago? "I didn't kill a woman."

"Sure you did, Felix," Detective McCullough said, "and you 'got busy' with her."

The detectives traded off like a pair of tag-team wrestlers. "And then you took some of her things, like her wallet and money," Brock said. "Maybe that diamond ring we found in your wallet."

"You know," McCullough added, "we'll find out if you took that ring from her."

"I didn't! I bought it from Al," Felix said, first to Brock and then turning to McCullough.

"Felix, Felix," Brock said. "There is no Al, is there? I don't know where you got that ring, but I'm going to find out. This has got to be weighing on you, making you feel bad. All that blood. The smell. The screams, even though you had her mouth taped. Did you tell Dolores you were going to cut her fucking head off if she screamed?"

"I didn't say that," Felix replied, tears springing back into his eyes.

"What did you say then?" McCullough asked.

"I didn't say anything!"

"You killed her and raped her without saying anything?"

"Yes! I mean no," Felix said, and buried his face in his hands. "I didn't kill anybody."

Detective Brock suddenly stood up so quickly that he knocked his chair over backward with a loud crash. He towered above the cowering young suspect and pointed his big finger. "Felix, I thought we were done with the lying," he said. "You just admitted that you attacked and tried to rape a young woman this morning. You killed and raped Dolores Atkins, didn't you?"

For a moment Felix was sure that the detective was going to hit him. He just wanted the detective to back away and quit yelling. "Okay, I killed her," he whimpered. "I killed Dolores."

Brock leaned forward with his knuckles on the table. "Thank you, Felix," he said. "I'm sure that felt good to get that off your chest, too. So tell me, how did you kill her?"

"What?"

"How did you kill Dolores Atkins?" Brock asked as he picked up his chair and sat down again. "Did you use your hands? A gun? Some other sort of weapon?"

Felix hesitated. He thought it might be a trick question, the sort his dad would try to catch him in to justify a beating. But the only thing that made sense was the same answer as it had been for the other woman. "A knife? Was it a knife?"

Brock tapped his notepad with his pencil. "You have to tell me, Felix. I can't play games with you."

"Then yes, I killed her with a knife."

"Was it the same knife you used in the attack on the other woman this morning?"

Felix relaxed. This was much easier. He nodded. "Yes, the same one."

"Where's the knife, Felix? Did you hide it somewhere?"

Suddenly Felix had an idea. The walls of the interview room were closing in on him. If he could just get out of the precinct house, he'd be able to think more clearly. "I can take you there. I can show you."

Brock looked at his partner and stood up. "Then what are we waiting for?" he said.

9

AHMED KADYROV TWITCHED AND SCRATCHED AT HIS arms as he walked along Watson Avenue. He was badly in need of a fix and had come to the right place even if it was still early in the morning. The avenue, which cut through the notorious Soundview neighborhood, was the biggest open-air drug market in the Bronx.

However, he wasn't just going to buy whatever meth one of the losers on the street was offering out of his pants pockets, cut with God knew what shit. He was heading to the apartment of a dealer one step up from the streets who sold a better product, if you were willing to pay for it. And Kadyrov was willing and able.

He felt the left side of his face—the swelling had gone down overnight but it was still tender and he had a nasty purple bruise. He'd slipped up with that bitch over near Mullayly Park. Distracted by the guy with the dog and then getting the arch of his foot stomped, he hadn't seen the elbow coming and it had rattled him pretty good. Stunned and panicked, he'd been lucky to get away and catch a subway into Manhattan and over to Brooklyn while he gathered his wits.

It had taken the last of his meth, which he shot up in a stall of a public bathroom along the Coney Island boardwalk, to feel right again. *Wish I'd cut the bitch*, he thought. But the next woman, a pretty Hispanic girl who'd fallen for his offer to help her move a box into her Bedford-Stuyvesant apartment, had paid the price. She'd apparently just cashed a paycheck, too, because her purse had more than two hundred dollars in it.

Although his eagerness to "help" worked with the Hispanic girl, Kadyrov had been finding it more difficult to lure young women into letting him into their confidences and apartments. Thanks to the meth he was losing both his looks and his charm.

Since the previous July, when he'd taken the violence to a whole new level—*What was her name? Oh yeah, sweet Olivia*—his life had been going downhill. He'd been arrested for an aborted snatch-and-go robbery of a Jewish diamond merchant in the subway that ended when the man's two huge bodyguards caught him before he could get away. Along with a beating from the merchant's men, he'd spent six months in the Tombs.

It could have been worse. In his struggle with the body-guards, he'd managed to get rid of his switchblade by tossing it under the subway platform. Getting caught with it might have prompted some ambitious detective to try connecting him with two recent knife murders near Columbia University. But instead, he just copped a plea to two misdemeanors, petty larceny, and possession of stolen property, and got a half year in lockup.

Forced to go cold turkey in jail, once he got out he jumped back into the drug scene. Crank made him the king of the world. When he was powering along on methamphetamine, he could stay up for days, fantasizing about all the great things he would accomplish, making grandiose plans. His self-confidence and self-esteem—neither of which existed without meth— soared; he believed that men envied him and women wanted him, and in the early days, some of them did. He was a sex machine, and his mind worked at a thousand miles an hour, displaying what he considered to be a dazzling wit and impressive intelligence, especially compared to those around him.

Crank also seemed to give him almost superhuman strength and alertness. Without it, he was depressed and just wanted to sleep all the time. He didn't like what he saw in the mirror. Why in the hell would he want to give up meth?

When he got out in March, Kadyrov started shooting up again with a vengeance. However, the more he used, the more he needed, and the more he needed, the more he changed.

His formerly olive complexion turned sallow and his skin had a dry scaly look to it—he'd even taken to wearing a long-sleeved sweatshirt to cover the scabs from his constant scratching. He was having problems with his gums bleeding and had lost a bottom front tooth when it just fell out one morning. And his hair, which he'd once taken such pride in, was thinning and had lost its luster.

Kadyrov considered his large brown eyes one of his chief physical assets. Only now, bloodshot and yellowed by jaundice, they burned with a sort of crazed intensity—at least when he was high—and constantly darted around, as if he expected an attack from any side.

The more significant changes, however, had been psychological, although he failed to recognize them. Speed still made him feel like he was on top of the world, but he was also more irritable and aggressive. Paranoia was a way of life. The mere sight of a cop car made him jumpy, and he suspected everyone of plotting against him. Thus he stayed increasingly to himself, except when preying on others or buying drugs.

As his physical appearance deteriorated so did the pride he once took in how he dressed, even if it had been for the purpose of luring his victims. He'd returned to his basement apartment in the South Bronx from jail only to find that his landlord had tossed all of his belongings out on the sidewalk and rented the room to someone else. That left him with the clothes he walked out of jail wearing, plus the tattered gray hooded sweatshirt he'd dug out of a Dumpster.

He lived most of the time on the streets or in various homeless shelters, so his bathing was infrequent, too. But Kadyrov didn't care. He desired two things in life—crank and sexual killing, each having become an addiction. Only torturing and murdering young women gave him the same sort of high he got from speed; indeed, each seemed to enhance the pleasure of the other.

The craving for both had increased while he was in jail. He'd only been out for two weeks when shortly after shooting up one afternoon, he spotted Dolores Atkins as she was entering the tenement off Anderson Avenue. He'd quickly made up his mind and bounded up the steps in time to catch the security gate before it closed and enter behind her. She was a little older than he'd thought at first glance but was a brunette and a close enough resemblance to his whore mother.

Dolores was clearly uncomfortable when he got on the elevator after her. And she avoided eye contact when he offered "please, to help" her with one of her bags. "No, thank you," she'd said tersely.

In the past, if his efforts to charm the women into gaining access to their apartments didn't work, he'd have moved on to a more cooperative victim. But there was something about this woman, maybe the way she summarily rejected his offer to help, that really made him angry.

He suddenly grabbed her by the throat with one hand as he held the blade of his knife to her neck with the other. Lack of proper nutrition, and a lack of interest in food when on meth, had caused him to lose weight from his already thin physique. But like many fellow users, he'd developed a sort of hard, rope-like musculature that could be astonishingly strong when he was high. He told her that they were now going to her apartment, where they were going to get busy. And if she screamed, he'd cut her fucking head off.

What he'd actually done was worse. "Slaughtered" was the word that reporter Ariadne Stupenagel had used, quoting her unnamed police sources. He liked the press coverage in all its macabre detail—it gave his "work" a sort of religious quality. The killing certainly released a lot of anger, so that after it was over, he was able to calmly clean himself up and then slip out of the apartment with no one the wiser.

Still, forcing women to take him into their apartments as opposed to talking his way in was a change in the way he liked to do things, and it made him uncomfortable. He recognized that he was taking a greater risk of being discovered.

Then there was the woman at Mullayly Park, which was yet another change and even more risk. Attacking her had been a spur-of-the-moment decision. He'd been out wandering the streets, wondering how he was going to score more meth when the last of his supply—one more hit—was gone. He wasn't really even interested in raping or hurting her; the bushes in a park weren't his style, at least not yet. Robbery had been the motivation, and it almost backfired.

Fortunately, the little Hispanic girl over in Bed-Stuy had taken care of both of his needs. The bloodlust was sated and he had enough cash to stay high for a week.

Time to party, he thought as he reached the six-story public housing complex off Watson Avenue. The building was an ugly, unimaginative box built of dull red bricks, just one of many similar public housing complexes and tenements that dominated Soundview.

The security intercom and locking gate had long since been destroyed by vandals, so Kadyrov was able to just enter the building and make his way to the stairs leading to the third floor. He walked down the long dark hallway—most of the bulbs had been removed or never replaced—and put his hand in his pocket, clasping his new switchblade. For many years, the Bronx's notorious Soundview section had been dubbed "the murder capital of New York" by the media; more than half the population of seventy-five thousand residents lived below the poverty level, and crime was a way of life for many of them. The knife made him feel safer.

He walked to the apartment on the far end of the hallway and knocked on the door. *"Quien es?"* a gruff voice behind the door demanded. "Who's there?"

"The police, open up," Kadyrov said. He could feel the occupant looking at him through the peephole. "It's Ahmed. Who the fuck do you think it is? I know you're looking at me, you dumb fuck."

The sound of bolts sliding and chains being unhooked came from the other side of the door. The door opened and a tall white man with a large protruding forehead rimmed by long stringy gray hair peered out. He was wearing a stained long-underwear top and frayed boxer shorts from which his long bony legs protruded like those of an ostrich.

"Watch your mouth, asshole, or next time I won't open the door, and you can buy some of that rat poison they're selling on the sidewalk," the man growled. "You got cash? No money, no honey, son."

Kadyrov held up the wad of bills he'd taken from his victim in Bed-Stuy. "Here's your honey, muthafugga."

The dealer glanced at the cash and then nodded. He turned and led the way into the one-bedroom apartment. He was carrying a big .357 Magnum revolver, which he now laid on the counter that separated the tiny kitchen from the living room.

The apartment was a filthy mess that smelled of mold, urine, and rotting food. The stained and threadbare carpeting was littered with trash and dirty clothes that looked like they'd been jettisoned on the spot and left to rot by their former occupants.

Dirty dishes, glasses, and porn magazines seemed to cover every usable space, and cockroaches roamed freely in and out of various food containers. The only art on the walls was a torn black-light poster of Elvis Presley.

The room was only nominally lighter than the hallway. The sole illumination was provided by a small window that was so dirty it might as well have been a gauze curtain. A heavyset woman with long gray hair sat in a sagging orange chair near the window, reading a magazine. She wore an old blue bath-robe over men's pajama bottoms and didn't even bother to look up when he came in.

"Hi, Lydia," he said without expecting much of a response. He didn't like her, and she didn't like him. She looked over her magazine at him and grunted.

"What can I do you for?" the man asked as he sank down into a large overstuffed recliner that appeared to have been salvaged from some alley Dumpster.

Kadyrov noted the pump-action shotgun within easy reach of the chair. When it came to methamphetamines, whose users tended to be violent, dealers didn't trust their customers any more than strangers on the streets.

Vinnie and Lydia Cassino were two of the only whites still living in the Soundview neighborhood, which was mostly popu-lated by blacks, Puerto Ricans, and Dominicans. Most of the other whites had long since fled, but the Cassinos had been there since the 1970s and stubbornly refused to move—even when Vinnie went to prison in the 1980s and '90s. They were both tough and known to carry, and if necessary use, guns. That along with Vinnie's connection to a good cheap source of crank, which the smaller dealers below him could cut with strychnine to increase profits, meant no one bothered them much.

Kadyrov sat down on the couch next to Vinnie's chair and tossed his money on the coffee table in front of them. "Two hundred worth," he said. "I should get a good deal too for that much cash."

"Two hundred bucks is shit," Vinnie said. "I'll give you a deal when you're buying an ounce at a time, not a couple of grams. If you and me didn't go back a ways, I wouldn't sell to you at all."

By that he meant that he didn't trust Kadyrov, who might just rat him out to the police if Vinnie cut off his supply of clean meth. And as a two-time loser, if he got busted again, they might put him away for life.

"Cheap bastard," Kadyrov complained as he pulled out his drug "kit," containing a spoon, a small container of water, and a syringe, from the belly pocket of his sweatshirt. "Just give me my shit."

Vinnie Cassino leaned forward, scooped up the money, and counted it. Pocketing the cash, he opened a wooden box on the coffee table and pulled out two small plastic bags of white powder. "You know I don't like tweakers shooting up in my pad."

"Well, unless you want me doing it in the hallway in front of your door, you'll break your fucking rule," Kadyrov replied as he continued with his preparations. "I'm not going to make it any farther than that."

The dealer didn't say anything more as Kadyrov tied the surgical tubing around his upper arm, mixed some of the white powder with water in the spoon, filled the syringe, and plunged it into a protruding vein. Ten seconds later, the younger man shook his head and smiled. "Now, that's more like it."

With his customer happy, Vinnie asked, "Who hit you?"

"No one."

"Looks like you got in a fight and lost." The dealer chuckled. "One of your 'girlfriends' fight back?"

"None of your business."

Vinnie shrugged. "You're right. And neither is this." He tossed a section of newspaper that had been folded to display one article in particular on the table in front of Kadyrov. The headline jumped out in large bold type:

POLICE ARREST SUSPECT IN
BRUTAL BRONX SLAYING

Kadyrov picked up the newspaper. He'd dropped out of school in the eighth grade and he'd never been much of a reader, so it took him a minute to get through the story. When he did, he laughed. Some loser named Felix Acevedo had been arrested for the murder of Dolores Atkins and the attack on the young woman in Mullayly Park. Apparently, he'd even confessed to the crimes. According to the story, the case was being reviewed by the Bronx DAO but charges were expected soon.

Looks like this might be my lucky day, Kadyrov thought as he read further. Acevedo's mother told the reporter that her son couldn't have committed such terrible crimes.

Kadyrov shrugged and pushed the newspaper back at his host. Oddly, he was mildly irritated that this Felix Acevedo punk was taking the credit for his work. With meth cruising through his brain, he was feeling all-powerful. Still, his paranoia cautioned him to be careful around Cassino. "So what's this shit to me?" he sneered.

"I guess that lets you off the hook for the Bronx deal," Vinnie said with a shrug. When Kadyrov didn't reply, he added, "I guessed that might be you. Maybe he'll confess to those two bitches in Manhattan, too, and you'll really be in the clear."

"I don't know what you're talking about," Kadyrov replied, though they both knew that he did.

Back in July, Kadyrov had gone to the Cassinos' apartment looking to buy, and at that time he had plenty of money, too. The dealer even remembered what his customer was wearing, because instead of one of his usual short-sleeve button-down shirts, he had on a blue, long-sleeved silk shirt that wasn't his style and was too big. "That's a nice shirt," he'd commented.

"Want it?" Kadyrov said, stripping down to his wife-beater undershirt.

Cassino figured that Kadyrov was changing his look more than being generous, but he liked the shirt and accepted the gift.

Kadyrov had also been wearing khaki pants, on which his wife noticed something. "What's on your pants?" she'd asked.

Kadyrov frowned and looked down. "What are you talking about?"

"There around the bottom of the cuffs, and some spots on your legs," Lydia said. "Looks like dried blood."

"You're crazy, it's just some dirt," Kadyrov answered, brushing at the stains before turning the subject to buying meth. He'd left soon after but not before using the bathroom and, the Cassinos noted, trying to spot-clean the stains from his trousers.

However, a couple days later when he'd returned for more drugs, another newspaper article had drawn his attention. He'd just shot up and was feeling confidence flow through his body when he noticed the main front-page headline of the news tabloid lying on the coffee table:

COLUMBIA U SLASHER STILL ON THE LOOSE

"That's me," he'd boasted, stabbing the paper with his finger.

Vinnie looked at the paper and then back at Kadyrov and scoffed. "Bullshit. You ain't got the stomach for that sort of work."

Insulted, Kadyrov had said more than he intended. "Screw you, I don't. I was just going to fuck her," he said. "Then rob her. But I'd tied her up and cut her clothes off when the older bitch showed up. She came at me like a fucking pit bull so I stuck her. But she kept coming, so I stuck her again, like four or five times. Finally, she goes down for good and just sort of lies there twitching and shit. That's when I remember the other bitch on the bed. I turn around and she's looking at me all bug-eyed and shit. She's crying and whimpering, and she won't shut up, even when I tell her I'm going to cut her fucking head off. But she just kept going. So I used her good and killed her, too."

Vinnie had looked at him with skepticism but his wife was

more convinced. "Jesus H. Christ, I think he means it, Vinnie!"

"Damn right," Kadyrov bragged. "And after that, I was cold as ice. My shirt was covered with blood, so I took it off and washed up. Then I got another one from the bitch's closet. That blue silk number I was wearing. Put my shirt in a bag and tossed it in a Dumpster in Harlem. Guess I didn't get all the blood off my pants."

"You're one sick puppy," Vinnie said to his customer.

"Just remember what I'm capable of," Kadyrov replied. He was starting to regret saying so much. "Some little bird calls the cops on your business here and you're going away forever. I go down, and you go down. Then ain't nobody going to be around to protect your old lady."

"Yeah, yeah, right, you don't remember telling us about those other women last July," Vinnie said. "You know, the one come at you like a pit bull so you had to stick her a few times. Then you fucked that other one and did her, too. You was bragging that you're the Columbia U Slasher."

"Fuck you. I never said nothing like that," Kadyrov retorted.

"Yes, you did," Lydia said, chiming in. "I was sitting right here. I also noticed those blood spots on your pants right after you done them gals."

"So you did that woman in the Bronx, too?" Vinnie asked. "Or is this guy telling the truth?"

"Whether I did or didn't, I think both of you should watch your fucking mouths," Kadyrov said threateningly, standing up. "And remember, snitches end up in ditches. Or maybe a little bird will start singing to the cops about what you do in this rat hole you call home."

Vinnie held up his hands. "Hold on, son," he said. "Ain't nobody snitching on nobody else. What you do on your own is your own business. And I don't stick my nose in another man's business, so long as he don't stick his nose in mine. Your money's good here, and that's all I care about. We cool?"

Kadyrov smiled. "Yeah, we're cool. Outlaws got to stick together, right?"

"Right, son," Vinnie replied. "And just to show you there's no hard feelings, how about another bump on me?"

"Now you're talking," Kadyrov said. "Care to join me?"

Vinnie smiled and picked up his own kit from the end table next to his chair. "Don't mind if I do."

Ten minutes later, Kadyrov was gone. He'd done so much meth he was practically bouncing off the walls and talking about "some big deals" he was going to put together. "Then I'll be buying ounces, and I better get a good deal or I'll take my biz somewhere else," he said, and left.

"That guy gives me the creeps, Vinnie," Lydia said after the door closed. "I don't care how much he was tweaking, what he did to those women was bad, real bad."

"It ain't our business, Mama," Vinnie replied. "If we started cutting the killers and creeps from our so-called clientele, we'd have no one to sell to anymore."

"Did you get that recorded?" Lydia asked.

Vinnie smiled and picked up the fake pack of cigarettes from the coffee table that held a small digital recorder. "Right here," he said.

After he saw the newspaper article about a suspect being arrested in the Atkins murder, he got an idea. He was pretty sure Kadyrov was the real killer, based on what he'd told them about the killings in Manhattan. He also knew that he'd be dropping by for drugs as soon as he could get the money together. "It wouldn't hurt," he'd told his wife, "to get a little something on him in case I ever need to pull an ace from my sleeve with the cops."

Vinnie pulled the recorder out of the cigarette case, pressed the rewind button for a second, and then played it back. "Whether I did or didn't, I think both of you should watch your fucking mouths. And remember, snitches end up in ditches. Or maybe a little bird will start singing to the cops about what you do in this rat hole you call home."

"It ain't much," Vinnie said. "Wish I'd thought of it the first time back in July."

"Well, he's by here every few days," Lydia said. "Maybe next time, you should get him really high—he'll get talkative again."

Vinnie winked at his wife. "That's what I'll do, Mama. We'll get his ass in a sling pronto."

10

ENTERING THE FORTY-EIGHTH PRECINCT HOUSE, DETEC-
tive Joey Graziani made a face as if he'd tasted something bad.
He hated working the Bronx, especially as his last assignment
had been at the Twenty-sixth Precinct on the Upper West Side
of Manhattan. Any NYPD detective worth his salt knew that
working any borough after Manhattan was a step down. Hell,
he'd have rather worked in Harlem than the Bronx.

Graziani knew he'd brought it on himself, though he thought
exile had been a bit extreme for his transgression. He considered himself to be a good cop—*Fuck that, a great cop,* he
thought—who had put his life on the line numerous times for
Gotham's taxpayers and his fellow officers. A lot of bad guys
were off the streets because of him. And he'd earned his detective's shield the hard way; he was the son of a Brooklyn butcher
with no "rabbi" to grease the skids to the high echelons of
NYPD officialdom.

He just got a little greedy, that's all. Working narcotics, it was common practice for the guys to "split the pot"—some drug dealer would get popped with $20,000 in ill-gotten gains, and maybe only $10,000 went on the official report and into the evidence locker. It was one of the few perks of a dangerous job— "hazard pay," so to speak.

Graziani's troubles arose when a coke dealer he busted turned out to be a midlevel operator the DEA had been watching for a year, hoping he'd lead them to "Mr. Big." Unfortunately for Graziani, the feds' snitch had just made a buy from the guy using bills whose serial numbers had been recorded. So when half of it went missing and was deposited instead in the bank account of Mrs. Graziani, his ass was in a sling.

The feds were pissed—not so much about the money (they had their own "hazard pay" system) but because of all the time they'd wasted with nothing to show for it. So they wanted Graziani's head. But the Patrolmen's Benevolent Association had stuck up for him and a compromise was reached. Instead of booting him off the force, they sent him to hell in the Bronx.

Graziani looked at the clock above the fat desk sergeant's dais. *Eleven.*

"Sleep in this morning, Graziani?" the sergeant said.

"Fuck you, McManus," Graziani said without stopping. Even if he hadn't been hungover, he would have been in a surly mood. He was ruggedly handsome with a perpetual tan, though the drinking was starting to sag his once-chiseled Italian features and the gray was a lot more prevalent than it had been a year earlier. But that didn't bother him as much as being forty-three years old with twenty years on the job and a career that had taken a giant step backward.

"Fuck you, too, Joey." McManus shrugged and went back to studying the racing form for the Meadowlands Racetrack. If Graziani wanted to be a prick, let him; he made no attempt to make friends with anyone at the Four-Eight, and the sergeant was more interested in the horses.

Graziani couldn't have cared less what McManus or anyone else thought of him and made no pretense that he was doing anything other than biding his time until he could get out of there. He didn't like the people of the Bronx; he didn't like his fellow officers. Everything was low-class to him and he'd been looking for a way back across the East River since the day he arrived. He figured it was going to take breaking a big case or maybe a commendation for heroism, but so far all he'd managed were a few minor-league drug busts.

As he got to his desk in the squad room, he noticed a small crowd, including some of the top brass, had gathered over in the corner of the large detective bureau room, where the guys in homicide sat. A lot of the attention was directed at Phil Brock, one of the older detectives. The mood seemed jovial, with a lot of back-slapping and handshakes, although, Graziani noted, Brock himself seemed more subdued.

"What's going on over there?" Graziani said to the young detective sitting at the desk across from his.

"You been on another planet this morning or something?" the younger man replied. He tossed the morning edition of the *Post* across the desks.

Graziani noted the headline:

POLICE ARREST SUSPECT IN
BRUTAL BRONX SLAYING

"This Brock's case?"

"It is now," the young detective, a red-haired freckled new-bie named O'Connor, said. "He caught a break on the Atkins murder—some asshole the guys in patrol picked up yesterday morning after he tried to jump some girl student in Mullayly Park. She made him at a lineup, then Brock stayed on him until he confessed to the assault and then spilled his guts about the Atkins murder."

Graziani felt his heart skip a beat and then quicken its pace. He had a theory about the Atkins case and the two Manhattan murders that had happened near Columbia University when he was still assigned to the Two-Six detective squad. He'd never shared his theory with anybody else, hoping against hope that if he kept his ear tuned to the drug world, he might be able to break both cases open. And that would mean a transfer back to Manhattan. The Atkins case appeared to be solved, but that still left Yancy and Jenkins.

He'd still been working Narcotics out of the Two-Six when the Columbia U Slasher struck that past July. After a couple of weeks with virtually no leads and the public, egged on by the press, clamoring for an arrest, the brass had put together a small task force comprised of the homicide detectives working the case as well as detectives from other squads.

Graziani had been sent over from narcotics because the

shrinks in the NYPD behavioral sciences unit thought there was a high probability that the killer was a junkie. Basically, they said there were two main reasons for their conclusion.

One, the perp robbed his victims but took only items that were easy to locate in purses or in plain sight on dresser tops, or took jewelry from the bodies. He was only after cash or items, like jewelry, that could be quickly converted into cash. But he'd missed a lot—including jewelry and money left in bedroom drawers—and avoided such items as laptop computers and cameras that a professional burglar would not have overlooked.

"But it wasn't like he was trying to get out of the apartment any too quickly," one of the homicide detectives working the case had commented. "He took his time raping and torturing his second victim, Olivia Yancy. And then he even washed up, stole a shirt—we're assuming he trashed the other due to bloodstains—and left like a ghost. This had more to do with rape and wanting to murder this woman than robbery or burglary. Getting a few bucks out of it to feed his habit was secondary."

Which brought the detective to the second reason the psychiatrists thought the guy was "either your run-of-the-mill psychopath" or "crazed on drugs—like meth . . . we all know how violent tweakers can get." And that was the level of violence.

"Not so much the older woman, Jenkins," the homicide detective said. "She appears to have surprised the killer after he subdued Yancy. We believe there was a struggle and he killed Jenkins in the course of that, but he didn't rape or maim her. But the younger woman, Yancy, was tied up, gagged, and defenseless. The shit this creep did to her after that went beyond murder. This was rage, plain and simple."

At that point, photographs from the crime scene had been distributed to the members of the task force. Even Graziani, who'd seen plenty of bloody rooms and bodies, was nauseated by the images. He agreed with the idea that the killer, if not simply a mad dog, was hopped up on methamphetamines. Any cop who knew the difference would rather take on five heroin addicts, who tended to be slow-witted and passive, than one speed freak. Meth addicts always seemed to be armed with guns and knives and were willing to use them. But it was the extreme nature of their violence that separated them from other violent criminals.

Up for days without sleep or food, paranoid and often delusional, meth users could be volatile, and when they went off, they tended to go berserk. It was as if they were releasing the demons of their drug-crazed and fevered minds. And because one of the effects of methamphetamines was to increase the amount of adrenaline in the bloodstream, they could be incredibly strong, quick, and hard to stop. The rule of thumb garnered from the streets was that when dealing with a speed freak carrying a knife, "shoot and don't stop shooting until the asshole isn't moving."

With the photographs fresh in their minds, the task force hit the streets. The guys in sex crimes questioned every deviant they could locate. Burglary checked out the pawnshops looking for the stolen jewelry and questioned the burglars they knew with a history of sexual assault. Graziani's main contributions had been to question the dealers and tweakers, especially the guys known for carrying knives. But everybody came up empty.

The psychiatrists had been convinced that the Columbia U Slasher would strike again. "This isn't the sort of rage that goes away," they said. "It may ebb after a killing, but it will build up again and have to be released. He may have been escalating to reach this point, and if so, he may continue escalating."

But months passed and there were no new murders that seemed to match this killer. The detectives assumed that either the psychiatrists were wrong and the Yancy-Jenkins murders were a one-time wrong-place, wrong-time incident, or that the killer had left the area, been killed himself, or was in jail for some other offense and wouldn't strike again until he got out. With nothing new to go on, the Twenty-sixth Precinct task force had been disbanded.

When Dolores Atkins was murdered nine months later, however, good fortune smiled on Graziani. He'd gone out for a beer with his only friend at the Forty-eighth, who happened to be the sergeant in charge of homicide, Jon Marks, a tall, good-natured cop with a receding hairline and a habit of snorting when he laughed. Actually, "friend" may have been a stretch. They'd been partners many years earlier while working uni-formed patrol. Graziani had actually saved Marks's life when he shot and killed a whacked-out biker intent on stomping Marks into the hereafter. So they occasionally went out for a few drinks though they didn't have much in common.

Over beers, Graziani had learned some of the facts about the Atkins case that weren't general knowledge to the public or even the rest of the detective squad. The brass had wanted to squelch loose lips from slipping information to the press, so it was supposed to be "need to know" only. But a third beer got Marks talking.

And as he talked, Graziani heard a familiar story. The killer got into the apartment with no sign of forced entry, and no one heard or saw anything. The victim had been gagged and bound faceup on her bed, and she'd been raped, possibly when she was dead or dying. She'd been robbed, but again only of easy-grab cash and jewelry. And the killer had used a very sharp knife and used it extensively.

"You don't even want to see the photographs of the crime scene," Marks said. "It was a bloodbath, and he took his time. Then when this guy got done, he washed up."

Graziani was convinced that Atkins's killer was the same lunatic who murdered Yancy and Jenkins. But he didn't say anything to Marks. Nor did he say anything over the weeks that passed, hoping the Manhattan homicide detectives back at the Two-Six wouldn't pick up on it either given that the brass at the Four-Eight kept such a tight lid on the details. He couldn't believe his luck that the Columbia U Slasher had reappeared in the precinct where he'd been exiled. If he could just figure out which tweaker liked to cut up women, Graziani would have his ticket punched back to Manhattan. *Maybe finally be promoted to detective first grade,* he thought.

Now apparently Brock had stumbled onto his suspect. *But that's only for the Atkins murder and this assault,* he thought. *I can still be the one who ties it to Yancy and Jenkins.*

Graziani stood up from his desk and worked his way over to where Brock was being congratulated. He spotted Marks and sidled up to him with a smile. "Hey, can I have a word with you, old buddy?"

"Can't it wait?" Marks replied. "We got the guy who did the Atkins murder. The captain and the assistant chief are here, and they're happy with the Forty-eighth detective squad right now."

"That's what I want to talk to you about," Graziani said quietly. "I think this could be even bigger than that."

"Okay, shoot, whaddaya got?"

Graziani shook his head. "Not here," he said. "Too many ears."

Marks looked back at the circle around Brock then nodded toward an empty office. "Give me a minute, and I'll meet you there."

When Marks entered the office, Graziani shut the door behind him. "You know I was part of the task force looking into that double homicide near Columbia last July," he said.

"Yeah, what about it?" Marks asked suspiciously. Although easygoing, he had a well-deserved reputation for not tolerating idiots, bigots, and fools. It was no secret that Graziani wanted back on Manhattan, preferably his old precinct.

"Well, ever since that night you and I went out for beers after the Atkins murder, I've been thinking that the same guy also did Yancy and Jenkins," he said. "Same MO—weapon, bloodbath, and cherry on top, the killer cleans up in the apartment after bloodlust."

"You think our perp is the guy?" Marks said doubtfully.

"I think there's a good chance," Graziani said. "I'd like to ask him a few questions before he's arraigned and gets a lawyer. Can we put the arraignment off until late this afternoon?"

"Yeah, shouldn't be a problem," Marks said.

"Do you know if a quickie indictment is in the offing?" Graziani asked.

"Not sure," Marks replied. "They had some assistant DA take a statement from him last night after Brock got him to confess. They have our reports; now it's up to them."

"Then I should do this quick," Graziani said.

The sergeant thought about it. "You know, I should probably call homicide at the Two-Six. It's their case."

Graziani felt his chance slipping away. "C'mon, buddy," he said. "I worked for the task force. I know the details of the case, stuff only the killer would know. You call the Two-Six and they'll take over the case. They're Manhattan and this is a double homicide. The Four-Eight probably won't even get credit for Atkins, not until they're done with him. The brass here won't be happy with that either."

Marks considered Graziani for a minute. He didn't believe that his old partner gave a lick about the Forty-eighth getting credit, but what he said was true. NYPD worked all five of the boroughs, but everybody knew that Manhattan got preference and everybody else was a red-haired stepchild.

"Okay," he said. "But I'm calling Brock into this with you. It's his guy. If you can make the case for Yancy and Jenkins, you'll both get credit for it."

Graziani laughed. "Hey, no problem. Not trying to hog the glory."

11

FELIX SAT DEJECTED AND ALONE WONDERING WHAT HE could say that would convince the police to let him go home. He glanced around. At least there wasn't a mirror in the room now that he was in the jail instead of the police station—just four stark walls. But there was still a camera mounted high in one corner aimed at the table where he'd been told to sit and wait.

When the door to the room swung open, he hoped to see his mother. She would probably scold him, but she'd let him know that it would be okay. Then they'd go home and she'd fix him something good to eat. He'd have even welcomed the glowering face of his dad, knowing he would receive a beating later, if they'd just let him leave.

After he took the detectives out to "find the knife," he thought they'd let him go. When he couldn't find it he figured they'd realize that he wasn't the man who attacked those women. It would be just like when he'd gotten in trouble for admitting to things he didn't do. But this time, they told him he was under arrest for murder.

Of course there was no knife, never had been. He'd just wanted out of that room, and the idea had come to him. He felt bad that he lied to the detectives. But once they were in the car—the detectives in front and he in the backseat wearing handcuffs—he thought he'd better continue to play along or they'd get mad.

Detective McCullough drove while Detective Brock sat in the passenger seat; they went to an alley near his home. They got out of the car and he made a show of looking under a Dumpster for the knife. The detectives had also got down on their hands and knees to help look.

"You sure this is where you left it, Felix?" Brock had asked when nothing was found. "Maybe this is the wrong alley? Or you left it somewhere else?"

Felix thought about it and agreed. He said that maybe he'd left it in Mullayly Park. But when it didn't turn up there, and the detectives were obviously getting angry, he claimed he couldn't remember where he put it. He hoped that they'd then let him go. But that's when they told him he was under arrest for murdering Dolores Atkins and put him in jail.

Of course, he had no idea who the woman was—though he now had everything he'd been told about her memorized. His ability to remember things was his "gift from God," his mother said, but now he wasn't so sure. He'd have rather not remembered some of the things they accused him of doing.

They reminded him that he could have a lawyer and that

he wouldn't have to pay for one. But he knew when someone didn't want him to do or say something—and although the detective had said he could have a lawyer, it was clear that Brock really didn't want him to have a lawyer. So he said no. And when the detective asked if he was still willing to talk to him, he politely agreed.

So they talked for a while longer before Brock said he needed to go to the jail. "Then they'll take you to court and probably appoint an attorney to represent you."

Although Brock had not let him go and had yelled at him some, Felix thought he was a nice man. When the detective took him over to the jail, he seemed like he even felt sorry for Felix, or like he had more questions but didn't know how to ask them.

As the detective turned to go, Felix asked if he would be allowed to go home in the morning. The detective furrowed his brow and looked at him for a long time without speaking. But then he shook his head. "I don't think so, Felix."

The horrible fact that he wouldn't get to go home in the morning either rattled around in Felix's head all night long as he lay terrified on his cell bunk. Jail was nothing like he'd seen on television. Here men screamed and yelled and cried and prayed all night long. There were sounds of struggle and sounds of sorrow.

Although alone in his cell, Felix had not been able to block out the sounds and had not slept. He'd gone to breakfast and then was allowed to return to his cell alone again, where he wondered what he could say to get himself out of trouble. Then he went to lunch, which actually wasn't bad, though a large man who sat down across the table kept making kissing gestures at him until the guard walked over. "You have visitors," the officer said as he escorted him to the interview room.

By "visitors," Felix hoped the guard meant his mother, so he was disappointed, though he tried not to show it, when Brock walked into the room accompanied by another man, who was younger and looked more like the detectives he saw on the television.

"Good morning, Felix," Brock said. "This is Detective Joey Graziani. He'd like to ask you a few questions, is that all right?"

Felix gave a worried smile. "Okay."

The new detective swung a chair around so that he could sit in it backward as he leaned toward Felix over the table. "Thank you," he said. He was smiling, but the way he looked at him reminded Felix of how a big alley cat looked at a rat just before he pounced. "But before I ask you my questions, I want to make sure that you understand your rights."

"I do," Felix said agreeably. "Detective Brock told me about them already. 'You have the right to remain silent. Anything you say can and will be used against you in a court of law. You have the right to an attorney. If you cannot afford an attorney, one will be appointed to you. Do you understand these rights as they have been read to you?' That's what you meant?"

Graziani glanced at Brock, who was looking at Felix with a frown, then shrugged. "Yeah, pretty much word for word. So?"

"So . . . what?" Felix asked, confused.

"So do you want an attorney present?"

Felix felt the detective tense when he asked the question.

"No?" he asked.

The detective smiled. Felix did, too. He'd guessed right.

"And you're willing to talk to me, is that correct?"

It almost wasn't even a question. "Sure," Felix answered. "I just want to go home. My parents will wonder where I am."

"Your parents have been told," Brock said, not unkindly.

"They have?" Felix cringed. "My dad's going to kill me." But then he brightened. "Is my mom here?"

"No, but maybe you can talk to her later," Graziani said. "Now I'd like to ask you a few questions. I know you already admitted that you killed Dolores Atkins, and I'm sure it was a big relief to get that off your chest."

It had been a big relief because it stopped the accusations and made Detective Brock happy. "Yes, I felt better," Felix replied.

"Oh, I'm sure," Graziani said. "Had to be a big relief to tell the truth. Keep that in mind when I ask you a few questions now, okay?"

"Okay," Felix echoed.

"Good, good. Do you remember what you were doing on One Hundred Fourteenth Street in Manhattan last July?" Graziani asked.

Felix scratched his head. "One Hundred Fourteenth?"

"Near Columbia University."

Looking over at Detective Brock, who'd remained standing and leaning against the door, Felix shook his head. "I don't understand."

"Just answer his questions, Felix," Brock said, but then looked away.

"Felix, over here," Graziani said, snapping his fingers in front of Felix's face. "I asked what you were doing on One Hundred Fourteenth Street near Columbia University last July."

"I don't think I was," Felix replied.

"Sure you were, Felix," the detective said, nodding his head. "I have a witness who says he saw you leaving the apartment building where Olivia Yancy lived."

"I wasn't in Olivia's apartment," Felix said.

"You're lying, Felix," Graziani said. "We showed a witness your mug shot; he's sure it was you he saw coming out of the apartment building. Don't bullshit me, Felix."

"Okay, I won't," Felix replied.

"You remember being in Olivia's apartment, right?"

Felix picked up on the detective's tone and nodded his head. "Yeah. I remember now. Olivia." This seemed to please the detective so much that he added to his story, "She's my girlfriend."

Graziani paused and tilted his head. "Your girlfriend?"

"Yes."

"So what? Were you guys having some sort of kinky sex and it got out of hand?" Graziani asked.

Felix, a virgin and worried he'd be asked about the act, replied, "No. We don't have sex."

"But you tied her up and put duct tape over her mouth?"

Felix glanced again at Brock, who was looking at the floor. "I guess."

"You guess?" Graziani said with a scowl. "Or you know?"

"I know."

"And you cut her clothes off with your knife," Graziani said.

Yet again, supplied with the answer, Felix agreed. "Yes."

"And what about Beth Jenkins?" Graziani asked, then when

Felix looked confused, he added, "The woman you stabbed when she came in on you and Olivia."

"I didn't stab her."

"Oh? Did someone else stab her? A partner?"

Felix shrugged. Somebody must have stabbed the woman. "I guess so."

"Who? Give me a name."

"I don't know," Felix replied.

Graziani looked hard at Felix and tapped his pencil on his notepad as if growing impatient. "That's because there wasn't anybody else, was there?"

"I guess not," Felix said, rubbing his eyes. He was tired and all these questions were giving him a bad headache. He had no idea why these police detectives kept thinking that he killed women, but he wished they'd figure out soon that he hadn't.

"So did you stab this woman, Olivia, who you had tied up on the bed?"

"No."

Graziani sighed. "Come on, Felix, remember what we said about how good it feels to tell the truth."

"Yes," Felix said.

"Then why won't you admit that you stabbed Beth Jenkins when she discovered you in the room with Olivia?"

Felix thought about it. The question seemed to imply that the problem wasn't so much that a woman had been stabbed but that he wouldn't admit to it. "Okay, I did it," he said.

"How did you stab her?"

"With a knife."

"Okay, but I mean, show me how you stabbed her. How many times?"

Felix made a slashing movement. "Twice."

Graziani frowned. "That's slashing, not stabbing, Felix. Now, think hard; how did you stab her?"

Felix made a poking motion and was rewarded with a nod from the detective.

"Okay, that's more like stabbing. How many times?"

"Twice" had not seemed to satisfy the detective, so Felix changed his answer. "Three?"

The detective pursed his lips.

"Four."

Graziani stood up and rested his knuckles on the table as he leaned closer to Felix. "So maybe you're not quite sure how many times you stabbed her. Is that right?"

Felix nodded. "I don't know how many times she was stabbed."

Graziani looked at him like he was getting mad. "You know what I think, Felix?"

"Yes. I mean no."

"I think you're lying to me about Olivia being your girlfriend."

Caught, Felix thought. He decided he'd better tell the truth. "She wasn't my girlfriend."

"So how did you get into her apartment? Did you break in?"

"Yes."

"How? We didn't see any signs of you forcing the lock."

Felix thought for a moment. "The door wasn't locked."

"So you just walked in."

"Yes."

"How did you get past the security gate at the front door?"

"Somebody let me in."

"They saw you?"

"Yes."

"Can you describe them? Man or woman? Old or young?"

Felix tried to imagine who might have let him in an apartment security gate. "An old man."

"So then you tied her up, put tape on her mouth, and cut her clothes off?"

That sounded like what he'd said so far. "Yes."

"Then Beth Jenkins came in and you stabbed her."

"Yes."

"And then you raped Olivia," Graziani said. "You remember that, right?"

"I don't remember that," Felix said. He pressed his fingers against his temples.

"Are you saying you blocked it out?"

Felix looked away from Graziani and saw that Brock was watching him again with that same questioning expression. He looked back at the first detective. "I must have blocked it out."

"Felix, I want you to really concentrate, okay?" Graziani said.

"Okay, I will."

"Good," Graziani replied. "Now, I want you to recall as best you can what you did to Olivia after you raped her."

"Okay, well, maybe I left," Felix replied.

"Maybe you left?" Graziani scowled and looked meaningfully at Brock.

"Felix, remember how relieved you felt when you admitted that you killed Dolores Atkins and got that off your conscience?" Brock said.

Felix hesitated. He didn't like this new detective; he acted like a bully. "Yes, sir."

"Then think about how much better you'll feel when you tell the truth here," Graziani said. "And the truth is, after you raped Olivia Yancy, you killed her. Isn't that right, Felix?"

Felix shrugged. "I guess."

Graziani sat back down in his seat and stared at the ceiling. "You guess," he said after a moment, "you fucking guess." He leaned forward to look his subject in the eyes. "Well, I guess I'm going to have to walk out of that door, Felix, and whatever happens to you after that will be your own damn fault. Do you want me to walk out that door?"

Felix panicked. He had no idea what would happen to him if the detective left, but it couldn't be good. "No. Please don't go."

"Well, then tell me the fucking truth," Graziani snarled. "What did you do to Olivia after you raped her?"

"I killed her."

Graziani smiled. "Well, now we're getting somewhere. And how did you kill her?"

There was only one answer that made sense to Felix. "With a knife," he said, making the same stabbing motion he'd imitated for Beth Jenkins.

"Was this the same knife you used to kill Dolores Atkins?" Graziani said. "The one you looked for with Detective Brock?"

"Yes. We couldn't find it."

"So I'm told," Graziani replied. "So tell me about the ring."

"The ring?"

"Yes, the little diamond ring that was found in your wallet."

Felix brightened. "I told Detective Brock I bought it for my girlfriend, from Al in the park."

"But you know what, Felix? I think you're lying about that. I think you took the ring from Olivia Yancy," Graziani said accusatorily.

Felix shook his head. "No, I bought it from Al. It's for my girlfriend."

"Your girlfriend Olivia?" Graziani asked.

"No. Maria Elena."

"Cut the crap, Felix," Graziani replied. "If you want us to help you, you need to start helping us. You cut the ring off Olivia Yancy's finger. What did you do with it after that?"

"I filed Al's name off," Felix replied.

"Bullshit!" Graziani exploded. Felix jerked back in his chair, frightened, as the detective continued, "Olivia's husband's name is Dale. That's what you filed off, isn't it?"

Felix blinked back tears. "I bought it from Al and filed his name off."

Graziani stood and acted as if he was going to leave the room. "That's it, Felix. No more joking around with you. You got the ring from Olivia and put it in your wallet. And if you don't fess up, any chance you have of us telling the judge that you cooperated with us will go out the window. Understand? We're looking at the fucking death penalty, Felix."

Swallowing hard, Felix struggled to speak and then started crying. "I bought it from Al for my girlfriend."

"Suit yourself, Felix," Graziani said. "Come on, Phil, let's leave him to his fantasy world."

The two detectives had almost reached the door when Felix yelled, "I took the ring from Olivia."

Graziani stopped and stood for a moment without turning. When he did, he was smiling broadly. "And whose name did you file off the ring?"

"Dale," Felix responded.

Graziani looked at Brock and smirked. "Well, thank you, Felix. I'm going to leave you for a bit. I need to make a telephone call to the New York district attorney's office, but we'll probably want to ask you some more questions later. Will that be okay?"

Felix sniffed and nodded his head. "Then can I go home?" he asked, looking from Graziani to Brock, who lowered his head.

"Sorry, Felix," Brock said. "But that's going to be a very long time from now."

"A very long time," Graziani repeated. "You're a murdering son of a bitch, and they're going to put you away for just about forever. . . . Hell, they're probably going to put you down like a mad dog, and I'll be there to watch 'em do it."

12

MARLENE PAUSED AT THE ENTRANCE OF THE HOUSING Works Bookstore and turned to face the massive dog who sat down on his haunches at her feet. The expression on his broad face seemed to express puzzlement at why their evening walk had been interrupted after only a few blocks.

"Sorry, Gil," she said apologetically as she tied his leash to an empty bike rack. The restraint was unnecessary, as the hundred-and-twenty-pound presa canario would have died before leaving any spot where Marlene left him. However, other pedestrians felt safer knowing the beast was not free to devour them should he be of that mind-set. "This shouldn't take long, and I'll make it up to you."

Trained as a personal protection dog, Gilgamesh was Marlene's baby. One of her pursuits since leaving the New York DAO many years earlier, after establishing and then selling a very lucrative VIP security service, was ownership of a security and bomb dog breeding and training facility on Long Island. The farm specialized in mastiffs and her current favorite, the presa. She loved the catlike movement and athleticism of the breed's thick, muscular body, as well as its fierce loyalty.

Gilgamesh was absolutely devoted to Marlene and her family. And while gentle under normal circumstances, he would, and had, killed to protect them.

Marlene was no longer active at the dog farm, which she'd left in the capable hands of her head trainer. And the fact of the matter was she'd been feeling a bit lost of late; her eldest child, Lucy, lived in New Mexico, and the twin boys were in high school and no longer put up with much mothering. With their belated bar mitzvah coming up, she'd recently started brooding over the fact that before she knew it, they'd be off to college and she and Butch would be empty-nesters. *Butch is at the height of his career,* she thought, *but what am I going to do that I find rewarding?*

Since giving up the dog farm, she'd been involved in dangerous battles with terrorists and criminal masterminds that seemed to follow her family like sharks follow blood in the water. And, as much as she hated to admit it and worried about her family, she liked the occasional adrenaline rush of fighting for her life, as well as doing something good for her community and country. But it was all sort of haphazard and not something she could do as a career. She did enjoy painting at her art studio in the building across the street from the family loft; however, it wasn't enough—not for her mind and, truth be told, not the level of excitement she needed.

Things had started to change a month earlier when she took

on the case of a man who'd been unjustly accused of a murder and was being railroaded by the unethical Westchester County prosecutor Harley Chin. Marlene had not only cleared her client, she had helped catch the real killer—a professional hit man who murdered the victim in order to cover up another homicide of a call girl committed by a New York State supreme court trial judge.

Solving two murders and nailing two killers, all while serving the cause of justice, had certainly filled her spiritual, mental, and adrenaline-junkie voids. She felt more energized and involved than she had in years. And now it gave her the idea for a new avocation combining her law degree—which she'd kept current with the New York Bar Association—with her knack for private investigation. True, she couldn't practice criminal law in Manhattan to avoid any appearance of a conflict of interest with her husband's position, but she could practice law in the remaining four boroughs of Gotham, each one a county of its own, and her private investigator credentials—which she'd kept since her days with the security firm—were good in Manhattan as well; she could always work with an attorney there.

The recent case had convinced her that there was a need for her services as well. A district attorney like her husband—who insisted that his prosecutors play by the rules and who believed that it was the duty of his office to seek justice, not win at all costs—wasn't the problem. Not that the New York DAO was infallible, but that sort of institutionalized ethics went a long ways toward preventing malicious or unwarranted prosecution.

Her husband was what the twins called "old-school," an anomaly. As a first-year law student at Yale she took to heart a maxim of America's justice system: it was better for ten guilty men to go free than for one innocent man to be wrongfully convicted. Yet there were self-aggrandizing prosecutors, like Chin in Westchester, as well as overzealous cops, politicized judges, and lazy defense attorneys, who didn't do their jobs, which meant that, regrettably, innocent people went to prison, and some were even sentenced to death.

And that's where her inspiration came in. It was no accident that many of those for whom justice was truly blind were poor or disenfranchised and could not afford "dream teams" of lawyers, private investigators, and bevies of expert witnesses. Indigent defendants accused of homicide in New York had two private attorneys appointed to represent them; such attorneys belonged to a pool of "qualified" trial lawyers who applied to be in the group. However, they were paid at a much lower rate than their standard fees, and the only way to make money was to take on as many cases as a judge would assign them and then bill as many hours as the courts would allow. All the while, they were also working on more lucrative cases in their private practices. As a result, the time and energy devoted to the case of an indigent person accused of murder could be less than adequate.

As Marlene had explained to her husband when broaching the subject the previous week after their meeting with Stupenagel, she thought that maybe she'd take on a few cases a year where she believed there was a legitimate question about an injustice being done. She'd work pro bono—a Latin term meaning "for the good," or more accurately "free of charge"—something she could easily afford as she'd made millions from the sale of the security firm, and the dog farm was quite profitable as well.

Although he'd teased her about whether he'd be comfortable "sleeping with the enemy," Butch had not objected to her idea. She knew he wouldn't. For one thing, he learned long ago that she was not easily dissuaded when she put her mind to something. But more importantly, he accepted that the job of the defense was to zealously and competently represent its client, and if the state couldn't prove its case, then even a guilty defendant should be set free. So if Marlene put his colleagues in the other boroughs through the wringer, then so be it; they'd better be ready for a fight.

She didn't have to wait for one either. That afternoon, Alejandro Garcia had called on her cell phone and asked if she could recommend a good attorney for a friend who was being unjustly accused of three murders. The irony was that when Marlene first met the then-budding rap artist, Garcia had been framed for a multiple homicide he didn't commit.

When she pressed him for more information about the case, Garcia told her that his friend Felix was the young man she'd been reading about in the newspapers, the one the media was calling the Columbia U Slasher, with barely an attempt to preface the word "murderer" with "alleged." He'd been arrested for the rape and murder of three women, two in Manhattan and one in the Bronx.

"Your husband's office just indicted him," said the former gang leader, who, although friendly with Butch, still had that street distrust of "the Man." "But I'll swear on a stack of Bibles, he didn't do it."

Marlene had frowned. Although she'd read about the arrest in the newspapers, she didn't recall Butch talking about the case after the Monday meeting he had with his bureau chiefs and assistant district attorneys who presented their cases. He didn't tell her about every case and had been preoccupied with some of the post–Jabbar trial fallout regarding jurisdictional issues with the feds. But the Columbia U Slasher case was fairly high-profile and he usually would have remarked on a case like that by now. *Maybe it's just such a slam-dunk case that it's not worth talking about,* she thought.

"If I remember right, the news reports were quoting anonymous cops saying he confessed," Marlene told Garcia.

"Shit, Felix will confess to anything," he replied. "It's sort of weird, and probably because his old man beats the shit out of him for nothing, but he'd tell you he flew one of the jets into the World Trade Center on Nine-Eleven if he thought it would make you happy—or at least get you off his back. He's been like that since I've known him."

"Doesn't he have an attorney?" Marlene asked.

Garcia had snorted with disgust. "No, Felix waived his rights," he said. "I'm sure they had him convinced it was the right thing to do from the jump. So now he's indicted for murder and won't get an attorney appointed until his arraignment. Even then, who knows if he'll get a good one and not some guy who talks him into taking a deal for somethin' he didn't do. He needs a good lawyer who'll fight. But his family doesn't have money, so I'm going to pay for it. That's why I'm calling you. See if you know somebody who'll fight for this kid."

Marlene knew that the New York DAO's assistant district attorneys, especially in the homicide bureau, were some of the best-trained and most skilled trial lawyers in the country. They were usually pretty damn sure that they were going to make their case at trial or they didn't go to the grand jury for an indictment. Still, Garcia was a friend and asking for a favor, so she suggested that they meet first and then, if warranted, think of which defense lawyer to bring on board for the Manhattan case.

Garcia seemed relieved when she agreed, particularly after he also suggested that he bring Felix's mother, Amelia, to the meeting. "She knows him better than anyone. I think if you talk to her, you'll understand how he couldn't have done this."

Leaving Gilgamesh moping on the sidewalk, Marlene entered the bookstore, inhaling the musty aroma of old books and the smell of fresh coffee from the café at the rear of the building. Long and narrow, with its two floors of walls covered with row upon row of used books, as well as an eclectic collection of record albums, the bookstore subsisted on these donated items it then sold. All profits went to the Housing Works organization, which provided shelter, health care, and other services to homeless New Yorkers living with the AIDS virus.

During the day and even into the early evening, the bookstore was usually packed with browsers, readers, friends just having coffee, and sightseers, as the iconic shop, to the disgust of the locals, had become something of a tourist attraction. On weekday nights the environs were much quieter, as they were now, with just a few people scattered about, reading in one of the old leather chairs, working on their computer at a table with a latte, or gazing along the walls of books searching for an overlooked gem.

Marlene had offered to meet Garcia and Amelia Acevedo farther north, but he'd suggested somewhere closer to where Marlene lived in SoHo. "We don't want to put you out," he said. "And to be honest, Mrs. Acevedo doesn't want to meet where someone she knows might see her and tell her husband. She has to take off from work for this, and he'd beat the hell out of her if he knew. The bastard sleeps all day, then drinks all night, gambles her money, and whores around while she's at work."

Marlene made her way back to where a bored barista made her a decaf Americano. She then took a seat in a nook and picked up a copy of *Atlas Shrugged* that someone had left on the coffee table. She flipped open the book and noted one of the lines: *The evil of the world is made possible by nothing but the sanction you give it.*

Just then the bell above the door rang and a small, dark-haired woman entered, followed by a young Hispanic man. The woman wore the sort of drab ubiquitous uniform found on the army of men and women who cleaned the offices of the high and mighty of Manhattan during the night and then disappeared back to their homes before daybreak. She looked frightened and out of place.

The man was also short but built like a fireplug, with a thick chest and muscular shoulders that supported a round, clean-shaven head. In his baggy New York Knicks jersey and lowrider jeans, Alejandro Garcia still looked like a kid from the streets of Spanish Harlem despite two platinum records and a major recording deal. He had big brown, soulful eyes that always reminded her of a deer's, though she'd seen them turn as hard, dark, and bright as obsidian when he was angry. He'd been the leader of the notorious Inca Boyz street gang, whose turf was most of Spanish Harlem. And yet a stint in a reformatory, as well as the guidance and love of the grandmother who'd raised him, helped him focus on his music and gradually allowed him to walk away from the hardscrabble streets.

Garcia spotted Marlene and revealed the Cheshire Cat grin that was his most charming feature. He steered the woman toward her. "I take it that's your trained bear tied up outside?" he said with a laugh. "I tried to be nice but he just gave me a look like he wanted to eat me. Don't you feed him?"

"Oh yeah, and Gilgamesh eats like a bear, too," Marlene replied, chuckling. "But he's a gentle giant . . . unless . . ."

She left it at that, which made Garcia laugh again. "Unless you sic him on some homeboy's ass. . . . Anyway, Marlene Ciampi, this is Amelia Acevedo. Her son, Felix, is my friend I told you about."

The three sat down and Garcia quickly filled in what he knew about Felix's confession. "I haven't seen him yet," he said. "I'm not next of kin or a lawyer. So this is mostly from what he told his mom this morning after his indictment and what the cops told her. The story is the cops picked him up for some other mugging, which I'm sure he didn't do either—just standing in the wrong place at the wrong time—and then they questioned him most of a day. To tell you the truth, I'm surprised he didn't admit to every unsolved killing in the boroughs. But none of this adds up."

"Like what?" Marlene asked.

"Like—and sorry, Mrs. Acevedo, but I have to be honest with Marlene here—Felix is what you'd call 'a little slow.' He was held back a couple of grades and still struggles with things like reading and understanding even when he says he does. He's not stupid; it just takes him longer to put it together than most people. There's one thing he's good at: if he hears something—like which trains to take and what stops to get off, or a rap song—he can spit it back out like he recorded it. But there's no room for mistakes. If he accidentally got off at the wrong subway stop, he'd be lost until someone else told him what to do. But the cops are saying this is the guy who supposedly slips in and out of buildings murdering women and disappears, until finally they catch him wandering around on the sidewalk on a Sunday morning. You believe that? Hell, the cops said Felix tried to run away and fell over his own feet. That makes sense, anyway, 'cause the guy's a klutz and blind without his glasses, which they lost, by the way."

"You say he has a habit of confessing to things he didn't do?" Marlene asked.

As a former assistant district attorney, she knew that with any major crime there were people who would step forward to confess when they didn't commit the offense. Sometimes it was for the publicity. Or sometimes they were mentally ill and harboring a guilt complex that made them feel as if they needed to be punished. But those people tended to turn themselves in or made statements to others hoping to be implicated. They didn't expect to be spotted on a sidewalk by the police and then try to escape.

Occasionally there was another type of false confession made during police interrogations. There wasn't a lot of rubber-hosing of suspects, no slapping a potential perp beneath a hot, bare lightbulb—defendants were well aware of their civil rights when it came to physical violence. But some police interrogators stopped just short of it—getting up in the face of the suspect, shouting, threatening, cursing, intimidating.

The U.S. Supreme Court had even ruled that the police could lie in order to secure a confession, such as telling a suspect that he'd been identified by a witness when the truth was that he had not. And some interrogators walked a fine line with techniques like sleep deprivation, hunger, and thirst—cases had been lost when defense attorneys successfully argued to a judge that crossing that line had constituted coercion or worse.

Whatever the reason behind a false confession, the police were supposed to keep secret some details about the crime that only the killer would know. It was a sure way to separate fact from fiction.

"Felix will say anything that will take the pressure off," Garcia replied, and told her about the incident between Maria Elena and her boyfriend at the Hip-Hop Club. He turned to the other woman. "Mrs. Acevedo, maybe you could tell Marlene more about Felix?"

Amelia Acevedo smiled timidly. Marlene observed that before a hard life had prematurely grayed Amelia's hair and lined her face, she'd been quite pretty. "Yes, ever since he was a young boy, if someone asks him, 'Did you do this?' he will say yes," Amelia replied. "He does not like people to be angry with him. His father is always angry with him. The other night Felix tried to deny that he took his father's beer, and then when my husband found the beer in the fridge, Felix then told him that he did it, which he did not do. That's when my husband hit him like this." She imitated a backhand blow to the right side of Felix's face.

"Has he been in trouble with the authorities—the police or at school—where he confessed to something he didn't do?" Marlene asked.

Amelia nodded her head emphatically. "Yes, the other kids at school sometimes do bad things and then blame him. They know he will say he did it. This happened at the school when that boy, I think his name is Raymond, threw a rock at the window of the grocery store. Felix was afraid when the police accused him and so he said he did it. He didn't want them to be mad at him. But then the police found out he didn't do these things."

Marlene thought for a moment before speaking again. "Forgive me, but I want to play devil's advocate here for a moment. I understand he sometimes confesses to things he didn't do, but what if he really killed these women? Do you have anything else to suggest that he didn't do it?"

Garcia shook his head and shrugged. "I don't think he could do it. The kid is a real sweetheart and just sort of naïve about the world. I mean, he wanted to give the coat-check girl a diamond ring he bought from some guy in a park—probably hot as hell— and he's too shy to even ask her for a date. But besides just not being the killer type, he's kind of skinny and not very strong."

He patted Amelia Acevedo's hand. "Sorry, Mrs. Acevedo, I like Felix but he can hardly walk without falling. The cops are saying he's this smooth cat burglar who gets into these apartments in the middle of the day, ties up these women, kills them without alarming the neighbors, then just calmly walks away, catches a bus or a taxi back to the Bronx? And nobody sees him? It just doesn't make sense."

Garcia looked at Amelia. "Tell her what you told me about Felix on the day of the murder in the Bronx."

"I do not remember last July when the two women were killed in Manhattan," she responded, "but I remember when that Bronx woman, Dolores Atkins, was killed because I saw it on television news before I went to work. My boy came home when I was watching."

"What was he wearing?"

"The same thing he always wears in the summer—a T-shirt, shorts, and basketball shoes."

"Did you see any blood on him? On his clothes? His hands?"

Amelia Acevedo shook her head. "No, nothing. And not when I washed his clothes later."

Garcia looked over at Marlene. "I don't know what was in the newspapers, but I've talked to a few people on the street who wouldn't shit me. They said there was blood everywhere. But Felix doesn't get any on him?"

Marlene frowned. "I haven't seen the crime scene photographs, but maybe he washed up or changed clothes."

"Talk to Felix sometime and then you tell me if you think he's so cool that after he cuts this woman up and did whatever else they say he did, he washes the blood off himself and his clothes," Garcia said. "Maybe he stopped at a Laundromat and then went to the Y to take a shower."

"Maybe," Marlene said with a laugh. "But it's just the sort of thing we'll have to look into should the prosecution try to make that claim."

Garcia grinned. "This means you'll take the case."

Marlene smiled back. "I can't represent him on the Manhattan beef, but I have someone good in mind, a real sharp lawyer, Alea Watkins. But let me look into this and the Bronx case some more and see what I can come up with."

Suddenly Amelia sobbed and reached over to grab Marlene's hands. "Felix is a good boy," she said. "*Gracias*, he is all I have to bring me joy."

Marlene squeezed the other woman's hands and smiled. "We mothers have to stick together. I'll do the best I can."

13

BUTCH KARP WAS WAITING FOR MARLENE IN THE LIVING room of the loft when she got home that night. "So how's Alejandro?" he asked, patting the couch in an invitation to join him.

"He's fine," she said, sitting down and curling up against him. "It's his friend he's worried about. I met with him and Amelia Acevedo, the mother of one Felix Acevedo, who is currently under indictment for murder with the New York DAO and may be facing similar charges in the Bronx."

Karp felt his wife hesitate. There hadn't been much time to tell him about the telephone call from Garcia that had precipitated the meeting. He furrowed his brow when she asked him why he hadn't spoken about the Yancy-Jenkins case to her before the indictment and he replied, "Well, I have to admit, I didn't know about it. Not that I hear about every indictment or that every felony—even murder—is brought before the bureau chiefs meeting on Monday morning for vetting. But still . . ." His voice trailed off.

"I told Mrs. Acevedo that I'd look into what's going on in the Bronx," she said now as she burrowed under his protective arm. "And I'm going to see if I can find someone willing to take the New York case pro bono."

"Really? You think there's something amiss?"

Marlene raised her eyebrows and he knew his studied nonchalance wasn't fooling her. She gave him a basic rundown of what she'd heard at the bookstore. "I think you might want to take a look at that confession," she suggested now. "I've got a gut feeling that something's not right about this."

"Not every confession is a fraud, Miss Hug-a-Thug Defense Attorney, even if this guy has a history of giving false statements," Karp said. "However, I've already called Pat Davis; had to leave a message, but asked to see him in the morning to brief me and bring the case file." Pat Davis was the deputy chief of the Homicide Bureau. "Can't have some fire-breathing defense lawyers and their friends in the press catching me with my pants down."

"Damn straight . . . especially if one of the fire breathers is your wife," Marlene said with a sly smile. "But why Pat Davis, not Tommy Mack?"

"Tommy's in the middle of a six-week trial," Karp said of the Homicide Bureau chief. "Meanwhile, Pat's been handling the bureau administrative duties. And as for getting caught with my pants down, there are exceptions to every rule, and if you play your cards right . . ." He winked. "But I believe we were talking about this friend of Alejandro's. Do you know who you're going to bring on as his attorney for Yancy-Jenkins?"

Marlene nodded. "I'm hoping to talk Alea Watkins into it. Then your people will at least know they'd better be prepared for a fight."

"Good choice." Karp pictured the attractive, middle-aged black attorney known for taking on the tough cases. "Sharp and aggressive. I wonder who we have working the case."

"I thought Guma was your point man on the Yancy-Jenkins task force," Marlene said.

"He was," Karp replied. "Or is. But he's been on vacation at a health retreat in the Catskills. He's not due back in the office until Monday, and it's only Wednesday, so I think I'll take a look at the case file and ask a few questions of Davis, including why I'm in the dark on this one."

Karp was still mulling over what Marlene had told him about Felix Acevedo as he walked to work the next morning, following his usual route east on Grand and then south on Centre to the monolithic Criminal Courts Building, which also housed the DAO. He smiled when he saw the owner of the newsstand in front of the building. The little man with the pointed nose and Coke-bottle eyeglasses spotted him at the same time and grinned as he hopped from foot to foot in front of his kiosk.

Dirty Warren was Marlene's first case in her new role of crusading defense attorney. He'd been framed for the murder of a Westchester County socialite and without Marlene's help would likely have been convicted—if the conspirators had not first had him murdered in jail to make sure the case was closed. He got his nickname because he had Tourette's syndrome, which afflicted him with various facial tics and caused him to lace his conversations with frequent and unexpected bits of profanity and odd sounds. But he was a genuinely good man who'd been a font of information about what was going down on the streets.

"Hey, Karp . . . son of a bitch whoop whoop . . . got a good one for you," Dirty Warren said, continuing his little dance, which was one of the manifestations of Tourette's.

"Take your best shot, and good morning, by the way," Karp replied as he came up to the newsstand. For years, he and Dirty Warren had played a game of movie trivia. Dirty Warren would ask some obscure question having to do with films, and Karp had to answer. So far the score was a zillion to none in favor of Karp, whose lifelong affection for movies had begun with his visits to the Kingsway Theatre in Brooklyn, where he grew up.

"This one should be easy, right up your . . . whoop . . . alley," Dirty Warren said. "Why would a scout . . . asshole balls oh boy ohhhh boy . . . watch the trial of a framed innocent man?"

Karp scratched his head, shuffled his feet, started to speak then stopped, and secretly enjoyed seeing the hope of victory grow in Dirty Warren's eyes. Then he dashed it. "Are you trying to mock me?" he said. "I thought you were my friend, but you're killing me here." He paused as if listening to a voice and said, "Ah, a little bird just gave me the answer."

The sparkle went out in Dirty Warren's eyes. Resigned, he said, "Just give me the . . . whoop whoop . . . answer, Karp."

"Well, she's there to watch her father, Atticus Finch, defend Tom Robinson in Harper Lee's *To Kill a Mockingbird*," Karp said.

"Damn it, Karp," Dirty Warren said. "I figured maybe you

wouldn't waste your movie-watching time on something so . . . fuck me bastard whoop whoop . . . so work related."

"*Au contraire,*" Karp replied. "Some of my favorite films are courtroom thrillers—for instance, *Twelve Angry Men*. A classic."

"Well, I told you it would be easy," Dirty Warren grumbled. He handed Karp a copy of *The New York Times*, but when his customer tried to pay him, he waved it off. "Your money's no good here, Butch. Not after . . . oh boy balls oh boy . . . what Marlene did for me."

Karp tried again to hand him the money. "I'm glad she did but that was Marlene, not me."

"The way I see it . . . asswipe bitch . . . you're a team," the little man said. "So like I said, you're wasting your time trying to pay me."

Karp held up the paper. "Well, then, thanks, Warren."

"Not a problem. Now, if I could . . . whoop whoop ohhhh boy . . . only beat you once, just once, I'd be a happy man." He scrunched up his eyebrows and squinted his baby blues at Karp through his thick glasses. "But no throwing the game out of pity."

"I have too much respect for you to do that," Karp replied with a grin. He turned and left the smiling news vendor hopping from one foot to the other.

In the elevator, Karp glanced at the large bold headline at the top of the *Times* and sighed. The headline and story the day before had been bad enough.

COLUMBIA U SLASHER ARRESTED

A nineteen-year-old Bronx man confessed Monday to the brutal murder of Olivia Yancy and Beth Jenkins, whose maimed and bloody bodies were discovered last July . . .

But this morning's edition made him grimace.

SLASHER CONFESSES, NEW YORK DA INDICTS

He found deputy Homicide Bureau chief Patrick Davis already waiting for him in the reception area of his eighth-floor office. He looked at his watch—seven thirty; their appointment wasn't for another half hour. But he knew that Davis was ambitious and always trying to impress, hoping for a promotion to the bureau chief's spot. It was now common knowledge in the office that Homicide Bureau chief Tommy Mack was being offered a judgeship but was undecided.

With respect to Davis, Karp felt that the jury was still out. There was no question that Davis was a top-flight trial lawyer and respected by his peers, including those with the defense bar. But he was thirty-five years old, and the man's age, or more accurately his lack of administrative experience and mature judgment in a leadership role, was worrisome.

"Good morning, Patrick," Karp said as his visitor shot up from his chair like a soldier when the commanding officer enters a room. "I hope I didn't forget what time we were meeting."

"Not at all," Davis said. "You just never know what traffic's going to be like coming through the Lincoln Tunnel, so I got started a little early. And wouldn't you know, it was smooth sailing. . . . But I can wait if you need to do some other things first."

"No, let's get started," Karp said, and nodded to the door leading to his inner office. At the same moment, the door to the hallway opened and a plump middle-aged woman entered the reception room. She seemed surprised to find them there and eyed the two men suspiciously.

Receptionist Darla Milquetost considered the office to be her domain as much as Karp's and didn't like surprise visitors who weren't on the calendar. "Good morning," she said, arching her painted-on eyebrows.

"Good morning, Darla," Karp replied cheerfully. He generally found her territorial imperative amusing. "I'm sure you know Patrick Davis?"

Milquetost gave the young man a tight smile. "Of course, I just didn't know we'd have the pleasure of his company this morning," she replied, and headed behind her desk, where she opened a drawer and dropped her purse in before closing it with enough force to rattle the photograph of Karp hanging on the wall.

Karp smiled at the display and turned on his heel to enter his office. "Please hold my calls unless it's an emergency."

"Certainly, Mr. Karp," the receptionist replied. She brightened at the thought of being able to tell anyone who called that her boss was not available. *And would you like to schedule a time to call back?*

Karp waited for Davis to pass him before closing the door

behind them. "Make yourself comfortable," he said, indicating the chair in front of his desk.

When Karp was seated, Davis handed over a thick file folder. "Here's the Yancy-Jenkins case file," he said. "It has everything the task force compiled plus the new stuff: a transcription of the defendant's confession to the detective in the Bronx—I believe his name is Graziani—as well as his transcribed Q & A statement to our ADA Danielle Cohn."

"I know Danielle," Karp said. "Good kid, but didn't she just get assigned to Homicide? How'd she catch a case like this one?"

"She was working the night chart on Monday when she got the call from Detective Graziani up at the Four-Eight in the Bronx," Davis said. "She's young, but she's very good; top of her class at Brown and Yale Law. Blazed her way through the criminal courts; tried a lot of cases successfully down there. Been with Homicide for six months and done well as second chair on a couple of murder trials and on her own with a reckless manslaughter. Still batting a thousand."

Davis stopped talking, realizing he was sounding like a used-car salesman. He shrugged. "Of course, I was going to talk to you about her co-counsel. If you think she should second-chair this one, too, that's fine by me. She'll understand; she won't like it, but she'll understand."

He doesn't like being second-guessed, Karp thought. *I don't suppose any of us do, but he has to see the logic. This case is going to get a lot of press attention and Alea Watkins is a tough, seasoned adversary. You can't hand a case like this over to a rookie.*

"We'll talk about that in a bit," Karp said. He didn't want to beat up on Davis; he might not be ready for the job right now, but someday he could be if he remained with the DAO. But he still needed to make his point; he felt that teaching his subordinates was one of his main functions as a DA. "Why didn't Danielle get in touch with the senior ADA who was supervising the night chart when she got the call? The Yancy-Jenkins murders were as high-profile as it gets and that usually requires an experienced hand."

"Well, for starters she wasn't immediately told that this concerned the Yancy-Jenkins murders," Davis said. "This Detective Graziani who called said he had a suspect who'd confessed to a Manhattan double murder. She only learned which case it was when she got there."

"Okay, that's for starters," Karp said. "But what's next? Why not call after she got there and learned which case this was?"

Davis dipped his head, but then to his credit he looked Karp in the eye. "Actually she tried to reach Terry Daley, the senior ADA who should have been on call, but there was a mix-up in the schedule and he wasn't home. Then she tried to call me, too, but I was late getting to the Yankee game and had rushed out of the house without my cell phone. I guess there was a concern by the detective that the suspect might lawyer up. So by the time I got home and got her message, she'd already gone ahead and questioned the suspect and got a separate confession."

The younger man hung his head again. "Sorry, I messed up," he said. "I shouldn't have been out of touch."

"Yeah, with this job we're pretty much on call twenty-four/

seven, or at least we have to make sure that the lines of communication are open," Karp replied. "But it happens, and it's one of those lessons we don't soon forget."

"True, true," Davis said, and smiled slightly as he pointed to his head. "It's now engraved in stone."

Karp chuckled. "Good. Then let's move on from here. Refresh me on the timing of these events. I take it the suspect confessed Monday sometime after our bureau chiefs meeting."

"Yes," Davis said, and pointed at the file folder. "You'll see how it breaks down in there, but essentially Graziani calls Monday evening and says he's got this guy who'd been popped in the Bronx on Sunday for an assault and ended up confessing to a murder up there. And now he's confessed to a Manhattan homicide. So Danielle then trots up to the Bronx jail and gets the whole story. Apparently, Graziani was working narcotics in the Two-Six when the Yancy-Jenkins murders went down. He did some work with the task force, so he was familiar with the details of the case. Anyway, he hears about this guy confessing to the Bronx homicide and gets a hunch to look at the evidence. Turns out, this guy—the perp's name is Felix Acevedo—was carrying a woman's engagement ring in his wallet with the inscription filed away. And Graziani knew that whoever killed Olivia Yancy took her engagement ring; in fact, the bastard cut her finger off to get it. So Graziani goes after this guy and pretty soon he gets the guy to confess to the Yancy-Jenkins murders. That's when he called the DAO and got Cohn."

"Okay, I understand all that," Karp said. "But why the rush to indict?" He knew it sounded a little harsh, like an indictment itself, but it might well be a question Alea Watkins would raise to get the case thrown out, and he wanted to see how Davis would react.

Davis bit his lip. "I didn't consider it a rush. It's pretty much a slam-dunk case. The defendant confessed first to Graziani and then gave a virtually verbatim Q & A statement to Danielle—plus he confessed to the murder in the Bronx. When you read the confession and the Q & A you'll see the guy is as consistent as a Swiss watch. Hardly a word of difference between what he told the detective and what he told Cohn. Then there's the ring. To be frank, I think his defense attorney is going to take one look at the evidence and beg us to plea-bargain the case."

Karp thought about what Marlene had said about her meeting with Alejandro and Acevedo's mother. His gut told him that it wasn't going to be anywhere near as much of a "slam dunk" as Davis thought, and he doubted that "Perry Mason Junior" Watkins was the sort to beg for mercy.

"What's the status of the Bronx case?" Karp said.

Davis frowned. "I'm not sure. I don't think they've filed an indictment yet. Maybe it's not as strong a case . . . I'm not familiar with all of the details. But I can find out."

Karp's brow furrowed and he shook his head. "I owe my old friend Mr. Bronx DA himself, Sam Hartsfield, a call. I'll let you know what he says."

Davis nodded but didn't reply. Karp knew that his young colleague was taking it hard. "It's okay, Pat," he said. "Under the circumstances, I understand how it all happened. I just want to review the case file, like we would have at the meeting, and make sure we didn't leap into something we're going to regret. I can't emphasize enough how vital it is for this office to not only believe that we can win a case but be convinced a thousand percent that the defendant is factually guilty *and* that we have the legally admissible evidence to prove it. Otherwise, we don't go forward. But that first threshold is factual guilt."

Davis squared his shoulders. "I'm aware of that, and I'm convinced he did it. The confessions are just too on point. And I don't see how the defense is going to keep them out of evidence."

Karp held the man's gaze for a long moment, then pursed his lips and nodded. "All right then," he said, and tapped the file. "I'll take a look at what we got. As far as personnel, I want Ray Guma as lead counsel; Danielle can second seat."

"Guma?" Davis asked, surprised.

Karp raised an eyebrow. He knew that a lot of the new young Turks in the office thought of Guma, who worked only part-time due to his health, as a relic. But Karp knew that he was as good as they came—smart and tough as nails in a courtroom. A brawler more than a boxer, but he got the job done and would be a good match for Watkins. "Yes, Guma. I don't know if you're aware of this but he was the DAO rep on the Yancy-Jenkins task force . . . the same one this Graziani worked with. He'll be able to spot any holes."

Davis twisted his lips. "Cohn isn't going to like it."

Karp scowled slightly to show that there wasn't going to be a lot of argument regarding this decision. "Then she can excuse herself from the case," he said. "If you're wrong, and the defense doesn't come looking for a plea deal—and I don't think they will—there's going to be a fight. Cohn can learn a lot from an old warhorse like Goom."

A few minutes later, Davis excused himself. When he left the office, Karp glanced down at the file on his desk. *Under the circumstances, I understand how it all happened.* He suspected the truth was that Davis wanted badly to close this case while on his watch. But if ambition meant taking shortcuts, it could lead to disaster.

14

BASEBALL PRACTICE HAD BEEN OVER FOR TWO HOURS, but the twins were still arguing when they got out of the yellow cab on the corner of Third Avenue and Twenty-ninth Street. They stood facing each other for a moment, tense and angry.

"You know Coach Newell told Chase to hurt him," Giancarlo said. "It was just practice and he slid into Esteban hard at second with his cleats up."

"Chase was just trying to break up the double play," Zak argued, and moved past his brother to the door of the Il Buon Pane bakery. The debate was momentarily interrupted when he opened the door and they were greeted by the smell of fresh-baked pastries and breads.

However, once Giancarlo recovered his wits and noted that they were going to have to stand in line anyway, he returned to the fray. "Esteban had already made the play," he said, "and, I might add, a frickin' great play—catches that one-hop blast up the middle, tags second himself, and fires over to first to double them up. He'd let go of the ball ten feet before Chase even got there. There was no reason to go into him like that."

"Coach Newell is just trying to get us to play hard-nosed baseball with the playoffs coming up," Zak said, getting more surly and defensive with each point his brother made.

"Esteban got hurt because of it," Giancarlo said. "That was a nasty cut on his leg from Chase's cleats."

"It looked worse than it was."

"Zak . . . come on . . . he was bleeding like he'd been stabbed."

Zak shrugged. "He should have seen Chase coming and moved."

"He wasn't expecting to get a cheap shot by his own team-mate."

"You'd think he would have learned by now."

Giancarlo stopped and stared at his brother in shock, then slowly shook his head. "Yeah, you're right," he said sarcasti-cally. "He should understand by now that a racist xenophobic coach and his little toadies would be looking for ways to hurt a seventeen-year-old because he's a Mexican. I mean, what a stu-pid wetback. What does he expect? Fair treatment? Maybe play a meaningless game without one of his own teammates trying to injure him? Dumb spic."

Zak scowled. Chase Fitzpatrick was the team's catcher—a big, not terribly bright redhead and one of Max Weller's toad-ies. "I'm very impressed with the 'xenophobic' adjective, but you're overreacting."

"*Overreacting!*" Other customers turned around or looked

up from their tables with disapproval at Giancarlo's shout. Although there was a constant hum of conversation in Il Buon Pane, people maintained a certain level of decorum meant to preserve the tranquillity of the place, and a shouting teenager wasn't part of it.

Giancarlo recognized this and immediately lowered his voice to an angry buzz directed at his twin. "I was the only one on the team to go out there to see how bad he was hurt. He was lying on the ground, Zak, holding his leg and bleeding. Coach Newell never even came over. He sent an assistant coach."

Zak rolled his eyes. "Newell was busy. He probably didn't think it was that bad."

"He high-fived Chase when he came back to the dugout!" Giancarlo said.

"I didn't see that."

"I did! So did a lot of other guys. And so did Esteban. The guy had tears in his eyes but didn't say a word, and by the way, thanks for getting my back like you said you would. I didn't exactly see you come out to help."

"You didn't need me," Zak replied. "And Coach Hames told me to keep warming up. Nobody was jumping your butt for helping Esteban."

"What about the crap I caught in the locker room after practice? 'Taco lover,' 'Bean Dip'—those were just a couple of names . . . all homophobic of course . . ."

Zak replied, "Sticks and stones may break my bones but words will—"

"Never hurt me. Yeah, I know," Giancarlo retorted. "But this time Esteban did get hurt. And I could be next. Max and Chase and their pals were all laughing about Esteban, then Chase said, 'Hey, Giancarlo, maybe now Coach will let you play short-stop for sliding practice.' Sounds like a threat to me."

"I'll kick his butt if he does," Zak blustered. "He's just a big, fat catcher."

"You're not getting the point—"

Whatever Giancarlo was going to say was cut short by the appearance of Moishe Sobelman. "Boys, boys, what are these hard words and angry eyes?" he asked, clapping a hand on each boy, though he had to reach up to do so. "It's a terrible thing when brothers fight. But come, let's discuss this over something to eat. Let me see, will it be your father's favorite, cherry cheese coffee cake, or could I interest you in something else today? A raspberry almond torte, perhaps? Of course, your mother will probably be angry with me for ruining your din-ners."

The twins immediately stopped sneering at each other and grinned at Sobelman. They happily followed him around be-hind the counter into the kitchen, where Moishe sat them down at a small table and took their orders. Neither ventured too far, however, from their father's addiction, opting only to try the blueberry cheese coffee cake.

Sobelman went out to the counter and then returned with the coffee cakes. He then sat down with a cup of coffee and waited for the boys to get well into their treat before asking what they'd been fighting about. He then listened patiently as each boy gave his side of the story.

"It's only six or seven guys, and we have twenty-five guys on the roster," Zak said in conclusion. "If something happens and those guys get kicked off the team, or Coach Newell loses his job, we'll have no chance to take state this year. Why should the whole team suffer for one guy?"

Sobelman looked thoughtful and then responded gently. "Indeed, why should the rights or happiness, or even the safety, of one person supersede what is best for many? Then again, I guess there is a question of what is best for many in the long run. It is a very difficult and often frightening decision to speak up for someone else, Zak. But let's look at this from the perspective of your report for your bar mitzvah class."

Sobelman got up and rummaged through a drawer. "In the 1920s, the Nazis were just a few thugs meeting in German beer halls. But they were loud and aggressive, and speaking out against them could even result in a beating. Still, they could have been easily stopped if the majority of Germans who didn't subscribe to their hateful views had said something, or at least voted against them." He picked up a piece of paper from the drawer and walked back to the table and sat down.

"You may have heard this; it was part of a speech given by Martin Niemöller, a German minister and philosopher," Sobelman said, and read from the piece of paper. "'First they came for the Communists, but I was not a Communist so I did not speak out. Then they came for the Socialists and the trade unionists, but I was neither, so I did not speak out. Then they came for the Jews, but I was not a Jew so I did not speak out. And when they came for me, there was no one left to speak out for me.'"

"I've heard that before," Giancarlo said. "When we were studying the Holocaust in a bar mitzvah class my dad was teaching."

"Good," Sobleman replied. "I'm glad you've heard it somewhere. But did your father tell you much about Mr. Niemöller?"

"No," the boys said.

"Well, it is good to know his history as well as his words," Sobelman said. "For instance, he was a submarine commander in World War I but later became a pacifist and anti–nuclear weapons activist. In the 1930s, he was staunchly anti-Communist and initially supported the Nazis' rise to power. Only when the Nazis made churches subordinate to the party did he balk and begin speaking out against them. He became very popular in Germany, which angered Hitler, who had him arrested in 1937. He spent more than a year in jail. When he got out, he continued to speak against the Nazis, which got him arrested again and this time sent to the death camps at Sachsenhausen and Dachau in 'protective custody.' He was, of course, treated better than the Jewish prisoners and so survived seven years in those hellholes until he was liberated in 1945. He gave his 'they came for the Jews' speech after that . . . which has, of course, become a popular treatise on the danger of political apathy."

"I understand your point," Zak said defensively. "But what does this have to do with a baseball team and one kid getting bullied a little?"

It was Sobelman's turn to shrug. "Maybe only to illustrate how horrible things like the Holocaust start small—a few evil men in a pub, or in a corporate boardroom, or a socialist workers' party meeting. These evil men believe they know what's best for everyone else. They say some things that make people uncomfortable, but no one does anything about it. People shrug and say, 'It's their right to free speech,' which is fine, but they don't counter it, or denounce it, with free speech of their own. The masses are mute. Perhaps they are too intimidated by the smear campaign that would be directed at them. Or maybe they're afraid of physical violence, even assassination. But deep down in their souls where they are frightened, they know they actually want someone else to make the tough decisions for them."

Sobelman reached across the table and set his hands on Zak's wrists. "Right now it's just a few bullies on a boys' baseball team. But tolerating this behavior now becomes a mind-set that will carry into the future. These bullies are the same sort of people who end up in those pubs and boardrooms and meeting halls. And those who witness the debasement of another human being and do nothing about it are the same people who may someday ask themselves why they didn't stand up when the evil men come for them."

"But shouldn't Esteban have to stand up for himself first?" Zak asked. "He never does anything about the crap he gets. He won't fight. He doesn't tell the principal."

"Certainly he has to defend himself," Sobelman said in agreement. "We Jews in Europe learned that the hard way. Except for a few anomalies like the uprising in the Warsaw ghetto and our revolt at the Sobibor camp, we allowed ourselves to be led like sheep to the slaughter."

Sobelman shook his head. "No wonder those of us who survived it, who want nothing more than to live a peaceful life in the manner that God has ordained for our people, swore that never again would we surrender without a fight. People who criticize the Israelis for their tendency to react harshly to threats might do well to remember that Arabs were not the first people to decide that Jews had no right to exist."

"So then you agree that this is really Esteban's problem?" Zak asked, thinking he'd scored a point.

"It's only part of the equation," Sobelman replied. "It's hard to face the world on your own. Still, if you won't stick up for yourself, you can't expect others to always fight your battles for you."

"That's what I mean about Esteban," Zak said. "Maybe he should tell his parents, and *they* should talk to the coach."

"That'll never happen," Giancarlo replied. "His parents are from Mexico. He's got a scholarship to a good school. They're probably more afraid to say something than he is. He's on his own. Even the other minority players aren't speaking up because they know they could be next. But you're wrong that he doesn't stick up for himself. Every time they knock him down with a pitch, he gets back up. They call him names; he smiles and plays that much harder. That's why I was worried they were actually going to have to hurt him to get him to quit. And now they may have done it, and nobody says anything."

"So what do you think you should do, Giancarlo?" the old man asked.

"I think we should tell Dad."

"So you want your father to fight your battles for you?"

Giancarlo furrowed his brow, surprised that the debate had taken this sudden twist. "I guess I was thinking this is the sort of thing that adults handle."

"Maybe," Sobelman said. "When there is no other choice,

maybe you will have to enlist your father's help. But if that is your first response, what have you learned from this experience? Rather than standing up yourself and saying this is wrong, and maybe suffering personal consequences, you'd rather some higher authority do it for you. Count on the government, perhaps, to make those tough decisions that you don't want to really know about. Just so long as the streets are safe at night and the trains run on time, eh? Oh, and of course, hope that when the crisis has passed, the government remembers to return your rights to you."

Zak nodded. "Right, so we don't tell Dad," he said. "Maybe I can talk to Max and Chase and get them to lay off . . . if Esteban comes back." He looked for approval from Sobelman. "How's that?"

Sobelman smiled and patted his hand. "You do what you think is right; you're almost a man now. But remember what I told you about the bar mitzvah being more than a right of passage. It is the day you become morally responsible for your actions in the eyes of God and man."

Zak sighed. "I was afraid you'd say something like that."

15

ALTHOUGH IT WAS ONLY MIDMORNING, MONDAY ALREADY promised to be an unseasonably warm day in the Bronx. It showed in the desultory attitudes of the youths hanging out on the northwest corner of Mullayly Park as they stopped talking and watched the attractive white woman approach.

She was petite but otherwise unremarkable, except that she was walking a dog that easily weighed as much as she did and looked like it could eat the local pit bulls for snacks. The youths hoped the pair would pass on by, but instead the woman and her dog walked right up to them.

"Are you Raymond?" she asked a tall black kid in front of the group.

"Who wants to know?" Raymond replied, trying to hold his ground and not look intimidated while keeping an eye on the dog, who he thought was staring at him like he was a leg of fried chicken.

Marlene noted the look and smiled. *Walk softly*, she thought, *but with a big dog, especially in the Bronx.*

It had been nearly a week since her meeting with Alejandro Garcia and Amelia Acevedo. She had been able to meet with Felix the following day in the company of Alea Watkins, who looked like an English teacher but fought in the courtroom like a barroom bouncer. She'd listened to Marlene's presentation and then said she'd be happy to take the Manhattan case. In the meantime, Marlene would work as a private investigator for Felix.

After his indictment, Felix Acevedo had been transferred from the Bronx jail to the Tombs, otherwise known as the Manhattan House of Detention for Men, which was situated at the northern end of the Criminal Courts Building complex. It was a massive gray building; if the exterior was cheerless and imposing it was even more oppressive within its cold stone walls, steel gates, and cell bars.

Marlene had wrinkled her nose at the smell of the place as she and Watkins passed through security and were escorted to an interview room. It smelled of unwashed bodies, splashed urine, industrial-strength cleansers, and the acrid aroma of fear.

Some of the latter was coming from Felix, who was waiting for them seated in a chair on the other side of a table. His head was down and he did not look up when they entered.

"Hello, Felix, my name is Marlene Ciampi and this is Alea Watkins," she said, standing before him. "Your mother has asked Ms. Watkins to represent you for your case in Manhattan and I'm going to help look into the allegations. I'm a friend of

Alejandro Garcia, so I hope you'll trust me and tell us the truth no matter what."

At the mention of his mother and Garcia, Felix looked up hopefully. It was then that the women saw that behind his thick glasses his left eye was swollen shut by an ugly purple bruise, and his upper lip appeared to have been split, requiring several stitches to close.

"Did that happen in here?" Watkins asked as they sat down across from him. The young man nodded. "Do you know who did it?" He dropped his eyes and didn't answer. "Are you afraid you'll get hurt if you tell us?" He nodded.

Watkins and Marlene exchanged glances. "We'll see if we can get you moved to a safer place," Watkins said. "In the meantime, are you okay with me representing you?"

Acevedo shook his head. "My dad will be angry."

The statement caught the women off guard. "Because you've been arrested?" Watkins asked.

Felix shook his head again. "Because lawyers cost money."

The women smiled. "That's okay, Felix," Watkins said. "We're going to help you for free. All you have to do is tell us the truth. Remember, we're your lawyers; anything you tell us is a secret and we won't tell anyone else without your permission."

Acevedo looked troubled. "I told the truth but they didn't believe me."

"Who didn't believe you?" Marlene asked.

"The detectives."

Marlene leaned across the table. "Were you telling the truth when you said you killed Dolores Atkins, Olivia Yancy, and Beth Jenkins?"

"They said I did."

"That's not what I asked you, Felix," Marlene said gently. "Did you kill those women?"

Felix looked frightened for a moment. Then he shook his head as tears sprang into his eyes. "I didn't kill nobody. I would never hurt no ladies." He looked around fearfully as if he expected the detectives to materialize. "They showed me horrible photographs and said I did that to those ladies. I just wanted them to stop. Now I can't sleep. I have nightmares. . . . And it's terrible in here. It smells bad and people are mean. And at night . . . at night . . . they scream and cry. Please, can I go home?"

It took the women a few minutes to get Felix to calm down. When he finally relaxed a little, Marlene asked him to recall everything he could beginning the night before his arrest. Although Alejandro had told her about Acevedo's special ability, they were both surprised at the detail of his recollections of what had happened, especially conversations. He seemed to recall these verbatim—from the confrontation with the coat-check girl's boyfriend to his conversations with Garcia and the police officers who arrested him.

The two women had not yet seen the transcripts of his alleged confession to Graziani and the Q & A statement he gave to the assistant district attorney; because of the magnitude of the investigation the DA was still gathering the voluminous police reports to give to the defense. Yet he repeated the back-and-forth between himself and the detectives as though he'd memorized lines from a play.

"I told Detective Graziani that I wasn't at Olivia's apartment and he said, 'You're lying, Felix. We showed a witness your mug shot; he's sure it was you he saw coming out of the apartment building. Don't bullshit me, Felix.'"

Marlene and Alea Watkins had exchanged looks at the mention of a witness claiming to have seen Felix leaving the apartment building. "What did you say then?" Watkins asked.

"I said, 'Okay, I won't.' And he said, 'You remember being in Olivia's apartment, right?'"

Acevedo sighed and slumped down in his seat. "I just wanted him to stop asking me questions so I told him, 'Yeah. I remember now. Olivia. She's my girlfriend.'"

Marlene and Watkins looked at each other in alarm. This was a new twist. "Your girlfriend?" Marlene asked.

"That's what he said, too," Felix replied.

"Olivia was your girlfriend?"

Acevedo started to nod his head but then stopped and covered his face with his hands. "I don't have a girlfriend," he said. "I don't know any Olivias. I hope Maria Elena will go out with me someday." He wagged his head sadly back and forth. "She probably won't now that I'm in trouble with the police."

Marlene reached across the table and patted his hand. "I'm sure she'll understand when we clear this up," she said, earning herself a shy smile. "But right now we need to know why you told the police that you killed these women."

Acevedo looked miserable. "Because they wanted me to," he said. "And they were angry at me. I thought it would make them stop being mad." He hesitated and looked at her with his one good eye. "Are you angry at me, too? What should I have said?"

"No, we're not angry, Felix," Marlene said, trying to reassure him. "We're not ever going to get angry, but we need you to tell us the truth, not what you think we want to hear. Okay?"

Acevedo brightened. "Okay."

That's when Marlene asked him about the ring. The details of the case against him had already been leaked to the press and then pontificated upon by the so-called talking-head TV experts, who focused on his confession and a mention of the engagement ring found on his person that had allegedly belonged to Olivia Yancy.

Acevedo smiled at the mention of the ring. "I told Detective Graziani I bought it from Al in the park. But he didn't believe me. He said, 'You know what, Felix? I think you're lying about that. I think you took the ring from Olivia Yancy.' I told him, 'No, I bought it from Al. It's for my girlfriend.' But he said I cut it off of Olivia Yancy's finger."

The thought that "Al" might be the killer who cut the ring from Olivia Yancy's hand quickly crossed Marlene's mind. Of course, if the cops were doing their jobs, they would have already checked that out and discounted the story. *But I still need to follow up,* she thought. *It wouldn't be the first time a detective got lazy when he thought he had a case wrapped.*

"Do you know where I can find Al?" she asked.

"I see him at Mullayly Park."

"What does he look like?"

"He's got a lot of pimples," Acevedo replied. "And white hair."

"White hair? Is he old?" Watkins asked.

"He's older than me but not old. I think it's not his real hair color."

"So he dyes his hair," Marlene said. "How tall is he? Is he fat or skinny?"

"A little taller than me. Skinny." Acevedo hesitated then spoke. "Am I giving the right answers?"

"Are you telling me the truth?" Marlene asked.

"Yes."

"Then you're fine," Marlene replied. "Was anybody else there when he sold you the ring?"

Acevedo thought about it. "No," he said. But he must have noticed the disappointment on Marlene's face because he'd quickly added, "But Raymond was there when Al told me I should buy it for my girlfriend." Acevedo scowled. "Raymond made fun of me. He said I didn't have a girlfriend. He might know how to find Al."

Which is what had brought Marlene and her dog to the park. "Well, Raymond," Marlene responded to the black kid's question. "My name is Marlene Ciampi, and I'm a private investigator working on behalf of Felix Acevedo, who you may have heard has been arrested."

A short Hispanic girl with heavy makeup stepped up next to Raymond. "Yeah, I heard that he cut up some women, which sounded strange to me. I mean, he's a wimp. I could kick his ass without hardly trying."

Marlene chuckled. "I bet you could. I don't believe he's guilty, either, but to prove it, I may need your help."

"How's that?" Raymond asked.

"Well, for one thing, does anybody remember Felix buying a ring from somebody named Al a couple of weeks ago?"

The Hispanic girl started to say something but Raymond stepped in front of her. "Maybe. But this ain't no tourist booth. Information here costs money."

Marlene reached in her purse and pulled out a twenty-dollar bill. "I need twenty dollars' worth of information," she said, holding the bill over Gilgamesh's muzzle. "But it better be good if you want to get paid without losing some fingers."

Raymond looked from the bill to the dog, who gave a low growl. "Yeah, I remember a dude was trying to get him to buy a ring. Felix said it was for his girlfriend, and I gave him shit about it 'cause he ain't got no girlfriend. The man's cherry, if you know what I mean."

"And this guy with the ring, do you know his name?" Marlene asked, handing over the twenty-dollar bill.

"It's something Spanish, like José," Raymond replied.

"It's Jesus . . . Jesus Guerrero," the girl said, correcting him. "He tried to hit on me, like I'd do that pizza-faced rat."

"How would I find him?" Marlene asked.

Raymond gave her a sly smile. "I sure can tell you how to find him," he said. "But it's going to cost you ten more."

Marlene dug in her purse for another ten dollars. "Okay, where's he at?"

Raymond laughed as he took the money and looked over her shoulder. "He's heading this way right now."

16

As he waited for Ray Guma to settle into his favorite chair next to the bookshelf, Karp considered what he'd gleaned from reading the Yancy-Jenkins case file over the weekend. And he was none too happy about it.

Reading for several hours at a time, he digested the entire case file, including the autopsies and toxicology reports, the transcript of the defendant's taped confession to Detective Graziani, and the Q & A statement subsequently given to ADA Danielle Cohn, as well as the initial police reports and supplemental detective investigative reports, known as DD-5s. All told there were some 1,500 pages worth of DD-5s, including a chronology of the events leading to Acevedo's arrest in the Bronx and subsequent interrogations.

Guma had dropped by the loft Sunday evening after arriving back in town and getting the news about Acevedo's arrest and indictment. Karp handed him the case file. "Let me know your thoughts tomorrow afternoon" was all he'd said.

Guma had just entered the office—after a quick flirtation with Darla Milquetost—and tossed the case file on Karp's desk. He then plopped down in the chair and pulled out an enormous cigar. He was no longer allowed to smoke the Diplimatico, both for health reasons and because smoking was not allowed inside any public building in Manhattan. But he still enjoyed chewing on stogies and complaining about "the meddling politically-correct antismoking Nazis."

"So?" Karp asked when his longtime friend and colleague quit admiring the cigar and stuck it in his mouth.

"So . . . I think someone screwed the pooch," Guma responded. "I didn't get to read the Acevedo stuff as carefully as I would have liked, but what I did is bullshit. I could start with the so-called confessions. I think it's pretty clear that Acevedo was led to the poisoned well, but why'd he drink the water? The detective got in his face—a little huffing and puffing and a few threats—and when he wasn't getting the answers he wanted, nothing physical or anything that could be deemed overtly coercive or inappropriate took place. And there's almost no pressure from Cohn when she took his Q & A statement, which is spot-on with what he told the detective. With very little prodding, Acevedo followed the detective's lead and then stuck to it with Danielle. I find that curious."

Guma stopped talking and placed the cigar back in his mouth, closing his eyes as though gathering his thoughts. *Or tired,* Karp thought. He noted how his friend's once thick and wavy dark hair was now thin and white, the formerly muscular baseball player's body thin and frail—all casualties of the cancer that had nearly killed him.

The night before, Guma had admitted that he felt old, which was unusual for him. The cancer had beat him "like a rented mule," he'd said, and he'd never regained the energy levels he had before chemotherapy. "But it's not that so much. It's this shit," he said, holding up the case file. "I'm tired of crime scenes and the tears of moms and dads, fathers, husbands, wives, and especially the children. Tired of all the wasted lives. Tired of the excuses and the senseless brutality. It's just wearing on my heart and soul."

Concerned, Karp said, "You don't have to do this anymore, Goom. You fought the good fight. You could retire."

"Yeah?" Guma asked. "Lay down the sword and fade away, forget about fighting the bad guys? Forget about justice? Could you?"

Karp smiled and shook his head. "No. Guess we're in this until they kick us out."

"Or we die with our boots on, whichever comes first," Guma said, laughing.

Tired or not, Guma's dark brown eyes were still bright with intelligence when he opened them again in Karp's office and said, "But there's a bigger problem than leading questions and threatening a suspect with the death penalty."

"The ring," Karp said grimly.

"Yeah, the ring," Guma said in agreement. "I figured you'd seen it and that was why you wanted me to speed-read the file."

"Yep," Karp replied. "There's nothing in the DD-5s to corroborate that the ring found on Acevedo is the same ring taken from Olivia Yancy. No report that says the ring was ever shown to her husband to confirm or deny. The single most important piece of evidence in the entire case against Acevedo and we have no idea if it's even true. It's a house of cards."

Guma raised a bushy eyebrow. "The press is going to town on this one, and someone is feeding them juicy tidbits, probably the 'hero' detective. They've got the public convinced that we've got the Columbia U Slasher off the streets. If this makes the media look like fools—more than the usual amount—they're going to be pissed. And it's not going to be fun if this falls apart."

Karp scowled and stood up. "I could give a rat's ass about the press. We've got a young guy locked up and charged with murder, and he could be innocent as far as we know because there's nothing in here"—he slammed a hand on the file folder—"that corroborates his guilt. I need some answers, and fast." Karp turned to look out the window onto the teeming sidewalks and streets below.

He turned back to Guma. "How many times have I said whenever we have a confession from a defendant or an admission of culpability that we need other evidence connecting the defendant to the crime?" he said. "That's the very basic rudiment of corroboration. And in a case like this—a high-profile case that serves as a window for the public to see into the justice system—we didn't even begin to check the provenance of the ring."

"You thinking what I'm thinking?" Guma asked, already starting to stand up from his chair.

Karp turned and nodded. "Go get the ring out of the evidence safe," he said.

"I'm on it," Guma answered, heading out of the office as Karp picked up the desk phone and punched in a number.

When a familiar voice picked up on the other end, he said, "Clay, do me favor, get a car and meet me and Goom out front in a half hour; we're going to take a drive up to Columbia University to see Professor Dale Yancy. Thanks."

Twenty-five minutes later, Karp and Guma walked out of the Criminal Courts Building and up to the curb, where a black sedan with tinted windows waited. They climbed in, Guma in front and Karp in back. Sitting in the driver's seat, Clay Fulton, the head of the NYPD detective squad assigned to the DAO, turned around. "Any stops along the way?" he asked.

Karp thought about it for a moment and nodded. "Take us to the crime scene first." Fulton stepped on the gas and not long after that Karp sat gazing up at the dingy ten-story apartment building where less than a year earlier Olivia Yancy and Beth Jenkins had been butchered. He imagined their terror and their helplessness, knowing they were going to die, anticipating the painful cuts and vicious blows. The killer raping Olivia even as she bled out.

With an effort, he pulled his mind away from the crime scene photographs indelibly fixed in his mind's eye, unclenched his fists, and looked around. The savagery was so incongruous with the scene surrounding him on a warm afternoon in May.

In many ways, the Morningside Heights neighborhood on the Upper West Side of Manhattan resembled a small town more than the urban jungle usually associated with Gotham.

Gentrified over the past four decades, the streets were lined with apartment buildings and row houses, but there were no skyscrapers in sight. And the street-level spaces were filled by small cafés, fresh produce grocers, florists, and boutique coffee shops.

In some ways, Morningside had a similar feel to the Lower East Side's Alphabet City with its more laid-back atmosphere and ranks of casually dressed pedestrians. Quite a difference from the hectic pace of the business-suited men and women in the Financial District and Midtown's Madison Avenue. Absent the glitz of the opposite end of the island, Morningside attracted a smaller percentage of tourists who were more likely to be students and faculty of one of a half dozen higher education institutions in the neighborhood.

In fact, Morningside Heights was sometimes referred to as "the Academic Acropolis" due to the number of educational institutions packed into the section of New York that ran north to south from 125th Street to 106th and was framed by Riverside Drive on the west and Morningside Drive on the east. Within those boundaries were Barnard College, Union Theological Seminary, New York Theological Seminary, the Jewish Theological Seminary of America, the Manhattan School of Music, Teachers College, Bank Street College of Education, and, of course, the neighborhood's biggest landowner and star resident, Columbia University.

Morningside was the sort of neighborhood where professors led informal discussions on the scientific questions of the day at the PicNic Market and Café or debated books and philosophy at the Greek restaurant aptly named Symposium. And jazz fans could find top-notch students and professors taking to the stage at the Smoke jazz lounge.

It was hard to imagine such a brutal crime had been committed there, and Karp wanted the guy who did it. *The right guy,* he thought before saying aloud, "Thanks, Clay. I just wanted to see this place for myself. Let's head over to the university. Darla Milquetost called and Mr. Yancy is in class, but he'll be done in thirty minutes and I want to catch him before he leaves."

Karp was quiet for a moment then addressed Fulton. "Clay, do you remember when we first met?" Karp asked.

"The LeRoi Rodriguez case, wasn't it?"

"Yeah." Karp reminisced, "I was brand-new to the DAO and working in the criminal courts under the inimitable Mel Glass. Man, he was special. But in my class of seventeen ADAs out of eight hundred applicants, I always figured that I was number seventeen. Everybody else seemed to have come from some big-name law school, including Fordham and St. John's. And *all* of them had more practical experience working in courtrooms than a grad of the Boalt Hall School of Law at UC-Berkeley whose professors were long on theory and short on practicality. Anyway, I knew I had some catching up to do, so when Mel would ask who wanted to volunteer to handle the competency hearings over at Bellevue Hospital, I raised my hand."

The hearings were held weekly in the psychiatric ward dayroom. They weren't to determine a defendant's sanity at the time of the alleged crimes—that might come up later at trial—but rather whether the accused was mentally competent to stand trial. As such there were two due-process issues: did the defendant understand the nature of the charges against him, and was he able to assist his defense lawyer in the proceedings?

Any given week there'd be fifty or so cases called one at a time into the dayroom, where a judge would read the recommendations of two staff psychiatrists on the competency of the defendant and make his ruling. The defense attorney, usually a Legal Aid lawyer, and the prosecutor were always present but only rarely objected to the findings or tried to introduce evidence or witnesses. In fact, it was all very informal; the judges didn't even bother to wear robes, and it was well known that they expected to be done by eleven thirty and at the golf course or racetrack by one. They did not like it when competency hearings did not run smoothly and quickly, so everyone—the judge, the lawyers, the court staff, and the staff at the hospital—made sure they went along to get along.

"Then the nightmare snafu scenario unfolded: the judge called the calendar and the psychiatric ward staff failed to produce a defendant, one LeRoi Rodriguez, a forty-one-year-old guy from Harlem who enjoyed cutting up the local prostitutes with a straight razor. He'd been arrested several days earlier with his bloody weapon still in his pocket only two blocks from a young woman whose face he'd mutilated.

"The cops thought Rodriguez was good for a dozen or more similar attacks. As you know, the psychiatric ward at Bellevue is a locked facility—no one just wanders in and out—so I was a little alarmed when Rodriguez was not produced during the calendar call. Even worse, the judge just shrugged and put the case over to a date in the following month. He then instructed the court clerk to call the next case. I was a little bewildered and said, 'Your honor, shouldn't we put out a second call and find out where the defendant is? I mean, this is a locked facility, where is he?' The judge shot me a dirty look and exclaimed, 'So are you some kind of wise guy or something?'

"'No, Your Honor,' I said calmly and respectfully, 'if the defendant is not produced on first call, it seems to me that before the case is adjourned we should make best efforts to locate him.' And, of course, as you guys know, everything I was saying was on the record. So the judge is hip with this too and gave me the 'don't fuck with me, troublemaker' look but then turned to the psychiatric ward guard who escorted the prisoners to the hearings. 'Mike, would you kindly go see if you can locate Mr. Rodriguez? Our young wiseass Mr. Karp does have a point that the defendant is here somewhere. So let's find him and get this over with.'"

Karp continued. "Mike sort of rolled his eyes, but it wasn't over. Turns out that there were two L. Rodriguezes: a Lorenzo Rodriguez, a young man who had been charged with jumping a subway turnstile at the Bowling Green Station and had his case disposed of at arraignment and was ordered released by the presiding judge. Unfortunately, a bureaucratic snafu occurred and the wrong Rodriguez was released, leaving the turnstile jumper in the Tombs while the brutal LeRoi Rodriguez was put back on the street, and it was discovered only when 'Mike' couldn't find him. Fortunately, when word went out, my friend here picked up LeRoi."

"He was on Lenox Avenue and had just pulled his razor on a girl standing on the corner waiting for the light to turn green," Fulton said. "Had him in my sights, ordered him to put the razor down, and was ready to pop him if he didn't."

Karp laughed. "Mel Glass kept me on that Rodriguez case and that's when we met."

Now it was Clay's turn to laugh. Guma grinned, too. "Whatever brought on that little jog down memory lane?"

Karp looked out the window of the car as they drove onto the university grounds. "Just that this justice business is not rocket science. It's common sense, thoroughness, preparation, and follow-through. There are enormous consequences at times when we fail to do what's necessary and professional in these cases."

Guma chimed in. "So now Big Daddy and the A-Team have to complete the follow-through."

When they arrived at Columbia's main campus, Karp watched Guma struggle for a moment to get out of the car. "You okay, Goom?" he asked.

Guma straightened his shoulders and nodded toward a pair of pretty coeds walking across the campus. "I was just remembering the good old days," he said with his patented Guma wink and grin.

"Yeah, sure," Karp replied. He'd seen the weariness and while he worried about his friend, he wasn't going to embarrass him by saying anything about it. "When was that? The Pleistocene Era?"

"Very funny," Guma replied as Fulton laughed. "Maybe when you're done catching bad guys, you can start a new career as a stand-up comic."

A passing student pointed them in the direction of Philosophy Hall and English lit professor Dale Yancy. They found him on the stage of an auditorium gazing at some one hundred students as he spoke:

Good name in man and woman, dear my lord,
Is the immediate jewel of their souls:
Who steals my purse steals trash; 'tis something, nothing;
'Twas mine, 'tis his, and has been slave to thousands;
But he that filches from me my good name
Robs me of that which not enriches him
And makes me poor indeed.

Othello, Karp thought. *The conniving Iago is speaking.* He thought of Felix Acevedo and wondered if his office had "filched" that young man's good name, as well as the underlying credibility of the justice system. *What was that other quote, the one from the honorable lieutenant Cassio after he was involved in that drunken brawl because of Iago and then dismissed by Othello? Oh yeah, "Reputation, reputation, reputation! O, I have lost my reputation! I have lost the immortal part of myself, and what remains is bestial." A good choice given the reason we're here.*

When class was over, Karp, Guma, and Fulton walked to the front and waited as Yancy spoke to several of his students and then turned and noticed them. He smiled tentatively. "May I help you?"

"Are you Dale Yancy?" Karp asked.

The smile disappeared. "I am. Why?"

Karp stepped forward and held out his hand, followed by Guma and Fulton. "My name is Roger Karp," he said. "I'm the district attorney for New York County. This is Assistant District Attorney Ray Guma and Detective Chief Clay Fulton, who directs the detectives who work for my office."

The professor relaxed and smiled broadly. "I'm sorry," he said. "I should have recognized you from the papers. I knew the face but for a moment thought maybe you were that bastard's attorneys. I haven't had much contact from the police or, to be honest, anyone from your office. I thought now that they've caught the guy, I would have heard more."

Karp grimaced as he pulled out his wallet and selected a business card. "Well, first, I'd like to apologize for that; it wasn't right and there's no excuse. However, from here on out," he said, handing over the card, "if you have any questions, day or night, please call me—my home number is on the bottom of that card along with the office number. And Ray Guma here will be handling your wife's case personally; he and Clay are also available to take your calls."

Accepting the card and another from Guma, Yancy gave Karp a puzzled look. "Thank you. I really appreciate that . . . I've felt a little lost in the system. But I'm sure you didn't come all the way up here just to introduce yourselves and give me your business cards."

Karp shook his head. "You're right," he said, "though it should have been done much sooner. But we're just trying to run down some loose ends. Make sure we get the right man for what happened to your wife and mother-in-law."

The smile disappeared from Yancy's face. "What do you mean 'right man'? Don't you have him? Didn't this Acevedo asshole confess?"

"Yes he did," Karp replied. "But I have a few concerns about his confession and some of the evidence."

"You're starting to sound like a defense attorney," Yancy said with a scowl. "What? Is his dad connected to the mob or something? He have an abused childhood and that's what turned him into a vicious animal who murders innocent women in their homes? And now you want to let him off over a few 'concerns'?" He turned and walked back to the lectern, where he started shoving his lecture papers into a briefcase.

"That's not what I'm saying," Karp replied evenly. "Mr. Yancy, I am truly sorry for what happened. I know you loved your wife. But does it matter to you that we get the right guy for her murder? Or will just any poor sap do?"

Yancy stopped. "Of course not."

"Well, if the wrong man is convicted," Karp said, "not only will an innocent man pay the price, it also means that the real killer is out there on the streets, thumbing his nose at the cops, at you, at me, at our entire system of justice. And let me be very clear about this: Guys like this don't stop killing. They like it. And I very much want whoever committed those crimes to pay for them. Now if I could just show you—"

Yancy cut him off as he whirled around to face him. "I don't need to see any more photographs," he cried out. "I came home that day and found my mother-in-law lying in a pool of blood and my wife lying on our bed, where she'd been—" He stopped talking and put a hand over his mouth as though he might be sick. When he recovered, his voice was barely above a hoarse whisper. "I see those images every night before I go to sleep. I don't need any more photographs."

Karp winced at the man's pain. "I understand. But I wasn't talking about photographs. I wanted to show you a ring and see if you can identify it."

Yancy scowled. "I've already seen one ring and it wasn't my wife's."

The other three men shot each other alarmed glances. "You were already shown a ring?" Karp asked.

"Yes, that detective—Graziani—he showed me a ring he thought was my wife's engagement ring, but it wasn't," Yancy replied.

There were more glances, only now they were angry. Karp pulled a sealed plastic bag from a manila envelope he was carrying, opened it, and removed the ring. "Would you look at this ring please?"

Yancy accepted the ring and shook his head when he looked at it. "That's the same ring Graziani showed me, and like I said, it's not my wife's ring. He said Acevedo confessed to taking it from Olivia, but it's not hers."

"You're sure?" Karp asked.

"I'm positive," Yancy said. "When I asked him what it meant, he said it wouldn't matter. He said maybe Acevedo took the ring from another victim. He said the guy's a serial killer and probably takes his victims' rings by cutting their fingers off. Like some sick calling card."

Karp pointed to the ring in the bag. "I just want to be sure about this ring," he said. "There's an inscription on the inside of the ring. You can make out the word 'Always,' but the rest of it appears to have been removed."

Yancy shrugged. "Hers never said 'Always' and the inscription area on this ring isn't long enough for what would have been there if it was my wife's ring."

"Which said what?" Karp asked.

A slight wistful smile came to the man's lips for a moment before disappearing again. "'Love goes toward love.'"

"From *Romeo and Juliet*," Karp said.

"Very good, you know your Shakespeare," Yancy replied, and then looked puzzled. "But I don't get it. Don't you guys talk to Graziani? How come you didn't already know this isn't her ring?"

"Could be a miscommunication," Karp replied.

Yancy looked skeptical. "Or maybe he just didn't tell you for some reason."

"We won't know until we talk to him," Karp said. "Did he ask you about the ring before or after Acevedo was indicted?"

"I believe Detective Graziani showed me the ring a day or two before Acevedo was indicted," Yancy answered, "because after the indictment I read about it in the newspapers and was irritated that no one bothered to tell me."

Yancy walked the men back to their car. As Karp got in the backseat, the professor leaned over to speak to him. "One thing I don't get: If he didn't do it, why'd Acevedo confess? Does he get a kick out of pouring salt on wounds?"

Karp looked troubled and shook his head. "Good question. But right now I'm focused on finding who killed your wife and mother-in-law and making him pay."

"So now what?" Yancy asked.

"We've got to go back and talk this over," Karp replied. "But whatever happens, I'll call you as soon as I know anything."

Tears came to Yancy's eyes. "This arrest really got my hopes up . . . that maybe someday I'd get some closure and be able to move on. If this other detective is playing some sort of game, I can't even think of the words to express the cruelty."

Fulton leaned from the driver's seat across Guma so he could look up at Yancy. "I can't speak for Detective Graziani. But I promise you, we will not give up until we've got the right guy and you get that peace."

As soon as they pulled away from the curb, Karp leaned forward to speak to Fulton. "Clay, do you know Graziani?"

Fulton shook his head. "Can't say I do," he said. "But counting all five boroughs there are some thirty-seven thousand sworn officers with the NYPD, so it's no surprise. You need me to reach out and find out what I can about him?"

"Yeah, I want his personnel file," Karp growled. "If you run into any trouble getting it, let me know, and I'll call in a favor with the chief. That son of a bitch withheld exculpatory evidence, and his ass is mine."

17

"HE'S HEADING THIS WAY RIGHT NOW."

Marlene turned around in the direction indicated by Raymond and saw a young acne-scarred man with peroxide-blond hair approaching on the sidewalk. He noticed Marlene's look and his street sense warned him to veer away from the woman with the monster dog. He suddenly changed course toward the interior of the park.

Stepping toward him, Marlene shouted. "Hey, I'd like to talk to you! I'm not a cop!" She might as well have said she was going to shoot him. He ran.

Marlene sighed and glanced down at Gilgamesh, who gave her a look that seemed to say, "How much of a head start shall we give him?" She nodded toward the running man. *"Prendere,"* she said.

Gilgamesh grinned and without a sound took off after the man, who peered back long enough to see the dog in pursuit.

He shrieked and didn't make it another twenty feet before Gilgamesh knocked him down. Crying out in fear, the man rolled over onto his back and put his hands up protectively while the dog simply held his ground, a deep growl rumbling in his massive chest.

Afraid to move anything else, the man only flicked his eyes over to see the woman walk up in no great hurry. "Don't let him bite me," he begged. The sweat pouring off his face was due more to fear than the hot and muggy New York afternoon.

"Then don't do anything he might interpret as unfriendly," Marlene replied. "I only told him to catch you, not have you for lunch. But as you have noticed, he's really fast, and if you do something stupid, he may react before I can stop him."

It was a lie, of course; Gilgamesh would not savage the man unless Marlene commanded him to *assalire*, the Italian word for "attack," just as *prendere* was Italian for "catch." But the man trembling on the ground didn't know that and for the moment Marlene was willing to let him remain ignorant.

"I want to ask you some questions," she said.

"I want a lawyer," he replied, keeping his eyes on the dog.

"I'm not a cop. I am a lawyer."

"Then I don't have nothin' to say."

"Okay, I'll leave you here to play with the doggie." Marlene shrugged.

"Take your fucking dog with you."

Gilgamesh growled and took a step forward at the man's tone. "He doesn't appreciate your language and neither do I," Marlene said.

"Okay, I'm sorry," the man answered. "What do you want?"

"Is your name Al?"

He looked relieved. "Is that all? Fuck no, my name is Jesus Guerrero."

"No, that's not all." Marlene continued. "I want to know if you sold a small diamond engagement ring to Felix Acevedo a few weeks ago."

Guerrero scowled. "I didn't sell nothin' to nobody."

Marlene looked down at her dog. "What do you think, Gilgamesh, is he lying?" The dog growled again and took another step toward the man. "He says you're lying."

The man scowled. "He's a dog. What does he know?"

"You've heard of bomb dogs and drug dogs, right?" Marlene asked.

"Yeah."

"Well, Gilgamesh is a lie-detector dog."

"That's bullshit."

"No, really, these dogs can smell a lie," Marlene said. "There's some sort of chemical odor the body gives off when a person lies. Dogs like this hate that smell. Drives them crazy. To be honest, even little lie-detector dogs can become hard to control, they hate it so much, and Gilgamesh is a big dog."

"He's damn big," Guerrero said in agreement.

"Then when I ask questions, you should try to tell me the truth," Marlene said, smiling. "Let's start over." She then pulled out a photograph of Felix Acevedo and showed it to Guerrero. "Do you know this man?"

Guerrero sat up and shrugged. "I might have seen him once or twice."

Marlene looked at her dog and gave him a hand signal out of Guerrero's sight. The dog growled. She turned back to Guerrero and frowned. "Once or twice?"

"Maybe more than that," Guerrero responded quickly, inching farther back from the dog. "I see him around. Mostly with those other punks in the park. He's kind of slow, but he's a pretty good rapper. His name is Felix." He looked at the dog and smiled slightly when there was no growl.

"That's better," Marlene said. "Gilgamesh believes you. Now, did you sell Felix a small diamond ring a few weeks ago?"

"Yeah, I might have."

"Where did you get this ring?"

"I found it."

Marlene signaled the dog, who suddenly tensed and bared his teeth. "Oh, bad one," she said. "You didn't just find it." She knew she was running the risk that if Guerrero was the real killer of Olivia Yancy, forcing this confession out of him might mess up the case for the cops. But her senses told her he was no more a murderer than her client.

Guerrero scooted farther away from the dog. "Shit, okay, I snatched a purse from a lady over by the old Yankee Stadium. There wasn't much in it. A few bucks, the ring, a credit card, and her driver's license."

"That right, Gil? *Rilassare*," she said, adding the Italian word for "relax" to the end of her question.

Gilgamesh sat down on his haunches and for the first time took his eyes off Guerrero. Marlene smiled. "Very good. Now we're getting somewhere."

"I remember the last name from the driver's license," Guerrero said helpfully. "Lopez. The same as my mom's before she married my dad."

"That's great," Marlene said. "You remember anything in particular about this ring?"

Guerrero thought about it and then shook his head. "Not really, except it was pretty cheap," he said. Then he brightened. "But there was some writing on the inside. A name and a word."

"I don't suppose you remember what it said?"

"The name was Al—that's why you called me that," Guerrero said, suddenly putting two and two together. "I told Felix that was my name so he wouldn't think the ring was hot. I don't remember what else."

Marlene reached back into her purse and pulled out two more photographs—these had been taken of the evidence by a defense photographer—and showed him one. "Can you tell me if the ring in this photograph looks like the one you sold to Felix Acevedo?"

"Could be. It was something like that."

"Here's another photograph," Marlene said. "It's the inside of the same ring."

Guerrero looked at the photo and shrugged again. "Looks like Felix filed the words off. I can't be sure but I think so."

"Did you steal the purse that same day?"

"Yeah, a couple of hours before I saw Felix. We done? I got to go."

Marlene thought about it and then nodded. "Yeah, except I need to know how to reach you in case I need you to testify about the ring."

"Fuck that," Guerrero said. "I ain't testifying or telling you where I live."

Marlene gave the dog a barely perceptible hand signal and Gilgamesh jumped up, bristling and growling at Guerrero. "Nobody's going to bust you for the purse snatching. Felix's life may depend on you telling the truth. So tell me how to find you, and just so we're clear, don't make me and Gilgamesh come hunting for you. He has your scent now, the smell of a liar, and it would be easy for him to track you."

"Okay, okay," Guerrero said. "I don't want nothin' to happen to Felix. He's an all right kid and everybody already picks on him. I live with my mom in her apartment building, the Hampshires, on the corner of 183rd and Southern, across from the zoo. But if she comes to the door, don't say nothin' to my mom about this. She thinks I'm a musician in a band."

Marlene laughed sarcastically. "She must be very proud. Now—not that I don't trust you, which I do about as far as you'd get from Gil if you lie to me—let me see your driver's license, and give me your mom's address again."

Grumbling but conscious of the dog, Guerrero stood and produced a driver's license. Marlene wrote the pertinent information down and handed it back. "One more thing: I need a photograph," she said, pulling a digital camera out of her bag. "Say cheese."

An hour later, Marlene stood on the sidewalk waiting for the couple pushing a baby stroller toward her. She left Gilgamesh in the truck so as not to frighten the couple, who she'd learned from a neighbor in their apartment building were out for a midafternoon walk.

"Excuse me," she said, addressing the tall, pretty woman, "are you Amy Lopez?"

The big, burly man accompanying the woman stepped in front. "Who wants to know?" he asked.

"My name is Marlene Ciampi; I'm a lawyer but right now I'm doing some investigative work for Felix Acevedo," she replied. "I just wanted to talk to Amy Lopez about a report she filed a few weeks ago about her purse being taken."

After leaving Guerrero, Marlene had called a friend with the NYPD records division and, after a little wheedling, got him to look on the computer and see if anyone named Lopez had reported a purse being stolen in the vicinity of old Yankee Stadium several weeks earlier. It was just a hunch, but it paid off. An Amy Lopez had reported the theft of the purse, and among the items she listed as its contents was "an engagement ring with the inscription 'Always, Al.'"

"You found my purse!" the woman exclaimed as she pushed her husband out of the way. "I'm Amy Lopez. Don't mind Al, here, he works as a court clerk downtown inside the Criminal Courts Building in Manhattan, and he's suspicious of everyone."

"You playing hooky?" Marlene asked Al.

"Nah, just taking some comp time off," he replied. "But Amy's right. Listening to that stuff all day, every day, has made me a little jaded. Sorry, I was being overprotective."

"Not a problem," Marlene said. "It pays to be cautious these days. And I thought I recognized you; you've been working at the Criminal Courts Building for a long time."

Al grinned. "Yeah, how ya doing, Ms. Ciampi, I thought that

was you, too, but it's been a while. Small world. Anyway, this tall drink of water is my wife, Amy, and the little guy is my son, A.J."

"Oh, he's a doll! What does A.J. stand for?" Marlene cooed.

"Alexander Jenner," Amy replied.

"Jenner? That's unusual."

"He was named for his aunt, Jennifer," she said sadly. "I'm afraid she passed away last December. A heart condition. She was my best friend, and we all love and miss her very much."

"I'm sorry," Marlene said. "I know how it feels to lose someone you love like that. Tears the heart right out of you."

"Thank you," Amy replied. "So you found my purse?"

Marlene shook her head. "Unfortunately, no, but did you also report that a ring was inside the purse?"

Amy nodded. "Yes, my engagement ring. I'm afraid I gained a few pounds carrying A.J. and it got a little tight. I took it off until I could lose the weight."

"Could you describe the ring?"

"Yes, it had a small diamond—"

"It wasn't that small," Al interjected.

Amy leaned forward conspiratorially. "It was maybe half a carat. That small," she said with a laugh, and put her arm around her husband. "But this two-hundred-and-eighty-pound bundle of love has more than made up for it in kisses."

"I'll take the kisses any day," Marlene said. She reached into her purse and took out the photographs of the ring that she'd shown Guerrero. "Would you mind taking a look at these?" she asked, handing the first one to Amy.

"That's my ring!" Amy replied. "See what I meant about the diamond?"

"Hey, it looked bigger in person," Al retorted.

"I'm sure," Marlene said with a laugh as she handed the second photograph to Amy. "Here's another of the same ring."

"Oh, he wrecked it," Amy cried. "It used to say 'Always, Al,' but it's all scratched out." Tears slipped out of her eyes and ran down her cheeks as her husband patted her shoulder.

"It's okay," he said. "I bet a jeweler can buff that up nice and inscribe it again."

"Sure he can, and now you'll have a story to go along with it," Marlene said. "Do you think you'd recognize the guy who snatched your purse?"

"In a New York minute," Amy replied. "He sat across from me on the train all the way from Spanish Harlem. The pizza-faced jerk waited until I was on the sidewalk then came out of nowhere and grabbed my purse. Believe me, I got a good look at him."

Marlene pulled the camera out of her purse and pushed a button before turning the screen toward Amy. "I'm going to show you six photographs of different men. Stop me if you recognize any one of them."

Amy looked at each photograph as it appeared but stopped Marlene at the fourth. "That's Mr. Pizza Face right there."

Marlene looked at the face on the screen. *Jesus Guerrero,* she thought with satisfaction. "Good," she said. "And if I need you to identify him for the authorities, would you be willing to do that?"

"You bet. Maybe they'll lock him up for a few years."

"Actually, I might need him as a cooperative witness," Marlene said. "I may want him to testify that he sold your ring to another man. It could save that man's life."

"Well, that's more important than putting Pizza Face in jail," Amy said, "though I'd still like to punch him. But hey, do you think I'll get my ring back?"

"You may have to wait until this case is resolved," Marlene said, "but you should be able to after that, and I'll help."

"Then I'm good with it," Amy said, and smiled. "It may be a small diamond, but it was my first. Thank you, Marlene."

18

VINNIE CASSINO SAT IN THE BACK OF THE SQUAD CAR weighing his options. He'd traveled to the South Bronx and a seedy apartment off Anderson Avenue to purchase several ounces of methamphetamine from his favorite dealer, only to learn the hard way that he'd been set up. Now he was looking at a felony drug possession with intent to sell, and they'd popped him with a handgun for an additional count. With two prior strikes against him, another could earn him the unwanted legal title of "habitual offender," or in the vernacular of the streets a "three-time loser," looking at life behind bars.

Time to play my ace, he told himself. "Hey, tell Detective Brock that I need to talk to him," he said. "Tell him he's got the wrong guy for the Atkins murder. The guy didn't do the two in Manhattan either, but I know who did."

The police officer driving the car looked in the rearview mirror at the scruffy, gray-haired drug dealer with the protruding forehead and rolled his eyes. "Yeah, yeah, whatever you say, Sherlock," he said in a tone that implied he was unimpressed by suspects trying to make deals on the way to jail.

"Listen, asshole, I'm telling the truth," Cassino said. "You'll be walking the two A.M. beat in Bed-Stuy if you blow this."

"Watch your mouth, punk," the officer snarled, "or maybe we'll stop in an alley for a little attitude adjustment before I get you to lockup."

"Go ahead," Cassino retorted, "then I won't have to say nothing to Brock, and I'll still walk. But if you got any brains, tell him to check and see if a blue silk shirt came up missing in the Manhattan killing."

An hour later, the police officer was talking to Sergeant McManus when he saw Brock. The officer weighed whether to tell the detective about the drug dealer. It was probably bullshit; then again, most of the scumbags trying to weasel their way to freedom didn't first offer something that could be checked out. He decided to pass the information on.

"Detective Brock, I'm Dave Drummond," the officer said. "This is probably nothing but I was detailed to haul a drug dealer named Vinnie Cassino down to booking after a bust this morning."

"Cassino? Doesn't ring a bell," Brock replied with a frown.

"Yeah, and this probably isn't anything but a line of BS," Drummond said, "but he was real insistent that I tell you that you've got the wrong guy in the Atkins case. He says he knows who did it."

"And I'm the queen of England," Brock snorted. "If it would get him a better deal, he'd probably tell me who killed Kennedy, too."

Drummond laughed. "Yeah, I'm sure he would. But anyway, he said to ask you about a blue silk shirt in the Manhattan case."

The smile faded from Brock's face. After Graziani connected Acevedo to the Yancy-Jenkins double murder, Brock asked for a copy of the Manhattan file to see if there was something in it that could help him nail down the Atkins case. The file contained a report on items the younger victim's husband had identified as missing—some jewelry, purses, and a blue silk shirt taken from his closet. He remembered that item in particular as it meant the perp had changed clothes after the bloodbath. It was one of the details that had been kept from the press as far as he could remember, but now some drug dealer knew about it.

"A blue silk shirt, you're sure that's what he said?" Brock asked.

"Yeah, positive," Drummond replied. "It mean something?"

"Maybe," Brock said, and patted the young officer on the shoulder. "You done good, kid, I'll pass my thanks on to your supervisor."

The young officer grinned. A commendation from a senior detective to the higher-ups could speed up the time it took to get his detective's gold shield. "No problem."

Twenty minutes later Brock was waiting in one of the interview rooms when Cassino was brought in. "You wanted to talk to me?" he asked.

"No, I think you want to talk to me," Cassino replied. "But I want a deal, or I ain't saying shit."

"What are you offering for this deal?"

Cassino's eyes grew shrewd and ratlike as he leaned forward. "You got the wrong guy for these killings. And I know who did it."

Brock shrugged. "Anybody can say that."

"That cop told you about the blue silk shirt or you wouldn't be here," Cassino said.

"What about it?" Brock asked.

"What if I told you the famous Columbia U Slasher wore that to my pad the day of the killings?" Cassino said. "That and that me and my old lady saw blood on his pants. There's more, too, but that's all you get for now."

"I'm interested," Brock said. "So who is this guy?"

Cassino grinned, revealing missing teeth and serious dental problems with those that remained. "Not so fast, Detective. I can tell you his name, but that won't do shit for you. Not without me and my old lady testifying, and what's more, I got a tape of him talking about that other woman, your case in the Bronx. But I ain't scratching your back until you or whoever has to fix this scratches mine."

"What are you going to want?" Brock asked.

Leaning back in his chair, Cassino smiled again as if he'd just concluded a big business deal. "I'm a two-time loser and if they get me on this latest charge, they'll put me away for a long time, maybe for the rest of my life," he said. "Either way, I don't like the idea of being away from my sweet Lydia for so long. So first things first, I'm gonna make bail, but I want these charges to go away, *and* I want the Crime Stoppers reward for giving this guy up. In exchange, you get me and my old lady on the witness stand pointing to that asshole in the courtroom, and you get my tape and the blue silk shirt."

"That's asking a lot," Brock said. "You've got to give me more."

"All right, I'll give you the fucker's name," Cassino replied. "Like I said, it ain't gonna do you no good without me, but at least you could start looking for him. His name is Ahmed Kadyrov."

"Know where I can find him?" Brock asked.

"Maybe," Cassino said. "Or at least where to start looking. But that's all you get until I get a deal."

"I'll talk to the higher-ups," Brock said. "But I can't promise anything."

"Then I can't either," Cassino said. "If I'm going away for a long time, I'm going to do it without a snitch jacket."

Two hours later, Brock sat in a booth in the Lino Tavern, a favorite hangout for cops working out of the Four-Eight off Van Nest Avenue. He was waiting to give Joey Graziani some unwelcome news and not looking forward to his reaction.

After sending Cassino back to his cell, Brock had looked up Ahmed Kadyrov and found a young man by that name with a record for crimes committed in Queens and Manhattan. He wasn't big-time, just a few burglaries committed when the owners weren't home during the day, but nothing too serious or anything that would indicate a sex killer. *People change,* he reminded himself, *and he was comfortable working daylight hours. He could have been surprised and things turned nasty.*

So far he had not told anybody about his conversation with Cassino. He felt obligated to tell Graziani first. He didn't particularly like the man; he'd been acting like a rock star ever since the news of the Columbia U Slasher arrest broke, and he declined interviews but somehow details about the crimes and the arrest kept being leaked to the press, with Joey Graziani as the man of the hour. He'd even gotten his wish and had been reassigned to the Two-Six detective squad in Morningside Heights to work the case. But there was still the brotherhood of the gold shield, and if Cassino's story checked out, it was going to mess up Graziani's case.

There was a chance that the other detective could redeem himself if he used Cassino's information to catch the real killer, even if it meant admitting that charging Acevedo was a mistake. *A chance, but not much of one*, Brock thought. The New York County DAO had indicted Acevedo based on Graziani's investigation and recommendations. Having to backtrack now would not only cause a great deal of embarrassment to the DAO, which the press would go to town with, but it would also present real difficulties in prosecuting a new defendant.

No, Graziani wasn't going to be happy about the news. *It's his own damn fault*, Brock thought with a touch of anger. He'd been sloppy and determined to pin the murders on Acevedo come hell or high water. *And that sort of thing reflects on all of us.*

Brock had seen it before, detectives who got so myopic about one particular suspect that they missed clues that could have prevented a mistake. Graziani had been so desperate to get out of the Bronx and saw Acevedo as his ticket, but if Cassino was right, he might wish he was back at the Four-Eight.

He was still thinking about the ramifications when he saw Graziani enter the pub and stand for a moment as his eyes adjusted to the dark room. He turned and spotted Brock, then walked over with a big grin as if they were old friends who hadn't seen each other in a long time. He held out his hand. "Hey, *paisan,* how ya doin'? Still enjoying the hellhole they call the Bronx?"

"I'm okay, Joey," Brock said, shaking the other man's hand without much enthusiasm.

Graziani didn't seem to notice or care. "Glad that you called, glad that you called," he said. "Been meaning to give you a jingle and ask why the Bronx DA hasn't filed on Acevedo yet. Can't get Hartsfield to move his fat ass?" He chuckled as a waitress walked up. "Couple of Brooklyn Locals work for you?" he asked Brock. "I'm buying."

Brock shook his head. "Nothing for me, thanks. I quit drinking ten years ago after wife number two left me."

"Good for you." Graziani smirked as he held up one finger to the waitress. "Though as my old man used to tell me, 'I don't trust a drinking man when I'm sober or a sober man when I'm drinking.' So why haven't you guys filed?"

Brock shrugged. "They're still putting it together. To tell you the truth, I'm starting to wonder if Acevedo is my guy."

Graziani frowned. "What do you mean? You got a solid case—in some ways better than mine, with a witness ID, and he confessed to the attempted rape and the Atkins murder." His voice was tense and the bonhomie was gone.

"Yeah, but I'm still bothered by a couple of things," Brock said. "For instance, the assault victim, Marianne Tate, described hitting the guy who grabbed her with her left elbow, striking him on the left side of the face."

"So?"

"So, Acevedo's face was bruised on the right side."

Graziani rolled his eyes. "Big fuckin' deal. It wouldn't be the first time a victim got mixed up. Or maybe he turned his head. It don't mean shit."

"Maybe," Brock said. "But I also talked to his mom, who said his dad hit him the night before he was arrested. She described it as a backhand blow to the right side of his face."

Now the other detective was scowling. "So what? Maybe the victim didn't hit him hard enough to cause a bruise. Or the mom is covering for her kid. He told the ADA the same thing he told me."

"Yeah, and my gut tells me that kid was just parroting everything we gave him," Brock said, "and he picked up on it real good. I looked back at my interview with him and it's clear he followed my lead. I knew better, but I wanted the killer, too. And you practically spoon-fed him the answers you wanted."

Graziani's eyes blazed and he started to say something but stopped as the waitress delivered his beer. He picked it up and drank half of it before setting it down again. "I didn't threaten him, didn't hit him," he said with his jaw clenched. "He was caught and he knew it. He was just hoping to get a deal if he cooperated. You're throwing away a perfectly good case on bullshit technicalities and your 'gut.' I'm glad the New York DAO wasn't so chickenshit."

Brock stared hard at Graziani for a moment. The guy was an asshole but this didn't mean he was a bad cop; they'd both made mistakes on this one. "What I think isn't your biggest problem," he said.

"What do you mean?" Graziani scowled.

Brock told him about Vinnie Cassino's accusations against Kadyrov.

"Bullshit," Graziani spat, and finished his beer. "He's just another scumbag drug dealer trying to cut a deal."

"He knew about the missing blue shirt."

"Maybe he read about it in the newspapers."

"I looked," Brock said. "I couldn't find a single story that talked about the shirt."

"Maybe he heard it from Acevedo," Graziani said. "Kid's probably a meth head and bragged about doing these women. Maybe Cassino heard about it but got him mixed up with this Ahmed Kadyrov. Or maybe somebody on the task force let it out. There must have been a hundred people who could have seen the investigation reports."

"Yeah, it's all possible," Brock said, unconvinced. "You ever hear of Kadyrov? He's got a rap sheet for a few B & Es in Manhattan and Queens."

"Never heard of him," Graziani said.

"Well, maybe if you tracked him down, and this Cassino has what he says he does, you still get the collar, and all else is forgiven."

"Yeah, right," Graziani sneered. He rubbed his face with his hand. "The DA and NYPD brass will throw me to the wolves. I'd be the guy who made them look like fools. I'll be pulling traffic detail in Staten fucking Island until I'm pensioned." Graziani stared at the ceiling for a moment, then shook his head and looked Brock in the eyes. "I don't believe Cassino. I *know* we got the right guy for this. The rest of this is bullshit. But if you let this out, a defense attorney will use it to jack up my case and put doubt in the minds of the jurors. And that means a psychopath gets off scot-free."

Brock tilted his head and shrugged. "Sorry. You know I have to turn in this report."

Graziani looked for a moment like he wanted to bust his beer glass on his colleague's head, but then he relaxed. "You didn't file the report yet?"

Brock hesitated; he didn't like Graziani to start with and liked him even less now. "Not yet," he said. "I wanted to give you a head start so that you could run this Kadyrov to the ground and figure out if Cassino is telling the truth. But I'm going to have to tell Sergeant Marks soon. We're supposed to meet with the assistant district attorney assigned to the Atkins case early next week."

Graziani thought for a moment, then he nodded his head. "You're right," he said. "I'm sorry; don't know what I was thinking. Can you give me a couple of days to find this Ahmed Kadyrov before you let the cat out of the bag? Maybe I can still make this come out all right. At least get the bad guy off the streets even if my ass gets fried for it."

Brock nodded. "Yeah, I can hold off for a few days. Maybe Kadyrov is connected to the Atkins murder, in which case you'd be doing me a favor, too."

"That's right, you'd owe me one," Graziani said, and signaled the waitress for another beer. He smiled. "You know, this might just work out fine after all."

19

Zak stared down from the mound at the catcher, who glanced over at Coach Newell for the pitch sign. Chase Fitzgerald nodded and grinned as he looked back at Zak and gave the signal. *High and tight.* A brushback pitch—a head-high fastball meant to intimidate a batter and move him off the plate.

Or in this case, he's hoping I'll hit Esteban or at least scare the shit out of him, Zak thought.

Coaches weren't supposed to be encouraging, or teaching, brushback pitches at the high school level. There was too great a chance of someone getting seriously injured. But Newell's ethics were always questionable when it came to getting an edge on the competition. And in this case it was no surprise that he was calling for it against Esteban Gonzalez even though this was just practice.

The coach's previous efforts to chase the young man from

the team had failed. Just three days after being cut by Chase Fitzgerald's cleats, requiring twelve stitches in his leg, Esteban had walked back out on the field as if nothing had happened. And though it was obvious that his leg was hurting him and he was limping by the end of practice, he'd kept up on the drills.

It was a gutsy performance. But instead of earning even Newell's grudging respect, the boy's perseverance seemed to anger the coach all the more. And now he was telling Zak to toss a beanball at him.

Zak shook the sign off and waited for a new signal. Fitzgerald frowned and looked back over at Coach Newell, who emphatically made the same hand signals, only this time he looked directly at Zak as he gestured. There was no question that this was a test. The coach's eyes said it all: *Are you with us or against us?*

Zak looked back at Fitzgerald, aware that Giancarlo was standing in the on-deck circle watching. He nodded to the catcher and went into his windup, then threw hard. The ball caught an inside corner of the plate for a strike. A great pitch and the third strike on Esteban, who smiled and shook his head in admiration as he turned to walk back to the dugout.

"Again," Newell bellowed from the dugout.

Zak and Esteban both looked at the coach and then each other. As the other boy stepped back into the batter's box, Zak saw a momentary look of fear on Esteban's face. But the fear was immediately replaced by resolve; he nodded at Zak.

Fitzgerald looked over at Newell and visibly laughed as he gave Zak the signal again for a brushback pitch. Zak reared back and threw. This time the pitch was high and inside . . . but about three feet over Esteban's head.

Coach Newell stormed across the field and up to the mound. "What are you doing, Karp?" he demanded.

"Pitching," Zak answered, his eyes not meeting the coach's.

"You ignored my signals," Newell growled.

"I'm not going to throw at his head," Zak stated as he looked the coach in the eyes.

Newell's face turned red, and he took a step toward Zak and appeared ready to yell. But the coach looked up and saw that the rest of the team had walked close enough to hear what he was going to say. Max Weller, Chase Fitzgerald, and Chet Anders stood together smirking. But others looked troubled and grim.

The coach held out his hand for the ball. "Hit the showers and see me in my office in fifteen, Karp," he said, and yelled over to where the other pitchers were throwing in the warm-up cages. "Worley, get your ass out here!"

Worley ran out to the mound. Glaring at Zak, Newell handed Worley the ball. "Let's see if somebody can remember the meaning of 'team.' Or if he knows better than the coach."

With that the coach turned and walked away. At the same time, Zak walked off in the direction of the locker room. He glanced toward his brother, who smiled and touched the brim of his cap in a salute. Zak rolled his eyes and with a quiet curse changed directions and headed for home plate.

"Give me the bat," he said as he walked up to Esteban. Without waiting, Zak grabbed the bat and gently pushed Esteban away. He then stepped up to the plate.

Sensing something going on behind him, Newell turned. His eyes bugged when he saw Zak Karp in the batter's box and his red face grew purple. But he said nothing, just signaled the pitch to Fitzgerald.

Zak saw Worley smile and knew what was coming. "You're screwed, Karp," Fitzgerald said, chuckling as the pitcher went into his windup.

Zak waited until just before Worley released the ball and stepped back out of the batter's box. But he wasn't trying to duck the pitch. He knew what the signal had been and knew where the pitch was going, which made it relatively easy to make contact and drive it up the middle of the field.

The ball skipped off the mound and caught Worley in the shins. The pitcher went down and began to howl. Weller and Anders rushed over to him. As Fitzgerald ran past Zak, he turned and pointed as he said, "Your ass is grass now, Karp."

Zak shrugged and tossed the bat over his shoulder and walked to the locker room. Fifteen minutes later, he knocked on the door of Coach Newell's office and walked in. The coach didn't look up from whatever he was reading and gestured to the chair across from him. "Shut the door and take a seat, Karp" was all he said.

Zak did as he was told and was left to sit for several minutes before the coach looked up at him. "You mind telling me what you were trying to prove today?" Newell asked.

"I don't think it's right to try to hurt someone," Zak said.

Newell acted as if he were shocked. "Hurt someone? Who said I wanted you to hurt someone? I asked for a fastball inside. Your opponent was crowding the plate. If you're going to have qualms about making that pitch, you're not going to get any offers to play ball in college."

"The signal was 'high and tight,' a beanball," Zak said. "I can pitch inside. But you can't ask me to take a chance of hurting someone, especially on my own team."

"Your own team," Newell repeated with a sneer. "Do you consider it part of being a good teammate to ignore your coach's instructions and then, in front of the whole team, treat him and your other teammates with disrespect? And do you think being a good teammate means trying to hit Worley? We're lucky he's only got a bruise or we'd be out our number-one pitcher going into the playoffs."

The coach stopped talking and looked sideways at Zak. "Or is that what you wanted?"

The hotter-blooded of the twins, Zak knew he had to control his temper. "I didn't mean to hit him. But he was trying to hit me."

"He was doing what I asked him to do, unlike you," Newell replied. "It's good practice for the pitcher and the batter. The pitcher gains the intimidation factor, and the batter learns to get out of the way."

"You did it because the batter was Esteban."

Newell's jaw set tight as he tried to stare Zak down. "I'm trying to mold a team here, Karp, to win a state championship," he said as if trying his best to be patient. "And if I have a player on the team who is a disruption or doesn't fit into what myself and the other coaches are trying to do here, then it's part of my job to weed him out."

"Esteban's a good player," Zak replied. "And he works hard."

Newell shrugged. "He's okay. But Weller's a team leader, and he's been around longer. Besides, those people are all about individual stats. They only see sports as a way out of the ghetto and couldn't give a shit about the team. I think he'd be happier playing for a public school where he'd have more of his people around to *habla español* and play like a bunch of prima donnas. We're fine without him; in case you haven't noticed, we're seeded second in the state and the playoffs start next week."

" 'Those people'?" Zak said. "You mean Hispanics?"

"I mean poor Hispanics who come here and don't even bother learning the language," Newell replied. "But they expect everything to be handed to them on a silver platter. Well, it ain't going to happen on my watch."

Newell picked up the binder he'd been studying when Zak entered the room. "You know what this is?"

"A lineup book," Zak replied.

"Damn right it is," Newell said, and pushed it across his desk so that Zak could see it. "And this particular page is the lineup for game two of the playoffs. You can see that at the moment, I haven't written anybody in as the starting pitcher. Normally, that would be your name there, but as of now you are suspended for conduct detrimental to the team."

"What conduct?" Zak asked, fighting to keep back tears.

"Disrespect and attempting to hurt one of your teammates," Newell replied.

"That's not fair," Zak exclaimed.

Newell leaned across his desk and fixed his eyes on the boy's. "I decide what's fair around here. Now, I don't need to remind you that these playoff games attract a lot of attention from college and pro scouts, and it would be a shame for them not to see you. But I will not hesitate to keep you on the bench if your attitude doesn't improve, and I mean pronto. Do I make myself clear?"

Zak dipped his head so that the coach wouldn't see the anger in his eyes. "Yes, sir."

"Good, now get the hell out of here," Newell said, and then softened his tone. "Glad to have you on board, Zak; you're going to have a hell of a career."

Giancarlo was waiting for Zak outside the coach's office. "Don't say anything," Zak said, looking at his brother. "I'm not in the mood."

Closing his mouth, Giancarlo fell in step with Zak as they walked down the hallway toward the exit. But he couldn't remain quiet. "I'm proud of you."

Zak paused. "Yeah? Well you know what you being proud of me means? It means that if my 'attitude' doesn't improve, he's going to bench me for the playoffs. Right now I'm suspended for conduct detrimental to the team."

"That's crap! We need to tell someone," Giancarlo sputtered.

"He'll say I misinterpreted what he wanted me to pitch and that I was insubordinate," Zak replied. "And that I purposefully tried to hurt Worley so that I could be the starting pitcher in game one. And this team will back him up, especially the upperclassmen; this is their chance for a state championship and they're not going to let me, or some Hispanic guy, screw that up for them. Besides, who are we going to tell? We're getting too old to run to Daddy every time something's not going our way."

The boys left the building and saw Lucy waiting for them in their mother's high-end truck. She was parked behind a beat-up economy car with threadbare tires and rust spots on the panels. As they approached, the passenger-side door of the beat-up car opened and Esteban got out and walked toward them.

"Great, now what?" Zak growled.

"Hey, Esteban, what's up?" Giancarlo said.

Esteban smiled at Giancarlo but held out his hand to Zak. "I wish to thank you," he said in heavily accented English.

Zak frowned. That's when he noticed another car in the lot containing Max Weller, Chase Fitzgerald, and Chet Anders. "I didn't do anything," he said without offering his hand in return, and walked on to where Lucy was waiting.

Esteban looked hurt and puzzled as he turned to Giancarlo. "I say something bad?"

Giancarlo shook his head. "Nah. He's just upset 'cause the coach got mad at him," he explained.

Esteban looked over to where Zak was crawling into the jump seat of the truck. He bit his lip and nodded. "I understand this," he said, and put his hand out to Giancarlo, who shook it. "Please to tell him *gracias* again for me when time is right, eh?"

"I will," Giancarlo said. "See you tomorrow."

The two boys split up and walked to their respective rides, both conscious that their teammates in the other car were watching. Giancarlo was surprised that Zak was in the back of the truck; usually he called shotgun and couldn't be budged.

"Well, hello to you, too," Lucy said as Giancarlo got in the front passenger seat and buckled his seat belt without speaking. "Don't tell me both of you are in foul moods. Grumpy the Dwarf hasn't said a word since he got in."

"Sorry, Luce, I'm fine," Giancarlo said, despite being able to see the boys in the other car mouthing words he couldn't hear but whose intent he understood. "Zak's just upset because the coach got on his case."

Lucy frowned. "Is everything all right?"

"I don't want to talk about it, okay?" Zak snarled.

"Not a problem," Lucy replied. "Maybe something tasty at Moishe's will put you in a better mood."

"What?" Zak asked.

"Did you forget? I'm supposed to take you to see Moishe for your report. Mom and Dad are both working late."

Both boys groaned. But their complaints ended the moment they walked into Il Buon Pane. They chose cherry cheese coffee cake and disappeared chattering happily to the upstairs apartments with Moishe.

When they were gone, Goldie motioned for Lucy to have a seat at one of the tables. *I will lock up and we'll have something to eat and drink,* she signed.

Lucy shook her head. *Thank you, but I really should be going,* she signed back. *The twins have cab fare and—*

There is something so important that you cannot spare a few minutes for an old woman? Goldie signed, and smiled, her blue eyes twinkling.

Lucy laughed. *Well, since you put it that way . . . but it will cost you another piece of that cherry cheese coffee cake.*

Good, good, a small price to pay for such lovely company, Goldie replied. She finished locking up and then scurried behind the counter, reappearing with two pieces of the coffee cake, which she set down on the table before sitting herself.

So . . . , the old woman signed, *when is the wedding?*

Lucy almost choked on her coffee cake at the unexpected, and unwelcome, question. It was a topic she'd been avoiding even with her mother. She didn't want to talk—even in sign language—about it now. However, Goldie was looking at her as if she'd asked about the weather.

"I just don't think the timing is good for getting married right now," Lucy said, picking her cup of tea up and taking a sip, hoping the discussion was over.

It wasn't. Goldie put her cup down and sat still for a moment, but then her hands began to fly. *I want to tell you a short story*, she said, *about when Moishe and I met. As you know, we were both survivors of concentration camps, and I met him shortly after the war in a refugee camp. I could tell he liked me—he kept hanging around, making eyes, and trying to speak to me, though I would only sign for him to keep his distance.*

Goldie sighed. *I was the least likely love interest imaginable. Not after what the Nazi doctors did to me in the camp when I was a young girl. It is the reason I could not have children, though I did not know it until much later. I did know that I did not want a man to touch me again . . . not ever.*

Taking another sip of tea, Goldie spent a moment gazing into the cup as though she could see distant memories. Then her hands continued with her story of the young man who refused to go away but stayed close and vigilant. At first she had seen him like any other man—after one thing only—but as she watched him she thought there was both an innocence and a sad, quiet strength to him that said he was different from the others. She hated to admit it to herself, but she felt safer when he was nearby.

Moishe would try to talk to me even though he knew that if I deigned to speak to him with my hands, he wouldn't understand. I should tell you that back then my hands spoke a combination of sign languages I had picked up in the concentration camp, as well as my own additions. But he kept trying . . . that young man would not give up.

Goldie smiled. *Finally one day he walked up and handed me a note. I dropped it to the ground and signed for him to leave me alone. He walked off and as soon as he did, I picked up the note and read it. It said, "I've decided that I love you and that I want to marry you. We will go to America and surround ourselves with children and grandchildren."*

I found a pencil and wrote a response and then stomped around our camp looking for him so that I could give him a piece of my mind. He saw me coming and though the men around him looked suddenly worried—I must have seemed like an enraged Valkyrie coming for the mortals—he just smiled.

The old woman laughed. *I think that is the moment I may have first realized that I loved him. But I gave him my note, which said, "How can you talk of love and marriage and bringing children into a world as evil as this one? You are a stupid man, and I am not interested." Not very eloquent but to the point. I saw the hurt on his face—and regretted my note. But all he said was, "That's okay. I'll ask again tomorrow." I told him not to bother, but the next day when I saw him walking toward me, I have to admit, my heart skipped a beat. He asked me to marry him again, and I said, "No. Love has no place in this world for me anymore."*

Day after day, however, Moishe returned and asked his question, the old woman told Lucy. *And day after day, I rejected him.* Goldie laughed again. *I believe that I must have a world record for the most proposals by one man. Finally, one day he came up to me, but instead of asking his question, he said good-bye.*

The memory brought tears to Goldie's eyes. *I pretended that I was only mildly interested but asked him where he was going. He said he was going back to Sobibor and that he would lie down there and die. I asked him why and he said—and I can remember his very words to this day—"If they can stop us from falling in love and marrying and having children . . . if they can convince us that the world is such a terrible place that there is no more room for love, then they have won anyway. Why not give them my bones to lie near those of my mother, sister, and father, and so many friends?"*

Goldie reached across the table for Lucy's hand. *I didn't know if he was just being dramatic, but suddenly I could not stand the thought of him leaving me. I pleaded with him not to go. I said that perhaps in the future there would be a better time to consider marriage, but it wasn't the right time.*

The old woman squeezed the young woman's hand. *And he said, "There is no right time for love, there is only now." Then, before I could stop him—or maybe I didn't want to stop him— he kissed me.*

Goldie sighed and fell silent. Lucy wiped at the tears rolling down her own cheeks. "Then what happened?"

Goldie spread her hands to indicate the bakery and all that it stood for and signed, *Don't you know? I married my prince and lived happily ever after.*

20

ALTHOUGH HE KEPT HIS EXPRESSION DISPASSIONATE, IN-
wardly Karp was seething as he waited for Gilbert Murrow,
Pat Davis, and Danielle Cohn to take their seats in his office.
Guma, Fulton, and Tommy Mack, the chief of the Homicide
Bureau, were already present, the former in his favorite chair,
Mack seated near him, and Clay leaning his big frame against a
wall.

It was midmorning, the day after his visit to Columbia University and Dale Yancy, a morning that followed a sleepless
night. *This could have all been so easily avoided*, he thought,
fuming, *with just the smallest bit of patience and attention to
detail. But everybody got caught up in the immediacy of the
now. The cop wanted the bust. Cohn wanted to take on a big
case. And Davis wanted to shine while he was at the top and
position himself for when Mack gets his judgeship.*

Perhaps, in the initial adrenaline rush of thinking he had the killer in front of him, Graziani had the blinders on so tight that he could see only Acevedo. But his withholding evidence that would have ruled out the ring used in support of Acevedo's indictment was not just a serious violation of legal procedures, it obstructed justice and inexorably led to false charges being filed against—in all probability—an innocent man.

Karp had looked at Graziani's personnel file, delivered earlier by Fulton, and saw a mixed bag. Graziani had received commendations for his service and risen in the ranks, though he seemed stuck at detective second grade. Part of that may have been the sorts of small issues that might show up in any detective's file—complaints about harassment, "police brutality," and shakedowns. But there was also the glaring accusation that he'd taken DEA-marked money from a drug dealer, which had gotten him transferred from the Two-Six to the Four-Eight without any other repercussions. *Probably thanks to the police union*, Karp thought. *The "thin blue line" mentality makes it tough on occasion to deal with the few bad apples.*

However, bad apple or not, Karp's own people had screwed up big-time, and that bothered him even more than Graziani. As the district attorney of New York County, he was responsible for the six hundred assistant district attorneys who worked for the busiest DAO in the country. Together they faced the daunting challenge of prosecuting those responsible for the fifty thousand violent crimes that occurred annually on the island of Manhattan, including approximately five hundred murders, fifteen hundred rapes, and a multitude of robberies, assaults, and kidnappings. And that didn't include the caseloads for tens of thousands of other types of nonviolent felonies, such as burglary, larceny, fraud, traffic infractions, and misdemeanor cases.

It was a monumental task, but he'd never believed that was an excuse for sloppy work or ignoring protocol. Since coming into office, he'd insisted on a system of checks and balances that his mentor DA Garrahy had employed but were abandoned or haphazardly enforced by subsequent administrations. Again borrowing from the old man's style, he'd also brought back what he thought of as the "institutionalization of virtue," in which the office, and the people who worked for him, would occupy the moral high ground in the administration of justice. And, as he'd been discussing with Guma and Fulton before the others arrived, not just because it was the right thing, but because "our whole system depends on keeping the trust of the public; if we destroy that trust by compromising our ethics, the whole system crumbles." Now, because of the callous disregard for the law of a rogue cop and recklessness motivated by the personal goals of two members of his staff, the system had been compromised, and he was angry about it.

Actually, Karp had been simmering since leaving Dale Yancy and then gone to full boil within minutes after Marlene arrived home that evening and greeted him with the now all-too-familiar "We need to talk."

After listening to Marlene and taking a stroll around the block to clear his head, Karp had called Tommy Mack and given him a brief rundown of what had happened. The homicide chief berated himself for getting distracted by the case he was prosecuting, which had gone to the jury that day, and not "riding herd better" on Assistant Bureau Chief Pat Davis and other members of his bureau. But Karp had dismissed the self-criticism; the lack of oversight was one of the disadvantages of insisting that he and his bureau chiefs try cases to keep themselves sharp.

"This one slipped through the cracks," Karp said. "Now the thing is to correct the problem and then make sure the cracks get filled in. I have an appointment first thing in the morning, but let's meet at about ten and have Davis and Cohn join us at about eleven."

He then called Murrow and gave him the same briefing. When he was finished, Karp's administrative chief groaned loudly.

"Spit it out, Gilbert," Karp said insistently, knowing what was coming.

Gilbert Murrow was a somewhat short and pudgy fellow who favored vests and round, wire-rimmed glasses that gave him the appearance of a research librarian. One of Murrow's roles was to act as Karp's liaison with the media; as such he sometimes complained that he was the only one in the office conscious of the fact that the position of district attorney was an elected one.

If there was a problem with the case, the press could be expected to make his life unpleasant. "At the risk of the slap-down I know I'm going to get," he said, "I was just contemplating how the media is going to react. They've been running Columbia U Slasher newspaper exposés and television specials since Acevedo's arrest. They've as much as convicted him. Now they're going to look like fools who sensationalized this, and who do you think they're going to take this out on?"

"Please spare me the rhetorical questions," Karp replied, annoyed.

"Us . . . and more specifically, you, the New York DA who persecutes innocent young men on a whim," Murrow said. "We'll all be pilloried, but they'll also use the tar and feathers on you."

"And my reaction to what the media says is . . . ?" He could feel Murrow slump into his seat even over the telephone.

"'Who gives a rat's ass.'"

"Right," Karp said. "But it's okay, Gilbert, it's your job to give one, and I appreciate it. But the day I run this office according to how I'm going to be treated by the media instead of what's right is the day I should be removed from this office."

Murrow sighed again. "Yeah, and you're right, but I had to say it. So what do you want me to do?"

Karp thought about it for a moment. His first reaction was to say "Our only option is to address this mistake as straightforwardly as possible and with transparency," then another thought crossed his mind and he hesitated. "I want to sleep on it," he said, and told his friend to show up in his office at eleven.

When the three new arrivals were seated, Karp looked from face to face, noting the apprehension on the visages of Davis and Cohn. Murrow just looked resigned.

"Okay, let's get started," Karp said. "I want to talk about the Yancy-Jenkins case, and the first thing I'll say is that in the end, I take the blame for this fiasco." He noticed Cohn shoot a quick glance at Davis. "Yes, 'fiasco,' and that's putting it kindly. But as I said, the buck stops here. Apparently, I have not adequately expressed that the way we conduct business in this office is nonnegotiable."

Karp let the comments sink in as the color drained from Davis's face and Cohn's expression went rigid. Guma studied his cigar as Fulton gazed up at the ceiling and Mack leaned forward with his elbows on his knees and hands clasped in front, as if praying that his subordinates could come up with some reasonable explanations.

Holding up two fingers, Karp stated categorically, "Let me emphasize again the gold standard around here. We need two things *before* we proceed with any case. The first is: are we absolutely, one thousand percent convinced that the defendant is factually guilty? Two: do we have legally admissible evidence to prove beyond any and all doubt that the defendant committed the crime?" He shook his head. "We didn't meet either one of those criteria in Yancy-Jenkins."

Karp then gutted the case, starting with his examination of the case file, noting the absence of a DD-5 regarding the provenance of the ring. He then moved on to the visit to see Dale Yancy, and finally the results of his wife's investigation. "Before I even get to the ring," he said, "I have several issues that should have raised red flags. Let's start with the confession. Where's the narrative?"

No one responded, so he went on. "Detective Graziani asked a lot of leading questions, particularly when the suspect didn't give the 'correct answer' to the original question or balked," he said. "All detectives do that to an extent to flesh out the details of a confession, but not until after the suspect has given a narrative—'Here's where I was, what I did, how I did it'—of what happened. But here there was no narrative against which we could have sought some corroboration. In fact, more often than not, Graziani provided the answers when he asked the questions."

Karp picked up the case file folder that was lying on his desk and turned to a page in the transcript he'd earmarked. "For instance, this is a passage where Acevedo has just told Graziani that the deceased, Olivia Yancy, was his girlfriend, which he later will admit was a lie. So Graziani asks him if he and Yancy had been having 'kinky sex and it got out of hand.' I'm reading now from page three of the transcript of the statement the defendant gave to Detective Graziani.

"Acevedo's answer: 'No. We don't have sex.'

"Graziani's leading question: 'But you tied her up and put duct tape over her mouth?'

"Answer: 'I guess.'

"Question: 'You guess? Or you know?'

"Answer: 'I know.'

"Question: 'And you cut her clothes off with your knife.'"

Karp stopped reading for a moment and looked at Cohn and Davis. "I'm sure you recognize that Graziani is supplying information to Acevedo that only someone with knowledge of the crime scene would have." When the two nodded he continued. "Graziani has just told, not asked, the suspect if he cut the victim's clothes off her with a knife. And Acevedo answered, 'Yes.'" Karp looked up from the transcript.

"He admitted the same things to me," Cohn pointed out.

"You're absolutely right," Karp agreed. "Nearly word for word."

"An indication of truthfulness," Davis suggested.

"Maybe," Karp conceded. "Or that he memorized what he was led to say."

"I wasn't leading him in the Q & A," Cohn said, "when I questioned him."

"You're right," Karp said. "Your Q & A was right out of the book. But it was already too late; he knew what to say."

"He's not like one of those guys who confesses to things he didn't do for the publicity," Cohn said. "He tried to run from the cops when they stopped him. And he first denied everything—the Bronx case, our case. He was trying to avoid being caught, not give himself up."

Karp nodded. "However, he didn't put up much of a fight. Basically, Graziani would ask a question, the suspect would answer, the detective would then tell him he was wrong and suggest what the correct answer would be, and Acevedo would agree."

"But isn't it normal for a perp to lie the first time they're asked?" Cohn asked.

"And maybe he's just not a good liar, or he feels guilty," Davis said. "So all it takes is a little push in the right direction."

"Could be," Karp replied. "But there's a difference between a push in the right direction and being told what to say. I've been informed that the defendant has a history of confessing to minor offenses at his school and possibly even misdemeanor vandalism."

"That's a long way from confessing to murder," Cohn said.

"Right again," Karp said. "But it's certainly something we should have checked out. Has anybody bothered to ask Detective Fulton if he could have one of his detectives run this stuff down?"

Silence. Karp thought for a moment before continuing. "I also have a problem with Graziani lying to Acevedo about there being a witness who saw him leave the Yancy apartment building."

"The U.S. Supreme Court has ruled that police officers can lie, or use trickery, to get a suspect to admit the truth," Davis said. "Cops do it all the time. Such as telling a suspect that he's been caught on surveillance video or that he left a fingerprint at the scene of the crime."

Karp pursed his lips and looked around the room. Tommy Mack had buried his face in his hands and was shaking his head. Guma grimaced, closed his eyes, and stuck a cigar in his mouth. Fulton was watching Davis like he expected him to burst into flames. But Murrow just shot the assistant chief and Cohn dirty looks; he knew who he had to blame for the coming media storm.

Very carefully, his voice clipped and hard, Karp leaned forward to look Davis in the eye and said, "I know what the courts have ruled and that it's common practice with cops and in a lot of DAOs, but there's a difference between what we can get away with and what's right. It's not even worth the damage it will do to you at trial."

"What do you mean?" Davis asked.

"When the detective eventually takes the stand, we have the obligation to present to the jury all the relevant facts and circumstances regarding the defendant's confession, including the detective's tricky tactics, if any," Karp said. "The defense will then attempt to focus the jury on the detective's deceit, trying to make a collateral issue into a giant big deal, maybe even the central focus. So instead of keeping the jury's focus on the defendant's guilt, the jurors may be led to equate the detective's deceit with everything done investigatively. We don't want the jurors thinking, *If he was capable of manipulating the defendant into confessing with lies, what's to stop him from manipulating us with lies?*"

Davis tried to respond. "I thought our job was to get at the truth. What's the harm if it accomplishes that?"

Karp had had enough and pounded his desk with his hand. "What harm?" he growled. "Damn it, Pat, what harm is there in lying to get at the truth? Are you listening to yourself? Lies and cheating to win a verdict are corrupting agents that eat at the foundation of the entire system. And that foundation is the public's trust, which will be further eroded: *You can't trust cops. You can't trust the district attorney's office. Who can we trust?*"

Pale and sweating, Davis started to mumble a reply, but Karp held up a hand. "Enough! I let this go on as a reminder that this case is a perfect example of why we bring such cases to the Monday bureau meetings, where we can ask these sorts of questions and make sure we've done our job professionally and thoroughly. But all of this back-and-forth now over missing narratives, leading questions, and the ethics of lying is moot. It's yesterday's news as far as I'm concerned."

Standing to look out the large window beside his desk at the busy street below, Karp then turned to face Davis and Cohn. "Now, does someone want to explain to me why no one in this office bothered to corroborate the single most important piece of evidence in this case, or noticed that the investigating detective apparently had not, either?"

"Acevedo confessed that he took it from Olivia Yancy," Cohn said weakly.

Karp glared at her for a moment before responding. "He was led to say that by Graziani and then he just repeated it to you. And nobody bothered to check it out—the only piece of evidence we had to ascertain the credibility and trustworthiness of the confession. Instead, we just went ahead and presented the case to the grand jury and obtained an indictment against Acevedo, who, as far as I can see, is an innocent man."

"He's not necessarily innocent because this wasn't the ring taken from Olivia," Davis argued. "Maybe he mixed up which ring he took from which victim."

"Unfortunately for that theory, his story checks out," Karp replied. "Acevedo bought it from a guy in the park who'd stolen it from a woman. And unlike our so-called evidence, this was corroborated. And the ring was the only thing that tied Acevedo to the murders of Olivia Yancy and Beth Jenkins."

"He was identified by an assault victim in the Bronx," Cohn said. "And confessed to that other murder—Dolores Atkins."

"Just as Acevedo's confession to Graziani and the Q & A with you is worthless," Karp said, "I suspect the confessions in the Bronx are as well. I have no idea about the validity of that witness's ID, but the way this case has plunged downhill, I'd strongly suspect that too."

Karp looked over at Guma. "So, Ray, what do you think we should do now?"

Guma inspected his cigar for a moment and shrugged. "I think we need to DOR the case," he said.

Karp nodded. "Yeah, I thought of that, and if dismissing the case on his own recognizance would get Acevedo out of jail, I'd agree we should do it right now. Unfortunately, it wouldn't do him any good. The Bronx DAO still has a hold on him for its cases, and he's not going anywhere. My thought was to hold off, at least until the Bronx DA decides what they're going to do, so we don't tip off the real killer that we're now still looking for him. Maybe he makes a mistake. In the end, the only way we recover from this is to catch and convict the son of a bitch who butchered those women."

Pat Davis stood up. "You'll have my resignation by this afternoon."

It took Karp a moment to consider the offer. "You do what works for you, Pat," he said. "You're a good attorney, and I'd rather not lose you. But I also can't let this one slide—there's too much at stake and quite simply, you knew better. So if you choose to stay, I'll be transferring you to the Felony Trial Bureau, where you'll work under close supervision for the time being."

Davis blinked back tears as his Adam's apple bobbed up and down; he swallowed hard and nodded. Karp turned his attention to Cohn. "Danielle, I believe your mistakes were the result of inexperience. Right now, you will be assigned to assist Ray Guma full-time on the Yancy-Jenkins case. And I hope you'll learn from this."

Cohn bit her lip and then bowed her head. "I will. And I look forward to working with Ray."

"We'll see if you still feel that way after actually spending a lot of time in his company," Karp said with a half smile.

"Hey, why am I always the fall guy . . . ," Guma said, laughing.

"Typecasting?" Mack replied.

❖   ❖   ❖

When the others left his office, Karp's intercom buzzed. "District Attorney Sam Hartsfield is on line two," Milquetost announced.

"Hello, Sam, what's shaking up north?" Karp said.

"My esteemed colleague the district attorney of New York County, Mr. Roger 'Butch' Karp, I presume." Hartsfield chuckled. "My belly shakes a bit but that's about the extent of it in the beautiful borough of the Bronx."

Karp laughed. While Detective Clay Fulton had played fullback in college and was a big muscular man, Sam "Dump Truck" Hartsfield had been the starting left tackle at Tulane, and he made Clay look svelte. His playing weight had been 310 pounds, and that had gone up considerably when he gave up the NFL for law school. He did, indeed, have a belly that shook.

"I believe you called," Hartsfield said. "How you doing, Butch? Long time no see."

"I'm doing well, Sam, thanks for asking," Karp replied. He genuinely liked Hartsfield. He was a few years younger than Karp, but Hartsfield had spent his formative prosecutorial years under legendary DA Francis Garrahy, and the old man's ethics were ingrained in him, too. The two men thought much alike when it came to how best to run their respective offices and the role of a district attorney in the system. Both were competitive men who'd played major college sports but understood that their job wasn't about wins and losses in the courtroom. The only game that mattered was justice. As a matter of fact, as cornball as it seemed to the young Turks entering the justice system, and even to the ring-wise old hands, Karp started every summation by reminding the twelve jurors "that a trial is a search for the truth. A sacred, solemn search for the truth under the rules of evidence."

"Good, good," Hartsfield said. "Your message said you had some questions about the Dolores Atkins case and the suspect Felix Acevedo?"

"That would be the one," Karp said. "If I can be blunt, what's the status of your cases?"

"Well, I believe we're set for a preliminary hearing next week," Hartsfield said. "I'm told that the lead detective, an old hand named Phil Brock, wanted to run down a few things."

Karp frowned. "I haven't read much about your cases," he said, "but I understand Acevedo confessed to the Atkins murder before he confessed to our double murder case?"

"That's correct," Hartsfield said. "And to the assault of another woman, too; the cops initially picked him up on assault."

"And don't you have a witness—the assault victim, if I'm not mistaken—who ID'd him in a lineup?" Karp asked.

"That's true," Hartsfield replied. "But it was a pretty shaky ID. At first she wasn't sure; then she thought it could be one of two guys—one a cop and the other our suspect. She asked if she could hear them repeat the threat he used; that's when she ID'd Acevedo and said she *thought* he was the one. But she admitted that she never really got a good look at him and I expect any decent defense lawyer is going to hit that hard. We didn't find any physical evidence on him, or in his things at his parents' apartment, that tied him to our homicide victim, Dolores Atkins. Not like that engagement ring; you have an ace on the table with that."

"How well do you know this detective Phil Brock?" Karp asked.

"Well, I've worked with him directly on a dozen cases over the years," Hartsfield said. "Nothing flashy, but methodical and doesn't cut corners. Avoids the press like the plague. Just does his job and does it well. He's got to be getting close to retirement."

"My kind of cop," Karp said. "They make the best witnesses on the stand, too."

"I agree," Hartsfield replied. He paused for a moment. "What's this about, Butch?"

Once again, Karp quickly explained what was happening with the Yancy-Jenkins case. "You might want to hold off on that hearing, Sam," he said. "I know you have a problem because of the witness's ID, but I think the confessions are pure fantasy. It might be worth it to let me and my guys sift through this before you end up having to dismiss the charges after the fact."

"Whew, I don't envy you the hell you're going to catch," Hartsfield said. "But thanks for the heads-up. You'll keep me in the loop?"

"Absolutely," Karp replied. "In the meantime, if you decide to dismiss, let me know. I don't want to unnecessarily tip off the killer, but I'd also like to get Acevedo out of jail if he's not the right guy for your cases either."

"You got it," Hartsfield replied. "When this is over, let's get together; been a while since we've had a chance to catch up. Maybe take in a Yankee game. I have some choice tickets to the Red Sox game in a few weeks if you'd be interested."

"That would be a pleasure," Karp replied. "Always get a kick seeing the Bronx Bombers beat up on the Sox."

21

GRAZIANI SAT IN THE SEDAN ACROSS THE STREET AND down a block from the aging row house in the Norwood neighborhood of the Bronx. It was a quiet neighborhood and the streets were nearly deserted at midnight.

The headlights of a car appeared from around a corner and moved toward him as he scrunched down in his seat. He'd driven past the row house before dawn that morning and saw the car that was now approaching parked on the street. So he knew that was where his target would park again.

Graziani glanced over at the alley on the side of the row house and thought he could detect the dark figure of a man within the general shadows. Suddenly a wave of nausea threatened to overwhelm him and he thought about calling the whole thing off.

Some part of him, a leftover vestige perhaps of that idealistic rookie cop he'd been some twenty-plus years earlier, was freak-ing out. He knew that he was crossing a line he'd never have imagined even two weeks ago. This wasn't taking money from drug dealers, shaking down pimps, or accepting envelopes of cash from businesses looking for a little extra "police protection." *This is a whole new ball game*, that rookie cop warned him, *but it's not too late.*

Not if you want to finish your career working the traffic division in the Bronx, Joey baby, a different voice said, this one belonging to the street-weary cop whose idealism had been drained away over the years like leaking oil from an old car. *And go ahead and stay a detective second grade. That's if you're lucky. It will probably get a lot worse if this Acevedo case blows up in your face after the shit that got you kicked out of the Two-Six in the first place. They'll "make an example" out of you and if they don't find a reason to kick you off the force and take your pension, they'll stick you in a basement cubicle, filing reports until you quit or stick a gun in your mouth.*

Graziani swallowed the bile that had risen from his gut and hardened himself to the task at hand. *It's the only way,* he told himself again. He wasn't going to let some dirtball meth dealer screw it up.

The other car pulled over to the curb and stopped. He glanced at the alley and saw the dark figure emerge and creep up behind the car. The assassin timed his approach so that when the driver opened the door and started to get out—and was at his most vulnerable—he moved quickly to intercept him.

Something silver in the assailant's hand flashed in the streetlight as he raised it and then plunged it toward the chest of the driver. It flashed again and again in rapid succession. The victim reached out with both hands for his assailant but then slumped back onto the seat of the car with his legs hanging out.

The assassin stood up and looked toward Graziani, who was nearly overcome with the urge to drive away as fast as possible. But he knew better than to assume that the job was done. Graziani picked up the .380 pistol with the silencer from the seat next to him and got out of the car. He walked down his side of the street until he was even with the murdered man's car and then crossed over.

Graziani ignored the assassin and peered inside the car. Detective Phil Brock lay back on the seat, his shirt dark and wet with blood from several knife wounds. He was still alive, his breath coming in ragged, bubbling gasps.

As Graziani started to stand back up, Brock raised his head. His expression changed from one of puzzlement to one of understanding and then scorn. "Just to get out of the Bronx?"

"'Fraid so," Graziani said as he raised the gun and shot the other detective twice in the head. The quick *pffft pffft* of the shots was lost in the night as Brock's body twitched and went still.

"Is the fucker dead?" Ahmed Kadyrov said, smiling as he tried to look in the car at the dead detective.

Graziani pushed him back and pointed the gun at his pale face. "He's a better man dead than you ever were alive, you piece of shit," he snarled.

"No, don't, man!" Kadyrov pleaded, throwing his hands up to ward off the bullet he thought was coming.

Instead, Graziani lowered the gun and stuck it in the top of his pants. He reached in and took Brock's wallet from his jacket pocket and the watch off his wrist. Finished, he started walking quickly toward his car, motioning for Kadyrov to follow him. "Don't worry, asshole, I'm not going to shoot you, as long as you do what you're told," he said as they walked. "But let me repeat what I told you earlier: I'd rather shoot a hundred dirtbags like you than the man I just had to kill, so if you fuck with me, I will shoot you without batting an eye. And don't think for a minute that you could turn on me and get away with it. I don't care how far you run; even if I can't get to you myself, I'm a cop, and someday, someone with a badge will coming looking for you."

Kadyrov looked frightened. "I get it . . . don't fuck with you," he said.

"That's better," Graziani said as they reached his car. He got in and rolled down the window to speak to Kadyrov. "Now, like I said, you got a problem with this friend of yours, Vinnie Cassino. It's what happens when you open your big fucking mouth and tell other scumbags that you killed three women. Take care of it."

Kadyrov nodded and the smile returned. "I'll take care of him *and* his little *sooka.*"

Driving to his home in Queens, Graziani tried to get the image of Brock's scornful eyes out of his mind. *Had to be done*, he reasoned, *it was him or me. Was going to choose a loser like Felix Acevedo over a brother cop.*

His mind flashed over to Kadyrov. He'd lied when he told Brock he didn't know him. He'd come across Kadyrov while working Narcotics in the Two-Six and knew him as a small-time burglar and sometime snitch who would sell out his own mother for enough "reward" money to buy another hit of meth.

What really bothered Graziani was that while working with the Yancy-Jenkins task force, he'd been going through case files of perps who did daytime burglaries and Kadyrov's file had come up. But he'd dismissed him as a poor candidate for a sex killer. The irony that he could have been the hero in all of this—without having to kill another cop or frame an innocent man—was not lost on the detective. *Him or me. It was him or me.*

Graziani reminded himself that he still didn't know if Kadyrov was the real killer. Nor did he care, which is what he told the drug addict when he tracked him down that afternoon with the help of a couple of meth dealers he put the screws to.

"But I will say that Vinnie Cassino is running around telling cops that you admitted to him and his wife that you're good for the murders," he'd told Kadyrov. "Personally, I don't believe it. I've got the killer and his name is Felix Acevedo. However, there's this detective who believes Cassino and is out to get you."

Kadyrov started to panic. "I didn't do it. But what do I do?"

"I don't think you have a choice," Graziani told him. "I know for a fact that other than me, the only people who are saying this are the detective and the Cassinos. If they were all gone, your problem would be gone too."

It took Kadyrov a minute to figure out what Graziani was saying. But when he did, he smiled, exposing his drug-rotted teeth. "So you want me to get rid of the problems."

Graziani shrugged. "That's what I would do if I were you."

"And if you were me, how would you get to this cop?" Kadyrov said.

That's when Graziani suggested that Brock might be persuaded to leave his apartment that night with a telephone call about a possible lead on the Atkins case, and he'd be vulnerable when he got back home.

Graziani had dropped the junkie off in the Norwood neighborhood after first driving by the apartment building and pointing out Brock's car. He then warned him that betraying him would be "the same as committing suicide by police officer."

Everything had then gone according to plan, except that the stupid junkie had left Brock alive so that Graziani had to finish him. He could still see the scorn in the other detective's eyes and hear it in his voice—*Just to get out of the Bronx?*

Graziani pulled up in front of the modest two-bedroom on Richmond Hill in Queens where he lived with his second wife. *At least for the time being,* he thought. She was fifteen years younger and tired of waiting for him to move up in the ranks and earn more money so that she could spend it. He suspected that she was having an affair but that everything would be okay again, like when they first met, if he was the hero who solved the Columbia U Slasher case.

In fact, when news broke of the arrest and he'd been photographed by television crews leaving the Four-Eight, they had sex for the first time in a month. And she even acted like she enjoyed it.

Graziani walked in the door of his home and poked his head in the bedroom, hoping, but his wife was asleep. *Doesn't matter,* he told himself as he went to the kitchen, opened the refrigerator, and took out a beer. *It's going to be all right once the Cassinos are out of the picture.*

The detective thought again about Brock and suddenly gagged on the bile that rushed into his mouth. He washed it down with a swig of beer. *Forget about it,* he thought, wiping his mouth. *You got it under control.*

22

MARLENE WAS READING THE MORNING NEWSPAPER WHEN
Ariadne Stupenagel called and asked if they could meet for
lunch. "I'm really busy, Ariadne," she said, trying to beg off.

"Too busy to talk to me about a call I got from a guy who says
he knows the identity of the real Columbia U Slasher?" Stupenagel asked.

Marlene was unimpressed. "As I'm sure you're aware," she
replied, "everybody in Manhattan who doesn't like their neighbor, or wants a piece of the Crime Stoppers reward money,
knows the 'real identity' of the killer. Besides, Felix Acevedo
has been indicted for the murders."

Butch had come home the night before still steamed from
his meeting with Davis and Cohn. He explained what had happened and his call to Sam Hartsfield. As hard as he'd been on
Davis, she knew Butch would be far harder on himself. He, like
his mentor Garrahy, was as committed to exonerating the inno-

cent as he was to convicting the guilty. And there was nothing that he abhorred more than unjustly accusing a citizen.

Marlene sighed. *He'll handle it,* she thought, *like he handles everything else. He'll accept responsibility, express his sincere regret, and move on. No excuses. No whining. And no blaming anyone else.*

"Yeah, well, rumor has it Acevedo may not be going to trial," Stupenagel replied.

"Where'd you hear that?" Marlene asked.

Stupenagel laughed. "Don't worry, Mama Bear, I'm not going to squeal. But that might make it even more important to listen to this guy. I understand lots of people would like to get their hands on that reward money, but what grabbed my attention was that he said his suspect was also connected to the murder of a detective in the Bronx yesterday. Cop's name was Phil Brock."

"I saw that," Marlene replied. She'd just finished reading the small story on page three about his death, which was being described as a possible robbery gone awry, given that the victim's wallet and wristwatch were taken. The murder had apparently occurred late the previous night and the newspaper had few other details.

"Not that I'm paranoid or anything," Stupenagel said, "but I'd rather have this discussion face-to-face. I *do* have my reasons."

Marlene knew that her flamboyant friend lived for drama. She also knew that Ariadne was a hard-nosed investigative reporter who knew when to be serious, and her tone said she was serious now. If she didn't want to talk on the telephone, the reasons were valid.

So they agreed to meet at Kaffe 1668, a trendy coffee shop on Greenwich Street in Tribeca. "Bring your truck, we may be going for a drive," she said, and hung up before Marlene could argue.

Dressed in shorts, a tennis top, and running shoes, Marlene easily spotted Stupenagel standing on the sidewalk outside the shop in a tight-fitting, cleavage-revealing, plum-colored mini-dress and matching plum lipstick and eye shadow and calf-high black boots with stiletto heels. They took a table in a corner, where Stupenagel told her friend about the call she got from "some guy named Vinnie, no joke. He said that he knows who did the murders and can prove it. But apparently he's in some hot water with the law and wants a deal out of it."

"Of course he does," Marlene responded. "These guys are always working some angle. But what was this about a connection to Brock's murder?"

"He wouldn't say much," Stupenagel replied. "Just that Brock was aware of this new suspect, which I find intriguing following on the heels of your husband going to dismiss the indictment against Felix Acevedo. Then Brock ends up dead? What if this wasn't a mugging? What if Brock was onto the new suspect and it got him killed?"

"A lot of questions," Marlene said in agreement. "So what do you propose to do with this information?"

"Well, this guy Vinnie got my name from that story I wrote about you and Butch—the Manhattan crime-fighting family," Stupenagel said. "And he wants to talk to you, said he also heard that you were working for Acevedo."

"Why not just go to the cops or the Bronx DA and try to work out a deal?" Marlene asked.

"I asked the same thing," Stupenagel replied. "He says he's afraid to go to the authorities without a middleman for 'insurance.' He thinks Brock told the, and I quote, 'wrong person,' but he thinks you can be trusted. Of course, I tried to get him to meet with me first, so I could get the story out of him. But he said you have to be at the meeting, and I can't write about it until he gets his deal. So I propose that we go talk to him and see what he has to say."

"When do you want to do this?"

"There's no time like the present," Stupenagel said, getting up from her seat. "Oh, by the way, Vinnie lives in Soundview."

Marlene rolled her eyes. "Of course he does. Maybe he could have picked someplace a little safer, like Afghanistan. And you are, of course, appropriately dressed for talking to junkies, dealers, and other assorted violent criminals. But who am I to complain? Should we stop by my place first to get bulletproof vests and Gilgamesh?"

Stupenagel laughed. "Nah, vests wreck my look, which takes more and more time every morning to achieve. And we have to drive separately anyway. I'm going to be on a tight time crunch and need to go from there to meet Gilbert. We're going to check out a few churches around Mount Vernon for our wedding."

"Churches? You? I thought you were more the justice-of-the-peace type," Marlene said, surprised and delighted.

"Well, I would have gone for the Chapel of Love in Las Vegas," Stupenagel said with a giggle. "But Murry wants to do the whole shebang. Oh, by the way, you are my matron of honor, of course, and I think my man wants yours to be best."

Marlene hugged her friend and kissed her cheek. "I thought you'd never ask. Okay, we'll take a chance and leave Gilgamesh at home if it will get you to the church on time."

On the way to the Bronx, Marlene called Clay Fulton at the DAO and asked what he knew about Brock's death.

"Not much," he replied. "Apparently the neighbors didn't see or hear anything. It looks like he was surprised as he was getting out of his car. Officially, it's being investigated as a robbery/homicide."

"Officially," Marlene repeated. "Which means unofficially there's something hinky about it. So spill it, Clay."

Fulton hesitated but then made her promise that she had to keep the information to herself. "When I heard about it this morning, I talked to Brock's sergeant in the Bronx," he said, "a good guy named Jon Marks. I knew that Brock was working on the Acevedo case up there, so I wanted to see if there was something I should be aware of. They're keeping it under wraps, but there are a few things that look suspicious. One is that Brock was stabbed and then shot."

"That usually means two assailants," Marlene said. "No one stabs someone and then shoots them, or vice versa."

"Right," Fulton said. "Not unheard of but rare. Anyway, this happened right in front of Brock's apartment building on a residential street, and no one heard any shots. Again, it was sometime after midnight, and the two shots were probably fired in quick succession—bang bang—so it could be that no one noticed. . . . Or the killer used a silencer."

"A hit," Marlene said.

"Maybe," Fulton replied. "The last thing is that according to Brock's cell phone log, he got a call about ten P.M. from a pay phone a few blocks from his house. He apparently was going somewhere, or was coming back from somewhere, a couple hours later and there just happened to be a mugger or muggers waiting for him."

"And, yeah, maybe he got set up," Marlene said. "But why?"

"Don't know; it's a dangerous job," Fulton said. "You make a lot of enemies. Why the interest?"

"I've heard something and am going to go check it out," she replied. "I'll let you know if it's worth looking into."

Marlene could feel the big detective frowning over the telephone line. "Be careful, Marlene. You sure you don't need a little backup?"

"Nah," she said, and then laughed. "Ariadne Stupenagel is going with, and we should be okay. It's the middle of the morning."

"Oh, well, if Ariadne's going then I pity the fool who looks at either of you cross-eyed," he said. "Still, you know where to reach me if things start to go downhill."

Thirty minutes later, Marlene and Ariadne stood on Watson Avenue. In the time it had taken to park, get out of their vehicles, and meet in front of the seedy six-story apartment building, they'd been offered every drug imaginable, as well as a dozen different lewd suggestions.

Marlene was less concerned about what the various thugs

and miscreants were saying than the way they were eyeing her purse. She was plenty capable of taking care of herself—she'd been more than just a figurehead for her VIP security firm—but she still found herself wishing she'd brought her dog or the Glock nine-millimeter she'd left at home.

Stupenagel, on the other hand, seemed impervious to the threat. In fact, she had said, "I'll put one of my stiletto heels through the back of your squirrelly head if you don't get out of my face, dirtbag," when one of the local pimps asked if she wanted to work for him.

When Marlene said, "Next time warn me if we're going into a war zone," Stupenagel scoffed. "I've been in worse places. Did I ever tell you about the time I tagged along with some ex-military types working for the CIA into Cambodia during the Pol Pot regime to confirm reports that the Khmer Rouge was carrying out a mass genocide? Now *that* was rough."

"Well, that's all very encouraging," Marlene replied while watching a group of young men who stood in a circle occasionally throwing suspicious glances at her and Ariadne. "But I don't see any ex-military types and that was thirty years ago."

The women entered the building, took the elevator to the third floor, and walked down a dark hallway that smelled like mold and urine. Coming to the apartment at the end of the hall, they knocked and soon became aware of a presence on the other side of the door as the occupant obviously checked them out through the peephole.

Various bolts and chains were moved and the door opened to reveal a tall, nearly bald white man in a wife-beater undershirt and threadbare boxer shorts who grinned when he saw them.

"Ladies," he said, and made an awkward flourish with his hand to indicate that they should enter, "welcome to our humble abode."

The women entered and the man closed and secured the door behind them. As he shuffled past them, Marlene noticed that his other hand held a large revolver. He placed the gun on the counter of the filthy kitchen they passed on the way to an equally unkempt living room.

"Lydia, we got company," he announced to a large woman with frazzled gray hair who stood in a tattered bathrobe near one of the windows that looked out onto the street. A shotgun leaned against the wall next to her. "See anything out there, my sweet?"

"All's clear, baby," Lydia replied, and nodded to the women. "Excuse the mess, I ain't had time to clean up lately."

"Ah hell," the man said with a wink at his wife, "she's got better things to do than clean. Ain't that right, sweet cheeks?"

"Now, Vinnie, these fine ladies don't want to hear your dirty talk," Lydia said, scolding him, though with a smile. "So which one of you is which?"

"I'm Ariadne Stupenagel," the reporter said.

"And I'm Marlene Ciampi."

"Your husband is the DA of New York, ain't he?" Vinnie asked, turning to Marlene.

Marlene started to say, "Yes, but I'm not here representing him—"

"Yeah, but maybe he helps me and I help him," Vinnie said, moving another shotgun off a filthy overstuffed chair so he could sit down. He explained his situation. "I barely got them to let me out on a hundred thousand bail. But that's not the big deal. The big deal is if I can't make this go away, they're going to send my scrawny ass to the joint for longer than I got left."

"So what are you selling?" Stupenagel asked to cut to the chase.

Vinnie grinned. "Well, I know who the Columbia U Slasher is," he said. "And I can prove it. That and he's good for the Atkins killing, too."

"And why should we take your word for it?" Marlene asked.

"Well, for one thing I got him on tape talking about it," Vinnie said. "But that ain't all; you go back to your husband and ask him if a blue silk shirt means anything."

"So what's this guy's name?" Stupenagel asked, prodding.

Vinnie shook a skinny finger at her. "Not so fast. This information has already got one person killed, and I don't aim to be next. I want a deal or I ain't talking. If I got to go to prison, I ain't going with a snitch jacket, which would get me killed sure as shit."

"Who got killed over this information?" Marlene asked.

"You know that cop that got whacked last night," Vinnie said, "that Detective Brock?"

"What about him?"

"I told him the name of the Columbia U Slasher a few days ago," Vinnie said. "Now he's dead."

Marlene shrugged. "What makes you think it's connected?"

"You tell me," Vinnie replied. "It wasn't just a mugging, was it?" He kept his eyes on Marlene's face and then smirked. "I knew it! It was a hit!" He looked at his wife. "What I tell ya, baby? The shit has hit the fan on this one!"

Lydia kept her eyes on the street below but nodded. "That's what you said, my man. That's what you said for sure."

Stupenagel looked at Marlene and raised her eyebrows. "You holding out on me, girlfriend?"

Marlene ignored her. "How do we know you told Brock anything of the sort?"

"Go talk to the cop who dragged my ass to jail on the drug beef," Vinnie said. "His name was Dave Drum, or something like that. I told him I wanted to talk to Brock about the Atkins murder. Ask him. And I tell you what, Brock sure perked up when I told him about that blue silk shirt."

"So what's this deal you want?" Marlene asked.

Vinnie smiled triumphantly. "You tell your husband I can hand him the son of a bitch who killed them two women," he said. "But with Brock getting whacked, the stakes have gone way up. First, I want the charges against me dropped."

"Those are Bronx charges," Marlene told him.

"Yeah, well, this is the same guy who did the Atkins murder, so I'd think your husband and the Bronx DA might want to cooperate," Vinnie said. "Second, I want a safe place for me and my old lady to live until the trial is over. If word gets out that I'm snitching, somebody's gonna stick a shiv in me just on principle. Third, I want the reward money for the killings in Manhattan *and* the Bronx. Me and Lydia is going to have to get the hell out of Dodge and we're going to need a bankroll for that."

"Anything else?"

"Yeah, Lydia ain't been able to visit her elderly mom in Yonkers," he said with a smile at his wife, "and she wants to take her a little something. But she needs a ride there and back. They won't visit long, and I'd surely appreciate it."

"I can do that," Marlene said, "but I can't promise anything else."

"Well, neither will I," Cassino replied. "This is all I'm saying until I got my deal."

Marlene controlled the urge to slug the drug dealer. "I understand, and isn't it fascinating how under certain circumstances we sometimes find the religious spirit to do the right thing," she said with a smirk.

Vinnie laughed. "Okay, okay, you get me just fine. The right thing is what's right for me and Lydia; ain't nobody going to look out for us. Ain't that right, sugar lips?"

"Damn straight, beautiful boy," Lydia said in agreement. "Got to look out for number one. Now, let me get my care package and we can be off."

23

The "spirit" luncheon for the baseball team was supposed to be a team-building event prior to the start of the playoffs that weekend. However, the players were buzzing with the rumor that the school's athletic director had taken Coach Newell to task for the injury to Esteban Gonzalez's leg. Apparently, Esteban's parents had complained about the treatment of their son and the AD was worried about a lawsuit.

"Coach called my dad last night," Max Weller told his cronies as they sat at their table while one of the assistant coaches spoke at the lectern about being "team players" and giving "110 percent" every game. "Newell said he's going to have to play that fucking beaner at least some innings." Weller made no attempt to lower his voice, nor did his pals disguise their curses and racial slurs.

Sitting at the table next to the complainers with two of the team's black players and other members of the varsity squad,

Giancarlo and Zak could overhear the angry conversation and see the hard stares directed at Esteban, who was sitting at a table otherwise occupied by the team's two student managers, an assistant coach, and two younger players brought up from the junior varsity team to get some playoff experience. He ate quietly with his head down and spoke to no one, nor was he spoken to.

As his assistant coach droned on, Coach Newell walked over to Weller's table, where he stood behind his senior shortstop. "How's my main man?" he asked.

"Okay," Weller replied sullenly.

"It's going to work out fine, son," the coach replied, leaning over and lowering his voice. "A lot can happen between now and the game." He stood up and tousled Weller's hair. "Chin up, champ."

The coach turned and saw the boys at the next table watching him. He frowned at Giancarlo but smiled at the other players and patted Zak on the shoulder as he walked past. "Get that arm ready for game two, Karp."

"I will, Coach," Zak responded with a smile.

"This is bullshit," Giancarlo said when the coach moved on.

"It's just talk," Zak replied. "Max is pissed that he's going to have to sit out some of the games, but I bet he's still going to start and this will blow over. Like I told you, Esteban's parents handled it. We don't have to get involved."

Giancarlo scowled at his brother. "Did you hear anything Moishe said about waiting for someone else to speak up when other people are being bullied and attacked?"

Zak scoffed. "Max and Chase and Chris aren't Nazis," he

said. "They're just assholes who will be gone next year. It doesn't matter what they say."

"It doesn't?" Giancarlo asked. He pushed away from the table, stood, and picked up his plate.

"Where are you going?" Zak asked.

"I'm going to sit with Esteban," Giancarlo said. He hesitated a moment. "You coming?"

Zak bit his lip but then shook his head. "If you want to make a scene, go ahead," he said. "I think you're just looking for trouble."

Giancarlo didn't answer and turned to walk over to Esteban's table. Esteban looked up, surprised, and smiled tentatively, but soon the two boys were laughing and talking animatedly. Zak, however, was conscious that when Giancarlo left, the boys at the table next to his had watched and reacted angrily.

"Hey, Zak, I guess your brother would rather sit with his boyfriend than his own kind," Chase said, taunting him.

Zak didn't respond but acted as if he found his own lunch fascinating and tried to carry on a conversation with the other players at his table. He cringed, however, when Esteban rose and headed in the direction of the hallway and the boys at the other table suddenly scooted their chairs back and got up. They headed in the same direction Esteban had gone.

When Zak glanced back at his brother, he saw that Giancarlo was looking at him. With a shake of the head, Giancarlo stood and followed the others out of the door. Zak looked over at where Newell was standing, hoping the coach was going to intervene, but while his eyes followed his senior players as they left, he remained where he was with a slight smile on his face.

Zak put his head down. Then he sighed and got up from the table.

"Where you going?" one of the black players asked.

"To save my brother from getting his ass kicked," Zak replied, and left to find Giancarlo.

In the hallway, Giancarlo saw the senior players head into the restroom and guessed that they were following Esteban. He walked down to the restroom and, taking a deep breath, he pushed on the door, only to find that it was partly blocked. He pushed harder and was able to get past Chris, who was standing guard but more interested in what was going on.

Giancarlo saw Esteban struggling in the grip of the much larger Chase and bleeding from his nose. Max stood in front of his victim with his hand balled into a fist as he snarled, "Now are you going to quit?"

"Let him go," Giancarlo yelled.

Max whirled around but then grinned when he saw who was speaking. "Well, if it isn't the spic lover. You looking for your sweetheart, Karp?" he said as the other boys laughed.

Giancarlo tried to push through to Esteban but Chris grabbed him from behind as Max stepped in front. "You want some of what he's getting?" Hatred radiated from his eyes.

At that moment, the bathroom door opened again and Zak walked in. "What the hell is going on?" he asked. He pushed Chris away from his brother and got between him and Max.

"Stay out of this, Zak," the older boy said, warning him.

"Not while my brother's here," Zak retorted.

"Take his punk ass and get out of here then," Max said, pushing Zak's chest.

"Don't ever touch me again," Zak replied. "Come on, Giancarlo, let's go."

Instead of leaving, Giancarlo shook his head. "Not without Esteban."

Zak stared hard at his brother. Then he smiled and shrugged before turning back to Max. "Okay, guys, you have a choice," he said. "You can let Esteban go and apologize to him and my brother, or I'm going to kick your asses."

"What? Are you nuts?" Max said, turning his head to smile at Chase, but doubt showed in his eyes when he turned back to Zak.

"Maybe," Zak said. "Oh, and you can quit the team and tell Coach Newell why."

"You're crazy," Chase growled, pushing Esteban to the ground and standing next to Max.

"Yeah, so how about it, Max? Would you like a shot at the heavyweight title?" Zak replied.

24

AHMED KADYROV WATCHED THE THREE WOMEN LEAVE the apartment from across Watson Avenue, where he waited for five minutes more to make sure they weren't coming back before entering the building. At first he'd been disappointed that Lydia Cassino wasn't going to be home with her husband. But the more he thought about it as he climbed the stairs to the third floor, the more he realized it would be easier to take care of them one at a time. He had no doubt that the woman was as potentially violent as her husband, and they were even more dangerous when together.

Kadyrov knew he was taking a big risk. Cassino had ratted him out to that detective he'd stabbed last night, and if the drug dealer had heard about the murder, he might be more on guard. But the other detective, Graziani, had told him that Cassino had evidence that could get him sent to prison for life, maybe even executed. He had to do something.

That damn blue shirt I gave him, Kadyrov thought with disgust.

He'd decided Graziani's plan was worth the risk. Just show up like he didn't know about Cassino's betrayal. He thought Cassino would see it as an opportunity to get more information out of him and make an even better deal with the authorities.

Which is exactly what Cassino decided when he answered the knock at his door, looked out the peephole, and saw Kadyrov standing in the hallway. The drug dealer felt a momentary surge of apprehension, but the weight of the big .357 in his hand made him feel better, and he smiled. If he could get Kadyrov to admit that he killed that detective, the Cassinos would have a free pass for life. The police would look the other way when it came to a guy who caught a cop killer.

Cassino stepped back and unlocked the door. "Ahmed, long time no see, brother," he said. "Come on in."

The unusually congenial greeting told Kadyrov everything he needed to know: the drug dealer was looking for more leverage for his legal problems. He smiled back. "Yeah, man, long time," he said. He held up a small red backpack. "I scored a bunch of good shit and need someone to help me move it."

Cassino's small-businessman's radar suddenly perked up. Here was a fine opportunity; he'd agree to help Kadyrov and then steal it when he turned the fool over to the cops. "I'm your man," he said. "How much?"

"Two ounces," Kadyrov said, patting the small green backpack he carried in his hand.

Surprised, Cassino asked, "Where'd you get it?"

Kadyrov grinned. Cassino's greed was leading him into the

trap. "I 'borrowed' it from some punk in Brooklyn who wasn't too careful about locking his doors," he said.

Cassino chuckled. "Can't be too careful," he said, turning to lead the way into the apartment. "A lot of criminals out there." He laid the revolver on the kitchen counter and shuffled toward his easy chair and the shotgun lying against its arm.

Kadyrov waited a moment and then reached into the backpack for his switchblade. He moved swiftly behind his victim and without hesitation stuck the blade into Cassino's back at kidney level.

The pain was so intense that Cassino couldn't even call out at first but clawed at the air in front of him. He gasped as his attacker withdrew the blade and plunged it in again and again. With every ounce of determination he had left, he turned and, stretching out his long arms, wrapped his fingers around Kadyrov's throat. "I'll kill you," he snarled, his eyes full of rage and agony.

Kadyrov was surprised by the man's strength and fought the urge to panic as he was being choked. In fear, he drove the knife deep into the left side of Cassino's potbelly and slashed sideways, the razor-sharp blade opening the man's gut. The grip on his neck loosened, and Cassino looked down as though surprised to see the blood soaking his overalls and then sank to his knees.

"Thought you could rat me out and get away with it, you son of a bitch," Kadyrov said as he backed away triumphantly.

"I ain't no rat," Cassino snarled weakly. "Where'd you hear that shit?"

Kadyrov grinned. "A little birdie told me. A birdie with a gold shield." He leaned closer and said, "I can do anything I want. And when your old lady gets back, I'm going to rape the shit out of her, if I can stomach touching that ugly bitch. Then I'm going to cut her up real slow."

Cassino cried out as he lunged forward, but Kadyrov easily sidestepped the attack and laughed as the drug dealer fell to the ground and lay on his side groaning. "Here's the deal, old man," the killer said. "Tell me where the blue shirt is and I'll make it quick for your bitch."

"Don't know . . . any damn blue shirt," Cassino gasped.

Kadyrov kicked Cassino, who could only grunt at the pain. "Sure you do," he said, "the shirt I took from the apartment where I killed them two bitches in Manhattan, same way I'm gonna do to that *sooka* wife of yours."

"Oh yeah, that shirt," Cassino spat, "fuck you, it ain't here. Gave it to a junkie."

Kadyrov kicked Cassino again. "I know you told that cop Brock about it," he hissed as the older man groaned and rolled over onto his stomach. "Now, where the fuck is it? Tell me or I'll take it out on your wife." But Vinnie Cassino didn't answer. He was dead.

In a rage, Kadyrov searched the apartment looking for the blue shirt. When he couldn't find it, he grabbed the .357 from the counter and stationed himself next to the window, waiting for Lydia Cassino to return.

As promised, Lydia Cassino did not spend a great deal of time visiting her "elderly mom" in Yonkers. In fact, she was only in the dilapidated wood-frame house for five minutes before she emerged and climbed back in Marlene's truck. "Let's go, honey," she announced. "Got to get back to my man."

On the way to Yonkers, Marlene had tried to appeal to Lydia as a woman, describing the outrages perpetrated on Olivia Yancy and Beth Jenkins. "I can't promise what kind of deal can be worked out for your testimony and the shirt," she said.

But before she could go on, Lydia interrupted. "Save your breath, sweetie," she said. "I feel bad for what happened to them gals, I really do. I know who killed them and he's a real scumbag; I'd like to shoot him in the balls myself and watch him bleed out. But I need my man with me, not rotting away in prison. And to be honest, I want that reward money so we can get out of that rat hole on Watson Avenue; it's getting so a decent woman can't go out on the sidewalks by herself anymore."

The two women didn't discuss the case anymore on the drive back into Manhattan. When Marlene let Lydia off in front of the building, the older woman leaned back in the window. "Get us that deal, sweetie," she said. "Then we'll all have what we want."

"I'll see what I can do," Marlene replied. She watched the woman go into the building. She then called her husband and told him about the Cassinos.

"Do you think they'd be willing to come downtown to talk to me about it?" Butch asked.

"I can ask," she said. "I'm still here, so I can drive them and you can get them a cab back."

Hanging up, Marlene got out of the truck and made her way through the sidewalk lurkers and was about to enter the

building when she heard a scream from above. The screaming stopped immediately but she recognized Lydia's voice and
rushed in and up the stairs.

Reaching the Cassinos' apartment door, Marlene banged on
it and shouted, *"Police! Open up!"* She stepped aside just in
time to avoid the bullet that passed through the door, blasting a
hole the size of a half-dollar in the wood.

*"The building is surrounded! Put the weapon down and come
out with your hands up!"* she shouted, and crouched down in
case the shooter started blasting at the wall.

There was the sound of something crashing in the apartment.
Then silence, followed by the sound of a window sliding open.
She realized what that meant—the fire escape—and started to
get up to give chase but hesitated. The Cassinos might need
medical attention.

Marlene lined up across the hall and then flung herself into
the door as hard as she could. She was gratified to hear the
sound of wood splintering but the door remained in place.
Backing up and then running forward, she battered the door
again. This time it gave around the molding, and on the third
attempt it crashed inward and she tumbled forward into the
semidark apartment.

Freezing in place, it took her a moment to realize that there
were two bodies on the ground in front of her. As her eyes adjusted she recognized Vinnie Cassino, who was lying on a dark
wet stain that she guessed was blood.

Too late, she thought. Then she spotted Lydia Cassino,
who groaned and tried to push herself up from the floor. She
peered at her husband and cried out. *"Baby! Oh, what's he*

done to you!" Lydia clawed at her husband's body and rolled him over.

Marlene moved and Lydia's head jerked up. Her face was a mask of rage and fear as she started to scramble for her husband's chair and the shotgun leaning against it.

Realizing the woman might just start blasting, Marlene vaulted to her feet and across the room in time to wrest the gun from Lydia's hands and toss it aside. She then slapped the woman hard. "Lydia, it's Marlene," she said. "What happened? Did you see who did this?"

The woman's eyes cleared as she recognized Marlene. "I didn't see him," she cried. "I came in and saw Vinnie . . ." Lydia looked at the lifeless body of her husband and an anguished sob escaped her lips. But the anger returned immediately. "I screamed and went to check on Vinnie and the son of a bitch hit me from behind. But I know who the murdering piece of shit was . . . Ahmed Kadyrov . . . the guy you're looking for." Lydia looked over at the window. "He go that way?"

"Yeah," Marlene answered as she dialed 911 on her phone. "A man's been stabbed," she then said into the phone, and gave the address. "Perpetrator: white male . . ." She looked at Lydia, who nodded and added, "Skinny. Dark hair. Not six feet," which Marlene repeated before continuing. "Last seen leaving the building from the fire escape."

As Marlene spoke, Lydia went over to the window and looked out. "Long gone," she said, picking up the shotgun and walking to the door.

"Where are you going?" Marlene asked, hanging up with the 911 operator.

"To look for the man who killed my man," Lydia said. Her face was grim in spite of the tears that leaked from her eyes. But then the façade cracked and she sobbed as she dropped the gun and covered her face. "Oh, Vinnie, what am I gonna do without you, baby?"

Marlene went over and wrapped her arms around the other woman. "I'm so sorry," she said. "You know there's only one way to get the guy who did this. Vinnie deserves it, and so do Olivia Yancy and Beth Jenkins."

Lydia broke the embrace and stepped back. She was breathing heavily and started to shake her head, but then she nodded as her shoulders sagged. "Come on, we need to go," she said. "The medics will take care of my Vinnie 'til I get back. But if we're here when the police show up, they might find some things and toss my ass in jail."

"Where are we going?" Marlene asked.

Lydia wiped her nose with the back of her hand and half-grinned despite her tears. "Why, to see my elderly mom in Yonkers, of course."

They started to leave the apartment but suddenly Lydia returned to her husband's body. She leaned over and removed something from the top pocket of his overalls. She then pressed her fingers to her lips and his head. "Mama's gonna take care of this for you, baby," she said. "Then I'll see you on the other side."

25

PREOCCUPIED BY KADYROV'S LATEST MESS-UP, DETEC-
tive Joey Graziani didn't bother to pick up the receiver when
the newspaper reporter called his number at the Two-Six detective squad that afternoon and left a message. "I need to talk to
you about the Yancy-Jenkins case," the woman, who had identified herself as Ariadne Stupenagel, said.

He started to erase the message—there were a lot of report-
ers who called wanting an "exclusive" interview with the heroic
detective who caught the Columbia U Slasher, an "officially
off-the-record, but . . ." privilege he gave only a select few he
trusted. However, what she said next made him stop and re-
consider. "I might have some information about who killed that
Bronx detective who was working on the Felix Acevedo case.
Phil Brock."

With his gut clenching, Graziani called the reporter back and
nonchalantly asked her to elaborate.

"I got a call yesterday from a guy named Vinnie Cassino," Stupenagel explained. "He said he told Brock something about the real killer in the Yancy-Jenkins murders in Manhattan and the Atkins case in the Bronx, and the next day Brock gets murdered. He said the only other person who could have known about what he told Brock would have been another Bronx cop."

"So why call me?" Graziani asked, trying to keep his voice calmer than his wildly beating heart.

"Well," she said, her voice trembling, "it was you and Brock who caught the Columbia U Slasher and I thought you ought to know. I mean, you could be in danger, too, and if something happens to me tonight, at least I told someone."

"Tonight? What's tonight?"

"I was supposed to meet Cassino this morning," Stupenagel told him. "He said he was going to bring me something that would prove the case against the 'real killer,' whatever that means; he didn't elaborate. And he said he wanted the reward money so he could get out of town. But he didn't show, so I thought it was all a bunch of bullshit until his wife called and said her husband had been murdered. But she still wants to meet tonight and give me this 'evidence.' Well, 'give' as in I give her two thousand dollars and she gives me what she calls 'the story of the century.'"

"You trust her?" Graziani asked.

"No," Stupenagel admitted. "To be honest, I'm scared. And that's really why I'm calling you. Even if she's legit, it means that two men have been killed over this already, one of them a cop."

Graziani thought quickly. "You did the right thing. If it's okay with you, I think I should tail you to this meeting tonight. If it's legit, then the worst thing that happens is she gets a couple thousand bucks out of the detective bureau kitty. But if there's a bad cop, and something goes down the wrong way, I'll be there."

"Oh God, I was hoping you'd say something like that," Stupenagel replied, the relief in her voice palpable. Then she hesitated. "I still get to break the story," she said. "I'm not risking my neck with no payoff."

Graziani agreed. "Of course. You'll deserve it."

Deserve a bullet between your eyes, he thought six hours later as he checked the chamber of the .380 before screwing the silencer onto the gun. *You and the Cassino bitch.*

The night was dark and the lighting sparse near the Soldiers' and Sailors' Monument in Riverside Park. It was easy to remain in the shadows as the tall female reporter paced about waiting for her meeting with Lydia Cassino. He shook his head; it was surreal, though necessary, that he was contemplating murdering two women with no more conscience than he'd feel killing a couple of alley rats.

Just to get out of the Bronx? The words continued to mock him. *No*, he thought, *now it's more than that*, and he was too far down the road to turn back.

The night before he'd met, as arranged, with Kadyrov at Grand Central Terminal. That's where he heard the story about Vinnie Cassino's death but that Lydia Cassino was alive.

"These other two women got there ahead of me," Kadyrov

said. "Probably from the city, slumming and looking for a little meth for a night on the town. So I had to wait until they left, but they took Cassino's ugly bitch wife with them. So I went and did Vinnie and waited for her to come back. She'd be dead too but the cops showed up at the door."

Kadyrov was adamant that Lydia Cassino had not seen him before he knocked her out. He saw her get dropped off and then hid in the bedroom until she was distracted by her husband's body. "Dealers are getting whacked all the time," he said. "It was just a robbery killing for all she knows. Somebody must have heard her scream and called the cops."

"Yeah, I checked," Graziani had replied. "Someone called nine-one-one. They must have seen you going down the fire escape, too, because they got a physical description. So what about the shirt?"

"I couldn't find it," Kadyrov said.

Graziani cursed the murderer. "That shirt can sink us both," he said.

"She'll get the hint," Kadyrov said. "Stay out of this or you'll get the same thing your husband got. And maybe they don't even have the shirt anymore. I went through everything."

"Yeah, well, that's too many maybes," Graziani said, handing Kadyrov an envelope. "I think it's time you took a little trip upstate. There's four hundred bucks and a bus ticket in there. As well as instructions on where I want you to stay so I can reach you. Do what you're told and there's more where that came from, and I'll keep our asses out of hot water."

Kadyrov reached out and grabbed the envelope, but Graziani held on for a moment as he looked in the younger man's eyes.

"Don't fuck with me, Ahmed," he said. "Get on that bus and you be where I can find you. Or if they don't get you for the Yancy-Jenkins murders, I'll kill you myself." He released the envelope. "And I know you're thinking, *They get me, I'll turn on him.* Just remember who's the cop here when it comes to your word against mine. You'd never live to testify against me anyway."

With the envelope clutched in his hands, Kadyrov disappeared into the bowels of Grand Central. Meanwhile, Graziani had spent another sleepless night wondering how to find Lydia Cassino and the blue silk shirt.

Then the reporter called with the answer. He was sure Lydia Cassino would be showing up with a blue silk shirt. A couple of bullets at close range, and he'd have only one more problem to deal with. And that would entail only a quick trip to upstate New York and another bullet for Ahmed Kadyrov.

Then the Acevedo trial would proceed unabated. He'd be a hero, doted on by the public, the NYPD brass, and his young wife. *It's all under control,* he told himself for the thousandth time as the small dark figure approached and walked up to Stupenagel.

The weight of the .380 in his hand was a comfort as he crept forward. He regretted that after tonight's business, the weapon was going in the East River, since it could tie him to Brock's murder as well as these women. He'd have to pick up another one to finish Kadyrov.

Graziani waited until the two women had talked for a moment. When the smaller woman handed Stupenagel a package, he moved. *The shirt,* he thought with satisfaction as he stepped from the shadows with his gun trained on the women.

"I'll take that," he said.

"What's going on?" the short woman exclaimed in fear.

"It's okay," Stupenagel replied. "He's a cop and he's with me."

Graziani snorted a humorless laugh. "That's right, we're together, but not for long, I'm afraid," he said as he trained his gun on Stupenagel's face.

The reporter looked stunned. "I don't understand," she said, and then a look of understanding came across her face. "It was you."

"It was him what?" the other woman cried out.

"He's the one who killed Brock and your husband," Stupenagel replied.

"As usual, the press gets it wrong," Graziani said. "If you want to be accurate, I finished off Brock when my boy Kadyrov messed up. But Ahmed is the one who sliced and diced that pig husband of yours, Lydia."

"Lydia?" the woman said, suddenly standing up straighter and looking him in the eyes as she smiled. "Actually, the name is Marlene Ciampi, you son of a bitch, and your ass is under arrest. Put the gun down unless you want the sharpshooter who has a nice little red laser light from his scope trained on the side of your head to pull the trigger. Clay, you want to come get this asshole?"

His mouth hanging open, Joey Graziani slowly lowered his gun at the sound of running feet. "How?" he asked.

"A little detective work," Marlene said. "I talked to an officer, Dave Drummond, who confirmed Cassino had wanted to talk to Brock about a blue silk shirt. Then you were seen talking to Brock at the Lino Tavern. My guess is you didn't like hearing that your case was about to go down the tubes, though to be honest, it was already finished. We found out about the ring, you dolt. But now it's over. Detectives working for my husband followed you to Grand Central, and they picked up Kadyrov as soon as you were out of sight. I just don't get it—was it really worth killing another detective, much less Vinnie Cassino and, what . . . two women?"

Graziani looked down at the sidewalk but he was seeing Brock's scornful face. *Just to get out of the Bronx?* Then the image of his wife in bed with another man came to him, followed by the image of himself in prison and what that would be like for a cop, especially a cop who killed another cop—even the guards would enjoy making his life hell. He raised his gun to shoot Marlene.

Instead, a rifle shot rang out in the night and Graziani's head exploded from the force of the fifty-caliber bullet, his gun striking the pavement only a moment before his body did. Even so, Clay Fulton kept his gun trained on the lifeless man as he kicked the .380 to the side. "Bag that," he told another approaching officer before turning to Marlene and Ariadne.

"Boy, I didn't like using civilians on that one," he said.

"Too much of a chance he might have seen Ariadne's photo in a newspaper," Marlene said insistently, repeating the argument she'd used earlier that afternoon in her husband's office. "And there was no way you were keeping me off this one."

The three looked down at Graziani. "I wonder what pushed him down this road," Marlene said.

There was a moment of silence before Stupenagel cleared her throat and responded. "I guess he just lost his mind," she said solemnly. "Too bad, he had a good head on his shoulders."

Marlene groaned. "Oh God, Ariadne! I'm going to try to forget you said that."

26

AHMED KADYROV SAT AT THE DEFENSE TABLE WATCHING
the twelve jurors as they filed back into the courtroom. He
hoped to see some small sign that they would declare him not
guilty. A faint smile, perhaps, from the pretty, young brunette
who he'd fancied thought he was attractive, to let him know
that after several months since his arrest, he would soon walk
out of the Tombs a free man.

What I'd do to you if I got the chance, eh, sooka? he thought,
staring at the brunette. But she merely looked him in the eyes
once and then turned her head toward the judge as a wave of
revulsion rippled across her face.

Next to Kadyrov sat Mavis Huntley, one of the two lawyers
who'd been appointed to represent him from a pool of attorneys qualified to argue death penalty cases. A slender blonde,
Huntley pretended throughout the trial that she actually believed he was innocent—smiling and laughing, or nodding in

agreement, at everything he said, lightly touching his arm on occasion. That was her job. However, he could tell that she was scared to death of him and was repulsed, despite her plastic smile. He wanted to kill her, too.

On the other side of Huntley was the lead counsel, Stacy Langton, who had achieved early success in her career and was noted as a top-flight courtroom strategist. Both of his attorneys' demeanor just prior to the arrival of the jurors reminded Kadyrov of refugees that he'd known from his childhood in Chechnya, shell-shocked and stupid as cattle as they fled the Russians and their burning villages.

However, when the jurors began filing in, Langton assumed an air of what she probably thought of as "quiet dignity." She nodded to the jurors with a half smile, as if to say she'd performed as had been required of her but understood if they had not been convinced. There was nothing anybody could have done, her body language suggested.

Kadyrov loathed Langton, too, and the judge, Timothy Dermondy, who was "prejudiced" against him, ruling against his lawyers and in favor of the prosecution at every turn. Of course he despised the jurors as well, especially the women, and had spent quite a bit of time during the trial fantasizing about what it would be like to rape and butcher each and every one of them.

However, for the moment, he was looking at them with puppy-dog eyes and a tiny, doomed smile, as if he could somehow persuade them at the last moment to alter the verdict he was sure they were returning with. But there was another reason for the pitiful look. Before the jurors entered, Langton had leaned over and said, "I think we have a good chance here," which they both knew was a lie. "But even if for some unfortunate reason they come back with a guilty verdict, we need to remember that we will go immediately into a death penalty trial, where we will be arguing to save your life. We're going to need at least one of those jurors on our side."

"Maybe I don't want to be saved," Kadyrov had replied. He didn't mean it. He was a coward and the idea of being strapped down and injected with deadly chemicals like some pound dog terrified him.

"You can't let yourself think like that," said Langton, who'd explained when they first met that she was taking the case because she didn't believe in the death penalty "for philosophical reasons. The state cannot prevent murders by murdering citizens, and in so doing give official sanction to the barbarism of inflicting death."

It all sounded like tripe to Kadyrov, who had no qualms about murdering. But if Langton believed it and could keep him from a similar fate, he was all for it.

Of course, the worst of his malevolence was reserved for the two men who sat at the prosecution table. The two men who were trying to kill him.

The old white-haired son of a bitch, Guma, stared somberly at the jurors. He'd tried to get Kadyrov to confess after his arrest at Grand Central and then laughed when he refused and demanded a lawyer.

"Good," Guma had said, smiling. "I want to take you apart in a courtroom so that the entire world sees what a piece of crap you are."

Next to him sat the worst one of all, the district attorney himself, Butch Karp, whose decision to take the case himself was further proof that the system had it in for poor Ahmed Kadyrov. When the defense lawyers originally approached Karp with the proposition that Kadyrov would plead guilty to two counts of murder in exchange for a sentence of life without parole, the district attorney had not even considered it for a moment. "He can plead guilty and face a death penalty hearing" was the only counteroffer.

It was so unfair. Even though he understood that his evil nature suggested that he deserved to die, he hoped to manipulate the system and count on good-hearted people who believed in "deterrence" and "rehabilitation."

During the trial, Karp had come after him like a pit bull in a dogfight. It started with the blue silk shirt, which his victim's husband, Dale Yancy, had identified on the witness stand as a shirt taken from the apartment by his wife's killer. It even bore the brand name as it had been recorded on the original police report.

Assistant Medical Examiner Gail Manning was called to the stand to explain how DNA skin cell analysis identified flakes of skin on the shirt belonging to Dale and Olivia Yancy, Vinnie Cassino, "and the defendant, Ahmed Kadyrov."

Under cross-examination by Langton, Manning agreed that if Kadyrov visited the Cassinos, "it was possible" that some of his skin cells could have been deposited on "anything in the apartment, including the shirt." However, on redirect by Karp, the AME explained that the only skin cells found on the inside material of the shirt were those of Dale Yancy and Kadyrov.

"And what does that say to you?" Karp asked.

"That the shirt was worn by Mr. Yancy and Mr. Kadyrov."

"And were you able to find any other DNA evidence on the shirt that would be of interest to this case?" Karp asked.

"Yes, using the chemical luminol I was able to detect trace amounts of blood belonging to Olivia Yancy on the inside material of the sleeves."

"Again, suggesting what?" Karp asked.

"Well, because there were no skin cells from Mrs. Yancy on the inside of the sleeves, it suggests that her blood was transferred there from the arms of someone who did wear the shirt, either Mr. Yancy or Mr. Kadyrov."

The most damning testimony had come from Lydia Cassino, and, in a way, her dead drug hustling husband, Vinnie. Not long after his arrest, Kadyrov heard that Graziani had been killed. His initial thought was that it was bad news, as he couldn't turn on the detective to try to save his own skin. But then again, he figured that with Graziani, Brock, and Vinnie dead, the only witness against him would be Lydia, and she had a rap sheet nearly as long as her husband's. It would be "he said, she said" and he was certain he would come off better in that exchange.

He was wrong. Lydia Cassino took the stand barely able to control her hatred for him, which at first he thought would be her undoing. He knew that his lawyer had made sure that she would not be able to voice her suspicions that he'd killed her husband. If in her anger she did, it would be grounds for a mistrial.

However, under Karp's deliberate questioning, Lydia stayed focused on her testimony. First she recounted how he showed up at the Cassinos' apartment after the Yancy-Jenkins murders wearing the shirt, which he then gave to Vinnie.

"I asked him, 'What's on your pants?', 'cause it looked like dried blood to me," she testified. "And he said I was crazy. But he went to the bathroom and washed it off."

Kadyrov returned to buy more meth a few days later, she said, and pointed to a front-page headline about the Columbia U Slasher. "He said, 'That's me.' My husband didn't believe him at first. But Kadyrov knew too much. He said he only planned to rape and rob that girl and had tied her up with duct tape and cut her clothes off with a knife when another woman—he called her 'the older bitch'—surprised him."

"Did he describe the attacks on Beth Jenkins and Olivia Yancy?" Karp had asked.

"Yeah, he said he stabbed the second woman four or five times," Lydia responded. "Then he said he told the younger woman, Olivia, I guess, that if she didn't shut up—he said she was crying and scared because she watched him kill the second gal—he was going to cut her fucking head off. . . . His shirt was all bloody so he took it off and got that blue silk shirt he gave to Vinnie."

Like fitting the pieces of a puzzle together, Lydia's recollections backed up previous testimony: that of the crime scene technicians who described how Olivia Yancy's body had been bound and her clothes removed with a sharp instrument— evidence that had been withheld from the public—and AME Manning's matter-of-fact description of the attacks, from the number of times Beth Jenkins was stabbed to the rape and near decapitation of Olivia Yancy.

Kadyrov kept his head down as Lydia quoted him talking about the rape, saying how he'd "used her good." But he'd felt the eyes of the jurors burning into him.

Karp was relentless as he asked Lydia to recall the time Kadyrov went to the Cassinos' apartment in the spring. The judge had ruled that Karp could not ask Lydia questions that would lead her to talking about the murder of Dolores Atkins in the Bronx. However, the prosecutor got her to describe how Kadyrov had shown up that previous spring with a large bruise on the side of his face—from that bitch in the park he'd tried to rape—and then threatened the Cassinos if they told anyone that he'd admitted to the Yancy-Jenkins murders.

Although reeling like a boxer who had barely stayed on his feet until the bell ended a brutal round, Kadyrov thought he might have survived Lydia's testimony and that of the other witnesses. However, the knockout punches were delivered when Karp introduced into evidence the recordings Vinnie Cassino had made.

First, Karp played the recording from the previous spring, in which the jury heard the conversation just as Lydia Cassino had described it. *"Whether I did or didn't, I think both of you should watch your fucking mouths. And remember, snitches end up in ditches."*

More damning still was Vinnie Cassino speaking from beyond death's door against the man who killed him. Kadyrov cringed as he heard himself snarl, *"I can do anything I want. And when your old lady gets back, I'm going to rape the shit out of her, if I can stomach touching that ugly bitch. Then I'm going to cut her up real slow. . . . Here's the deal, old man.*

Tell me where the blue shirt is and I'll make it quick for your bitch."

"*Don't know . . . any damn blue shirt,*" Cassino gasped on the recording. There was a grunt of pain, then Kadyrov's voice: "*Sure you do, the shirt I took from the apartment where I killed them two bitches in Manhattan, same way I'm gonna do to that sooka wife of yours.*"

Kadyrov knew he was already down for the count when Karp threw one more punch by calling a language expert to the stand. Having already established that Kadyrov was originally from Chechnya, the relentless district attorney asked the witness if *sooka* meant anything in Chechen.

"Yes, it means 'whore,'" the expert replied.

The fight was over before my damn attorneys said a word, Kadyrov thought while the jurors settled themselves and turned expectantly toward Judge Dermondy as the court clerk took the jury's verdict paperwork to the dais. Kadyrov leaned over in front of his attorney, Mavis Huntley, who froze in fear, and motioned to Langton that he wanted to say something to her privately.

"I hate both of you," Kadyrov hissed without changing his woeful facial expression. "I would kill you if I could."

Huntley whimpered slightly. But Langton blinked twice, then shrugged and leaned back in her chair with her half smile still glued to her face. "Don't think there's going to be much chance of that, my friend," she said under her breath. "Though I'm still going to try to save your miserable life."

Not if the penalty phase goes as well as your defense strategy, Kadyrov thought as he leaned back and turned to look at the judge.

Even if Karp's barrage had not been enough to have the fight stopped on a technical knockout, his defense attorneys' counterpunches had been weak at best. Of course it was beyond Kadyrov's ego to acknowledge that they had precious little to work with.

Langton's strategy had been based on two possibilities: The first was that Felix Acevedo was the real, and confessed, killer. The second was that if Acevedo wasn't the real killer, the district attorney was running around "willy-nilly" accusing innocent men and "changing his mind on a whim."

Langton had started by calling Felix Acevedo to the stand and then going over his confession to Graziani, followed by the statement he'd given the prosecutor Danielle Cohn, who Kadyrov knew was the pretty brunette sitting behind the prosecution table. *She looks like my sister,* he thought absently as he glanced over at her.

Of course, his attorney's direct examination of Acevedo concentrated on those aspects that made Felix look guilty: the confessions to the murders in Manhattan and the Bronx; the admission that he'd assaulted the woman in Mullayly Park, from whom he'd allegedly received the bruise shown in his booking photograph; and, of course, the ring he claimed to have taken from Olivia Yancy.

Langton had also noted the "nearly identical" answers Acevedo had given in his confession and the statement given to Cohn. "And that's because, Mr. Acevedo," the attorney said, raising her voice as she spoke to the obviously frightened young man on the witness stand, "it's the truth, isn't it? You could repeat it word-for-word because you didn't have to make anything up. Isn't that true, Mr. Acevedo?"

"Yes," Acevedo had replied as the defense attorney smiled at the jury triumphantly.

The victory was short-lived. It took much less time for Karp to take the confessions apart than it had to read them into the record. He started by getting Acevedo to recite from parts of the confession where he told Graziani he bought the ring from a young man named Al at Mullayly Park.

"Why did you eventually tell Detective Graziani that you took it from Olivia Yancy?" Karp asked.

"Because Detective Graziani told me I did," Acevedo said, hanging his head, "and I wanted to go home."

"Did you take the ring from Olivia Yancy?"

Acevedo shook his head. "I bought it from Al."

Karp had grimaced and raised his voice as he'd stalked up to the witness stand, holding up the plastic bag containing a small diamond engagement ring. "Come on, Felix! You took the ring from Olivia Yancy!" the prosecutor thundered. "You *admitted* it to Detective Graziani! You *did* take the ring from Olivia, didn't you?"

"Yes, I took it," Acevedo cried out. It might have seemed like theatrics, but even Kadyrov noted the genuine terror in the young man's voice and eyes.

Karp had then softened his voice and smiled. "It's okay, Felix," he said. "Sorry I yelled. Just tell the truth. Did you take this, or any other ring, from Olivia Yancy?"

"No."

"Did you kill Olivia Yancy?"

"No."

"Did you kill Beth Jenkins?"

"No."

"Did you, in fact, kill anyone? Or assault anyone?"

"No."

"Then why did you tell Detective Graziani and Miss Cohn, sitting behind the prosecution table there, that you did?"

"Because I wanted to go home," Acevedo said, wagging his head sadly back and forth.

Karp dissected and dismissed the rest of Acevedo's false confession in much the same fashion. At the prosecutor's direction, Acevedo would read his first honest responses to the detective's questions. Then Karp would ask, "Why did you change your answer if it wasn't true?"

Then Acevedo would answer in one of two ways: "Because Detective Graziani wanted me to" or "I wanted to go home." Karp would follow this by again angrily accusing Acevedo of not telling the truth, at which point the young man would again admit to crimes he didn't commit.

At one point in his cross-examination of Acevedo, Karp suddenly asked if anyone in the gallery had a book they'd brought for reading when court wasn't in session. After overruling the defense objection, Judge Dermondy allowed him to accept a book from a member of the audience.

As Karp walked over to stand in front of Acevedo, he smiled, shook his head, and laughed inwardly when he looked at the title, *Rush to Judgment* by Mark Lane. *So much for spontane-*

ous courtroom drama, he thought. He then read a page aloud from the book.

Karp looked up and held the front of the book out so the witness could see it. "Mr. Acevedo, have you ever seen this book before?"

Acevedo hesitated as if he wasn't sure of the answer he was expected to give. But then he replied, "No."

"Have you ever read it?"

Acevedo shook his head. "No. I don't like to read. The words get jumbled up."

"Your Honor, for demonstration purposes I ask that this book be deemed People's twenty-eight for identification," Karp said. He then walked over to the jury box and handed the still-open book to the jury foreman before turning back to the witness stand. "Mr. Acevedo, would you please repeat what you just heard me read from this book? And, Mr. Foreman, would you please follow along on page one fifty-three?"

Acevedo repeated the words; it was clear to everyone in the courtroom that he had it down. When he finished, the jury foreman looked surprised and nodded his head before handing the book to the juror next to him.

Meticulous as a surgeon, Karp cut away at the defense's case. He asked Acevedo to read from the transcribed statement he gave to Detective Brock about how he received the bruise on his face from a backhand blow by his father. Then Karp called Marianne Tate to the stand as a rebuttal witness after first getting Dermondy to allow Kadyrov and Acevedo to be seated on either side of a court officer in a pew behind the defense table.

"Miss Tate, do you see, here in this courtroom, the man who attacked you?" Karp asked.

Tate looked out over the gallery and then fixed her gaze on Kadyrov. "That's him," she said, pointing to the defendant.

"You're sure?" Karp asked. "The man sitting in the second row with the green shirt?"

The woman nodded. "I'm positive."

"Your Honor, the record should reflect that the witness has identified the defendant," Karp said. "Now, Miss Tate, what if I told you that you originally identified the young man in the blue shirt sitting to his right as your attacker?"

"I recognize him, too, but from the police station. I thought he might be the one back then," she admitted. "But now that I can see them both clearly, I am sure it's the other man."

Karp continued. "Miss Tate, could you demonstrate how you fended your attacker off?"

With Karp describing the action for the court stenographer, Tate showed the jury how she used her elbow to strike the "assailant" behind her. "And you struck him hard?" the prosecutor asked.

"Hard enough for him to lose his grip and let me go," she answered.

Karp dismissed Tate and then re-called the assistant medical examiner, Gail Manning, to the stand. She was shown a blowup of Acevedo's booking photograph depicting the bruise on his face.

Taking the photograph over to the jury, Karp then said, "Ms. Manning, there has been testimony that the young man in that photograph received the bruise on his face from an elbow strike. Based on your observation of that photograph, would you agree that the bruise was the result of such a blow?"

Manning shook her head. "No. In my opinion, the bruising was not caused by an elbow."

"Please explain," Karp said.

"If the bruising had been caused by an elbow, I would expect to see one larger point of impact," she said, turning to address the jurors. "As you can see in the photograph, although there is a general area of swelling and discoloration, there are three small, dark purple spots within the general area, and, somewhat fainter, a fourth. Note they are generally aligned vertically on the side of this man's face."

"Do you have an opinion regarding what sort of blow would have caused that particular pattern?" Karp asked.

"Yes, based on the pattern, I would say that the bruise was caused by knuckles, as would be expected from a backhand blow," Manning answered.

Karp had then called Jesus Guerrero to the stand to admit that he stole a purse containing a small diamond engagement ring. "Whose purse did you take?" Karp asked.

Guerrero shrugged. "I don't know her, but I remember her last name was Lopez because that's my mom's maiden name."

"What did you do with the ring?" Karp asked.

"I sold it to Felix in Mullayly Park," Guerrero said.

"Did you tell Felix your correct name?"

"No. I told him my name was Al because that was the name on the inside of the ring."

Kadyrov didn't even bother to look up anymore when Karp called Amy Lopez to the stand to describe how she'd been robbed. "Can you identify this ring?" he asked, handing her the plastic bag.

Lopez looked at it for a moment before gazing back up at him with tears in her eyes and a smile on her face. "Yes, this is my engagement ring," she said. "Can I take it home now?"

The closing summations were more of a victory lap for Karp. Langton insisted that the defense's case was enough to "throw a cloud of reasonable doubt" over Kadyrov's guilt based on the confessions and subsequent indictment of Acevedo.

However, Karp had shrugged off Acevedo's confession as "a pack of lies, manipulated out of a young man who will, as you heard, admit to anything to avoid confrontation and to escape an uncomfortable situation."

"Acevedo's indictment," he said, "was a mistake that never should have happened. Because of a failure in my office to adhere to good practices an innocent man was accused of a heinous crime and deprived of his freedom. For that, I am truly sorry.

"However, ladies and gentlemen of the jury, what matters here isn't whether a mistake was made regarding Felix Acevedo," Karp had said in conclusion. "The only thing that matters here is that the evidence against Ahmed Kadyrov is overwhelming. There is no cloud of reasonable doubt. There is no doubt at all. He is . . ."

". . . guilty of the murder of Olivia Yancy," Judge Dermondy read to the court, "and guilty of the murder of Beth Jenkins."

27

KARP HAD SEEN TO IT THAT FELIX ACEVEDO WAS RE-
leased from the Tombs as soon as Kadyrov was arrested. Sam
Hartsfield had then announced that the charges against Acevedo in the Bronx were "without merit" and dropped.

Even so, Karp had expected Acevedo and his family to react
angrily, even file a civil lawsuit, which Felix's father, through a
well-known "celebrity" attorney, had vociferously threatened.
But the lawsuit never materialized.

Instead, Karp one day received an unexpected visit from
Amelia Acevedo, who thanked him for looking more closely at
the accusations against her son. "I know it hasn't been easy,"
she said, referring in part to the media storm that, as expected,
had followed, even though it was much less than Murrow
had originally feared. There were a few editorials questioning
"what's going on over at the Manhattan DAO" and a prominent
defense attorney railing on television that "never again" would

the public be able to trust a confession. However, the arrest of Kadyrov and the death of Graziani—with the ensuing "cop kills brother cop" exposé by Stupenagel—had quickly distracted the pundits and press corps.

Amelia said she was having a much harder time forgiving the police detective who'd nearly cost her son his freedom, if not his life. "I know he is dead and in God's hands now, and as a Christian I'm supposed to forgive him," she said. "But what he did seems even more evil because he was a policeman."

Karp still wondered about Graziani. There was no question of his guilt both in trying to frame Acevedo as well as in the murder of Brock. Not only had Marlene and Stupenagel recorded him at the Soldiers' and Sailors' Monument, but ballistics had matched the bullets found in Brock's head to the gun Graziani had with him at Riverside Park. But what could have pushed him that far over the line?

According to Fulton, who'd talked with Sergeant Jon Marks at the Four-Eight Precinct in the Bronx, it was common knowledge in the detective squad room that Graziani had been unhappy with his transfer from Manhattan. Karp suspected that the detective had not started off intending to dishonor his gold shield. Graziani probably initially believed that he'd caught the killer and had fudged on the confessions, thinking he could make it stick later. Then when the case started to fall apart—beginning with Dale Yancy saying the ring didn't match—he'd panicked and pretty soon found himself too far down the road to turn back, including killing another detective.

Even if the Manhattan case against Kadyrov had inexplicably imploded, the Bronx DA would have had a hold on him for the murders of Dolores Atkins, Detective Brock, and Vinnie Cassino, the latter based on the same recording that Karp had used during the trial with Kadyrov boasting he'd taken the blue silk shirt from the apartment where he'd "killed them two bitches in Manhattan."

The Manhattan case had, of course, not imploded. By the defense attorneys' and their clients' faces after final summations in the guilt phase, Karp thought the metaphor of a lopsided heavyweight fight may have occurred to them. The only difference was that in a prizefight, the referee inside the ring would have probably stopped it. But Karp had kept raining blows, right down to connecting Kadyrov's Chechen childhood to the things he said to women he attacked.

After the guilty verdict, Judge Dermondy announced that the trial would now move into the death penalty phase, which would be run much like a regular "trial within a trial." The prosecution would first present its case of "aggravating factors"—essentially the reasons why Kadyrov "deserved" death over life in prison. Then the defense would present its case of "mitigating factors"—the reasons why he should be spared. After that, the order would be reversed, with the defense giving its summation followed by the prosecution. The jury would then weigh the aggravating factors against the mitigating, and whichever proved more convincing would decide Kadyrov's fate.

There were two main aggravating factors Karp and Guma concentrated on. The first was that Kadyrov had committed the murders while in the commission of other felonies—burglary and rape—to eliminate the witnesses. The other was that the murders had been particularly heinous and inhumane.

Guma handled presenting the evidence for the aggravating factors. The first was easy to prove. Items had been taken from the apartment and the bodies of the victims, making it a burglary. AME Manning had been re-called to the stand to describe in much more detail than she had during the guilt phase the sexual assault on Olivia Yancy.

Under Guma's careful questioning, Manning testified that in her examination of the crime scene, it was evident to her that "from her position on the bed, Olivia Yancy had a clear view of the assault on Beth Jenkins."

"Is there anything that would cause you to doubt that Ahmed Kadyrov murdered Beth Jenkins before raping and killing Olivia Yancy, as was testified to by Lydia Cassino during the guilt phase of this trial?" Guma had asked.

"No. In fact, there are indications that Olivia Yancy struggled for quite some time before she was murdered," Manning replied. "Such as deep bruising, and even cuts, from where she struggled against her bonds, and hemorrhaging of the blood vessels in her eyes. It would make sense that she struggled to get free as she watched her mother being murdered."

"Can you estimate the length of time it took Ahmed Kadyrov to kill Beth Jenkins?"

Manning pursed her lips and thought about the question for a moment. "Again, there is evidence of a struggle, which means that she wasn't stabbed in rapid succession or she would have collapsed on the spot. In fact, of the five stab wounds she suffered, two would have been almost debilitating; the other three might have killed her eventually, but she would have been able to fight. So it stands to reason that she received the two worst blows near the end."

"All of which—the screams and curses, the vicious blows, the blood and terror—would have been easily visible to Olivia Yancy as she struggled against her bonds?" Guma asked.

"Yes."

"And all of this would take how long?"

Manning shrugged. "I'd estimate several minutes from the start of the attack to her collapsing to the floor. It would have taken another five or so minutes after that for her to bleed out, lose consciousness, and die."

"Dr. Manning, what would it be like to watch someone bleed out?" Guma asked.

"Well, the body twitches and spasms," Manning said. "Until the victim loses consciousness, they may cry out, groan, or otherwise indicate extreme pain. The victim may even go quiet for a moment and then suddenly resume more spasms and sounds. Not pleasant to watch."

With Manning still on the stand, Guma then turned to the attack on Olivia Yancy. Soon many of the women on the jury and some of the men were weeping as the assistant medical examiner described how she was able to determine that the young woman was raped "before and after death."

Although soft-spoken and unemotional in her delivery, Manning held nothing back in her description of Olivia Yancy's death. "The killer was astride her while she lay prone on the bed, her wrists bound behind her. He then pulled her head

back by the hair—we were able to determine where hair fol-
licles had been pulled out from being yanked—and then cut
her throat from her left to right."

"How deep?" Guma asked.

"Enough to sever almost all of the structures of her neck—
muscles, trachea, veins, arteries—and most of the way through
her spinal cord."

"And what sensations would the victim have experienced?"

"Well, the first is physical pain. Imagine cutting yourself with
a very sharp knife," Manning replied. "Only this goes deep
through the muscles and the windpipe and into the spinal col-
umn. But even with a sharp knife, it's not easy to cut through a
human neck, and there was some sawing and tearing."

Manning paused and needed a moment to regroup as she
reached for a cup of water on the witness stand. Sitting at the
prosecution table, Karp felt for the woman. He'd known her for
most of his career and was aware that behind the doctor's scientific demeanor was a woman who felt deeply for each victim
and had made it her life's work to bring them justice.

Guma waited for her to gather herself and then asked gently,
"Please continue."

"Yes, well, when the trachea—what we sometimes call the
windpipe—is severed, the victim suffers the sensation of being
suffocated, because there is not enough air being pulled into
the lungs, as well as drowning, due to the blood that is draining
into the airways."

"And would the victim have been aware of what was happening to her?" Guma asked.

"I'm sure she was," Manning replied. "This was not a particularly fast death. I'm sure she experienced a great deal of terror, as well as enormous pain and suffering. She was certainly aware of the sexual assault prior to having her throat cut and may have still been alive, possibly conscious, during the sexual assault afterward."

Guma, who had never been afraid to show his emotions in a courtroom, turned with his eyes blazing to Kadyrov. "Are there any other atrocities committed by this defendant on Olivia Yancy that you haven't discussed yet?"

"Yes," replied Manning, who dabbed at her eyes with a tissue. "The victim's ring finger on her left hand was severed in order for the defendant to remove her wedding and engagement rings."

"And other than the obvious disgusting nature of that act, what stands out about it to you?" Guma asked.

Manning took a deep breath and then let it out with a sigh. "Judging from the blood loss," she said, "she was still alive when he cut it off."

During the mitigation phase of the sentencing hearing, Kadyrov's attorneys pulled out the usual litany of mitigating factors, including that he was on drugs at the time of the murders and that he suffered from a "mental defect" that had caused him to act out.

The "mental defect" excuse was discussed at great length by two psychologists and a psychiatrist, who pointed to X-rays and CAT scans of Kadyrov's brain and said "abnormalities" in certain spots could have caused him to act psychotically. Therefore, executing him would be "tantamount to executing a disabled person for acts they could not stop."

Karp asked the psychiatrist if anything on the X-rays or CAT scan proved that the supposed abnormalities "caused him to stalk, assault, rape, and murder" the two victims.

"It's possible, in my opinion," the psychiatrist said.

"And it's just as possible you're wrong," Karp said. "Essentially, you were asked to look at these pieces of so-called evidence and then guess as to their impact, if any, on the defendant in light of the charges he faced?" he asked.

"Objection, Your Honor," Langton said. "The defense isn't asking for anyone to guess; we were asking for an expert opinion."

"Sustained. Mr. Karp, perhaps you should rephrase your question," Dermondy said.

"Very well, Your Honor," Karp said, turning back to the psychiatrist. "It's fair to say, Doctor, that there's no scientific certainty underlying your opinion."

"No, there's no certainty," the psychiatrist said. "It's just based on my experience."

"Well, isn't it fair to say that not all people with X-rays and CAT scans showing those same so-called abnormalities go out and rape and murder innocent women?"

"Certainly not all," the psychiatrist responded.

"Then it's fair to say your analysis could be mistaken?" Karp asked.

"I'm not infallible," the psychiatrist admitted.

The psychiatrist had also testified about the effects of methamphetamine on the brain and the personality of users. "First, it gives the user a sense of empowerment," he said. "But over time it also tends to cause paranoia, as well as violent mood swings."

Karp shrugged it off on the cross-examination. "Was the defendant forced to use this drug?"

"No," the psychiatrist admitted. "At least not to my knowledge."

"Did this drug cause him to boast to the Cassinos about what he'd done?" Karp asked.

"Again, it tends to make the user feel powerful—"

"Powerful about murdering two women in cold blood? And did this drug cause him to try to hide what he'd done, including threatening people he told and allowing an innocent man to be indicted for his crimes?"

"I would say that had more to do with him fearing retribution."

"So washing up immediately after the killings, changing shirts, would be indications he knew right from wrong?" Karp asked.

"Yes."

"As would threatening people he told?"

"Yes."

"So essentially what we know is that he took methamphetamine for his own pleasure and while possibly on the drug tortured and murdered two women?"

When the psychologists and psychiatrist were gone, the defense called in two experts to discuss Kadyrov's "tormented" childhood in Chechnya. The first, a Russian history professor at Columbia University, testified about the Russian military's brutal behavior in Chechnya after the latter declared independence. He detailed the systematic genocide perpetrated on the civilian population, "which included wholesale raping of women and mass executions."

The second expert had testified that a child who had experienced watching his mother and sister being raped and murdered by Russian troops "could be expected to show signs of post-traumatic stress that could include acting out violently, even many years later." During his examination of the defendant, the expert said, he'd noted that Kadyrov "went so far as to identify more with the soldiers that committed the atrocities than with his own family members."

Karp limited his questioning of the experts so as not to give them greater weight than he felt they deserved. As if only mildly curious, he asked each if there were any studies that "proved" that "all, or even many, people who experienced what the defendant experienced as a child became murderously violent many years later after they were removed from the environment."

"I believe there is anecdotal evidence to support this view," the second expert replied.

"Would it be fair to say that by far most people who experience even such horrors as you've described in Chechnya do not end up becoming murderers themselves?" Karp asked.

"That's probably fair," the expert admitted.

After the expert left the courtroom, there was a short, quiet, but heated conversation at the defense table. Then, sounding resigned, Langton rose to call Ahmed Kadyrov to the stand, obviously against his attorneys' wishes.

For nearly an hour, Kadyrov wept as he described the rape and murder of his mother and sister and how that came into play in Olivia Yancy's apartment. He claimed that he had not intended to harm either woman and had merely bound Olivia to keep her from escaping when her mother showed up.

"She attacked me," he cried. "I was frightened and fought back. Suddenly she was like the Russian soldiers and I was defending myself and the girl on the bed. I don't remember stabbing her, but then she was lying on the floor with blood everywhere."

"What happened then?" Langton asked.

"I turned to the other girl, and I don't know, my mind snapped," Kadyrov said. "Suddenly I was Russian soldier and she was my mother. I felt rage and . . . after that I blacked out. The next thing I know, I am standing in front of mirror trying to wash blood from my hands."

Kadyrov buried his face in his hands and cried in great racking sobs. But when he looked up, hoping to see some measure of pity in the jurors' faces, he found none.

"Mr. Kadryov, you made a great show of crying on the stand," Karp said. "Can I ask you how many times you cried for these women you butchered?"

"Many times."

"Really?" Karp asked. "Did you cry when you saw the terror in Olivia Yancy's eyes, or as you told the Cassinos, did you tell her to shut the fuck up or you were going to cut her head off?"

"I was thinking I was Russian soldier."

"And did you cry as you were raping Olivia Yancy while her mother lay dying on the floor?"

Kadyrov didn't answer. He just sat there, stone-faced, as Karp took another step toward him.

"I know you want us to believe that you thought you were a Russian soldier," Karp said sarcastically. "But did you cry when you yanked her head back and sawed away at her neck? Or as she drowned in her own blood?"

"No. I—"

"And long after you were no longer thinking you were a Russian soldier, like when you were at the Cassinos' apartment and boasted that you were the Columbia U Slasher, did you cry then?"

"No. I could not show weakness."

"Nor, apparently, compassion or remorse. And how about later when you went to the Cassinos' apartment to try to get the blue shirt back so that it couldn't be used against you in court, did you cry then?"

"No, I was frightened."

"More frightened than Beth Jenkins or Olivia Yancy?"

"Objection," Langton shouted.

"I withdraw the question," Karp said. He glared hard at Kadyrov, who blanched. "You didn't cry at all for these women, did you, Mr. Kadyrov? Instead, you enjoyed murdering and raping them, didn't you?"

"Objection! The witness has not said that."

"No, you haven't yet, have you, Mr. Kadyrov," Karp said, continuing. "But you liked seeing the terror, hearing their helpless cries, knowing that they were aware they were going to die at your hands, didn't you, Mr. Kadyrov?"

"Your Honor, I've objected!" Langton shouted.

"*Sit down,* sooka!" Kadyrov screamed from the stand. He stood and faced the jury as the court officers started to move toward him, but Karp extended his right arm and motioned for them to stop.

Spitting, Kadyrov yelled, "If you vote to kill me, you'll have my life on your consciences. I'll haunt your sleep and will be in the shadows watching you for as long as you live."

Calmly, without batting an eye, Karp said, "Sit down, Mr. Kadyrov, your threats have the impact of a feather. We're not through with you yet. Your Honor, no further questions, but I do want to call a rebuttal witness."

"Your Honor, I am calling Moishe Sobelman, whose experiences as a child are not just similar to those of the defendant but greatly exceed them in horror," Karp told the court. "The defendant just gave us a sob story about how the atrocities he committed against Olivia Yancy and Beth Jenkins are somehow excusable in light of what he experienced as a child. Mr. Sobelman is an expert in his own right regarding the murder of family members by soldiers acting under the guise of military authority, as well as how someone might cope with such an experience."

Dermondy thought about it for a moment, then shrugged. "I'm going to allow it, Mr. Karp, but let's not overdo."

"Thank you, Your Honor," Karp said, and turned to the back of the courtroom, where in a moment Moishe Sobelman entered.

Carrying himself with dignity, the little man made his way

to the witness stand and took the oath to tell the truth. Then, under Karp's questioning, he told the story of Sobibor, the Nazi death camp—the deaths of his mother, sister, and father; the horror of working as a *Sonderkommando*—until at last he came to his days as a partisan and the capture of the three German SS officers whose car had broken down.

The old man paused to wipe at his eyes and blow his nose. "I played the part of judge, jury, and, may God forgive me, lord high executioner. With my anger raging inside, I decided that the punishment must fit the crime."

The courtroom was absolutely still as Sobelman finished his story. But Karp had another question. "Mr. Sobelman, what did the Nazis do at Sobibor after you escaped?"

"They murdered everyone who remained and then bulldozed the place and tried to make it look like farm country," Sobelman replied. "As if it had never happened."

"And why do you think they did that?" Karp asked.

"I think they knew that they had gone beyond the boundaries of all civilized society," he said. "And that they knew what their punishment would be if the world found out what they had done there."

"And what would that punishment have been?"

Sobelman blinked and then lifted his chin. "The same as what I meted out to Hans Schultz. For some evil, there is only one answer. And that is to be cast beyond the circle of all humanity. For some evils, only death is justice."

EPILOGUE

KARP HANDED THE CRIME SCENE PHOTOGRAPHS TO THE jury foreman and stepped back. The photos depicted the brutal outrages Kadyrov had inflicted on Olivia Yancy and Beth Jenkins. Now the jurors, as well as the police officers and crime scene technicians who'd been called to view that horrible outrage, would have the visual result of the defendant's inhumanity indelibly imprinted in their minds' eyes.

The photographs were not admitted in the prosecution's case-in-chief. Judge Dermondy had ruled that their prejudicial impact against Kadyrov had outweighed their probative value. But during the sentencing phase, the prosecution had more latitude. The AME's vivid descriptions of the physical impacts, the sheer devastation of two individuals, was graphic and horrifying. Yet the photos, by any civilized measure, were emotionally appalling.

From experience, Karp knew that time would help those

images fade, but he also knew that they would never go away entirely. He also believed that the administration of justice required that good people—cops, attorneys, and private citizens called to serve on juries—do their jobs thoroughly and witness evil's work so that evil could be stopped.

"Understanding does not mean that we forgive or excuse the brutal, vicious, methodical, and inhumane horrors he perpetrated on two innocent women." He was well into his final summation and had set the stage for asking the jury to sentence a man to death. It was not a request he took lightly, and it was one he made rarely, believing that the death penalty should be reserved only for the worst of the worst whose inhumanity and depravity demanded no lesser punishment.

Beginning with "Life was good," Karp had led the jurors back through each brutal moment of the attacks on Olivia Yancy and Beth Jenkins, as well as the defendant's attempts to get away with what he had done. Now it was time to bring it home and, as Moishe had stated so eloquently, cast Ahmed Kadyrov beyond the circle of humanity.

As he waited for the photographs to circulate among the jurors, Karp glanced back at the gallery, where his wife and twin boys sat behind the prosecution table. He looked at the cast on Zak's hand and, despite the pathos of the moment, noticed that his sons were maturing from boyhood into young men.

Zak had broken his hand knocking Max Weller to the ground in defense of his brother and Esteban Gonzalez. The blow that broke his son's hand had also busted Weller's nose, which would have been enough to take both boys out of the playoffs even if there had been no further repercussions. But, of course, word got out to the parents and athletic director, who launched an inquiry. The result was that Weller and his cronies were kicked off the team, and more importantly, Coach Newell had been fired.

Missing their top two starting pitchers, as well as several key players, the team had been drubbed out of the playoffs, though starting shortstop Esteban Gonzalez had received an honorable mention to the all-tournament team for his play. With a new coach, the boys were already looking forward to a better run the next season.

The injury had been hard on Zak. He had to undergo two surgeries to make sure the bones in his hand set right. But he'd been assured by the surgeon that after he got the cast off, in a few more days, and went through rehab, he'd be back in time for spring training. And what he gained in both his self-respect and his brother's adulation was impossible to quantify, but it could be seen in the way he carried himself.

Like a man who knows he made a difficult choice and did the right thing, Karp thought.

Seeing his boys in the gallery reminded Karp of his other child, and he smiled slightly. Lucy was back in New Mexico, happily preparing for her wedding in the spring. Her fiancé, Ned Blanchett, had arrived in New York about a week after Kadyrov's arrest. He couldn't talk about where he'd been or what he'd done—though it had obviously, from the strain that was evident in his face and eyes, been a rough time. Former FBI agent and antiterrorist operative Jaxon and U.S. Marshal Jen Capers had come to Karp's office a few days later to let him know that Amir al-Sistani, the mastermind of the attack on the

New York Stock Exchange, who'd been allowed to leave the country by the State Department, had been "reacquired" and was back in federal custody.

When Lucy announced that the wedding was back on and was leaving with Blanchett for the airport, Karp had asked her, "What about your concerns that this is not the right time?"

Lucy smiled and replied, "A very wise woman told me there's no right time for love, there's only now. I think I should follow her advice."

"I think you're right," Karp replied.

"Mr. Karp, we seem to be dead in the water; do you care to continue?" Judge Dermondy's voice broke through the reverie.

"Yes, thank you, Your Honor," Karp quickly replied. He looked at each juror, saw their ashen faces and the tears in their eyes. "When I began this summation, I raised the questions 'Aren't all murders horrible?' and 'Isn't the taking of any life equally reprehensible?' And the answer, of course, is yes. So then we come to how to differentiate between a murderer who deserves life in prison and one who deserves to be executed."

Karp walked slowly over to the defense table and stood looking down at Kadyrov, who kept his head bowed. "As you are well aware, we just went through an exercise that establishes the legal reasons that a killer may qualify for the death penalty—the aggravating factors," he said, turning back to the jurors. "But those are really just an attempt by civilized society to quantify how to reach such an important decision.

"I'm sure you are aware of the debate that surrounds the

death penalty. Alleged experts face off in debate challenging each other with respect to whether or not the death penalty serves as a legitimate punishment model. For example, is it a deterrent, or not? Is it a form of cruel and unusual punishment, a violation of the eighth amendment? And philosophically, should the state be in the execution business?"

Karp shrugged. "But I leave that for the academics, editorial writers, and policymakers to debate," he said. "I am not asking you to sentence the defendant, Ahmed Kadyrov, to death to keep him from killing again or as a deterrent to others. I am asking you in the name of the people because it is the only answer that justice will allow."

Pointing to the photographs that the jury foreman now had back in his hands, Karp continued. "Forgive me for asking this of you one last time, but I want you to put yourself in Olivia Yancy's place on that terrible day. You're facedown on your marriage bed. Your wrists are bound behind your back, your ankles bound together. Your clothes have been cut from your body, and then your mother, sixty-year-old Beth Jenkins, walks in. You can only watch helplessly, in terror and in horror, while she is stabbed repeatedly as she fights for her life. As she collapses to the ground, the killer turns toward you, and when you cry out, he tells you to stop or he's going to cut your fucking head off."

Karp turned back toward Kadyrov. "And you know in that moment what your fate is going to be. It doesn't matter if you stop crying and ignore the terror; there's not going to be any mercy. He's told you what he's going to do. So you can only watch, the fear growing, as that man, his knife dripping with the innocent blood of Beth Jenkins, walks toward you. He is a beast. In his eyes, no compassion, only rage and lust and . . . perhaps more terrifying than all the rest, enjoyment. You know you are going to die. He knows you are going to die. And you both know that it will not be a quick death."

A woman in the jury cried out, but Karp ignored her. "The defendant is enjoying this so much that he is sexually aroused. Blood and fear and death are his real drug of choice. And when he has acted out his lust, he sits astride you and you feel him grab your hair and yank your head back."

Karp paused and looked at the floor for a moment before going on. "You know what's coming even before you feel the first bite of the knife at your throat," he said. "What goes through your mind? Do you think of your husband and how he will come home to find the women he loved most in the world slaughtered? Do you think of the children you will now never bear? Is there time to regret the joy of the long life you had a right to expect but that is being stolen from you?"

Feeling the emotion rise in him, Karp let it form his words. "Then the agony as the blade cuts deep into your neck and the unspeakable horror when you can't breathe and you begin to drown in your own blood. And how long do you remain conscious? Long enough that you are aware that this beast, this inhuman creature, is so thoroughly pleased that he degrades you again? That he satisfies his lust in your dying body?"

Karp let the anger ebb as the jurors and many in the gallery reached for tissues to dab at eyes and stifle cries. "I just said that I was asking you to vote for the death penalty," he said quietly. "But in a way, that is not true. Would it offend your common sense if I suggested to you that it was the defendant who made this choice for you? That when he committed these unspeakable acts, he knew that there could be only one response from civilized society?"

Walking over to the prosecution table, Karp picked up two photographs that had been introduced during Moishe Sobelman's testimony. One showed the death camp; the other showed what appeared to be seemingly quiet and peaceful farmland.

"Why did the Nazis at Sobibor bulldoze that death camp and try to hide what they had done?" he asked. "It was because they knew that what they had done there went beyond the bounds of all civilized society. That if good people in the world learned of the atrocities they'd committed, there could be only one answer, and that would be to wipe them from the face of the earth as thoroughly as they eliminated all traces of Sobibor. All traces, except the memories of the very few who escaped and survived to bear witness to their atrocities, who held the murderers accountable."

Karp put the photographs back down and pointed at Kadyrov. "That man seated there, the one who wept on the witness stand and blamed his actions on others, also knew that the decisions he made on that horrible July afternoon—the depravity of the pain and suffering and terror he inflicted, and the joy he took in that—would leave civilized society only one answer, too."

Karp continued to point until, as though against his will, Kadyrov raised his head, terror on his face. "Yet he continued to think that perhaps he could manipulate the system and convince you, the jurors, that it really wasn't his fault, to make good, honest people question whether sentencing him to death was the right thing to do," he said. "And, in doing so, hoped to make a mockery of the system and of you, because he knows, as well as you and I know, that there is only one way to respond to evil of this magnitude, and that is to eradicate it."

Slowly, Karp lowered his hand and shook his head. "Ladies and gentlemen, I am asking you to invoke the death penalty because it is the only answer to his evil. The defendant knows it. He chose it as surely as he chose to follow Olivia Yancy into her apartment that day. He asked for this, not me." For several moments, Karp stood facing the jury, looking from one face to the next.

As Karp returned to his seat, Kadyrov sat unmoving, staring straight ahead. But what he saw wasn't the courtroom but a brightly lit sterile room that smelled of ammonia, deadly chemicals, and fear. A room where they would strap him down and he would die. And when he woke again, it would be dark and cold and forever.